Iphigenia Murphy

Iphigenia Murphy

SARA HOSEY

BLACK
STONE
PUBLISHING

Printed in the United States of America

First edition: 2020
ISBN 978-1-982618-29-2
Young Adult Fiction / Coming of Age

1 3 5 7 9 10 8 6 4 2

CIP data for this book is available
from the Library of Congress

Blackstone Publishing
31 Mistletoe Rd.
Ashland, OR 97520

www.BlackstonePublishing.com

For all the girls that nobody looks for.

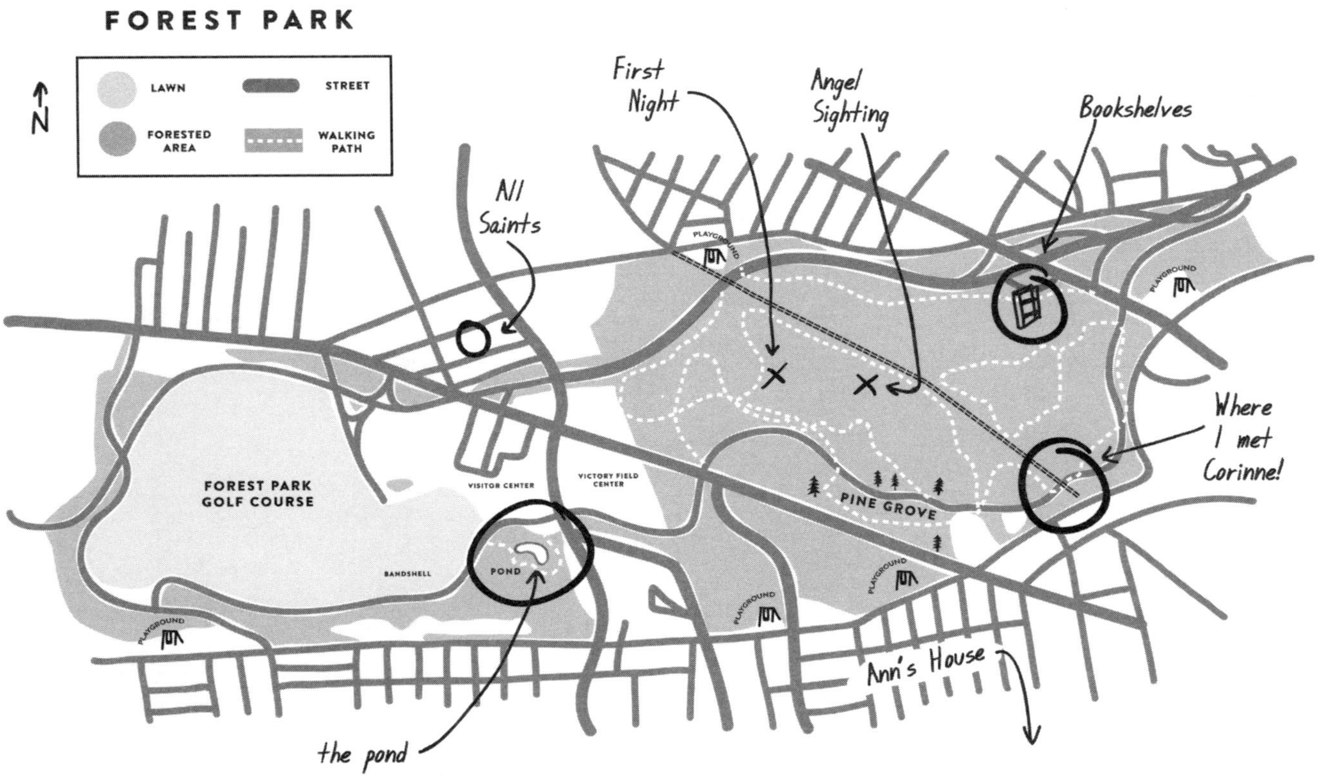

FOREST PARK
N
LAWN
STREET
FORESTED AREA
WALKING PATH
All Saints
First Night
Angel Sighting
Bookshelves
Where I met Corinne!
PLAYGROUND
PLAYGROUND
PLAYGROUND
PLAYGROUND
PLAYGROUND
FOREST PARK GOLF COURSE
VISITOR CENTER
VICTORY FIELD CENTER
PINE GROVE
BANDSHELL
POND
Ann's House
the pond

EWS

DAILY CRIME BLOTTER

A shooting took place early this morning in Forest Park, Queens. The victim, who appears to be homeless, is in critical condition at Booth Memorial Hospital. Anyone with information should contact the police at 1-800-577-TIPS.

PART I:
GETTING GONE

CHAPTER 1

On the couch that was also my bed in the apartment I'd lived in all my life, I sat, sucking my thumb, thinking of the terrible things he'd said to me, using them to ignite a small fire, to get myself warm and moving, to get myself going, to get myself gone.

But, cold and numb, I sat listening hard to the noises: the train rumbling down Roosevelt Avenue, a bus squealing its brakes and then its tired engine sighing and heaving back to life, the water running in the pipes over my head and then the padding footsteps of our upstairs neighbor, my stepmother's whistle-snores through her bedroom door.

My empty stomach churned. Vaguely, I knew that if I sat there long enough, someone would wake up, emerge bleary-eyed, and ask me what was going on. *What's that stupid look on your face, Iffy? Answer me.* Sucked teeth. *Dumb skank.*

I took my thumb away from my mouth. I touched my eye and my clammy fingers stayed there, gently exploring. It was sore from where I had fallen against the edge of my stepbrother's dresser the day before.

My backpack sat on the floor beside me. This morning, I'd

gotten up and packed—clothes and underwear and bathroom stuff. I'd folded and stowed my sheet, gone to the bathroom and brushed my teeth and hair. But then, when it was time to leave, I sat back down on the couch, cold and quiet inside.

Remembering myself, I reached for the straps of my backpack.

There was a flutter and then a scratching noise from across the room; my stepmother's bird was moving under the rust-colored blanket draped over its cage. I felt something moving inside me too—maybe something kindling in me as I thought about my stepmother. Although she'd often loudly insisted on her love for them and spent quite a bit of money buying them, my stepmother averaged about one parakeet every three months. A pretty short life expectancy, right there. I honestly wondered whether she realized that they were unhappy. That their cage was too small and too dirty and that they were neglected. That she was killing them. Did she not know that? Or did she just not care?

There was a noise from my stepbrother's room, something falling, maybe a sneaker or a beer bottle kicked from the bed. Then, a low moan. *Layla's still asleep.* I almost smiled. Something was warming inside me.

Layla was a neighborhood girl, and she and my stepbrother had been running around for weeks behind the back of her scary-as-hell boyfriend, Oscar. It was late when they'd come in last night and I'd been sleeping on the couch when the door clicked open. My whole body had tensed, then relaxed when I realized Layla was with him. They went straight back to his room. Through the thin wall, I could hear them fooling around, and then playing video games, and then fooling around again, for hours.

I'd lain awake for the rest of the night, listening to the pounding *Mortal Kombat* music and Layla's murmured *Oh, Marcos*. I would have put my headphones on, except I needed to save my batteries. But lying there, I had resolved to follow through on the scheme I'd come up with.

And hearing the bird, thinking of that scheme, finally I jumped from the couch, moving decisively around the apartment one last time.

I took a piece of loose-leaf out of my backpack, went into the kitchen and scrawled a note: *Staying at Lizette's. Be home on Sunday. Iff.*

I slapped the note down on the kitchen counter and grabbed one of my stepmother's Pop-Tarts, knowing that'd piss her off. Thinking better of it, I grabbed a second packet and shoved them both in my hoodie pocket, carefully returning the empty box to the cupboard. Now *that* would piss her off.

On a roll, I went and opened the kitchen window. I took the three short steps back to the living room and undraped the birdcage. Tweetie flapped its little wings and looked at me. I eased open the sliding gate and stuck my pointer finger in; even though we didn't interact a whole lot, the bird seemed to sense what was happening and hopped right on to my finger.

I carried the bird carefully back to the kitchen, one hand cupped around it as though I was holding a lit candle, and I set my hand out the window.

That bird didn't hesitate. It got gone.

I watched it perch on the neighbor's fire escape before setting out for real and flapping down 83rd street. "Good luck," I whispered.

I had no idea if that bird would make it through the summer, if it would live to see 1993, or if it would fly south or find a new family or what, but its odds were a lot better out there than they'd ever been in here.

And I was right behind it.

I redraped the cage and headed to the door. They probably wouldn't even notice that cage was empty 'til tomorrow. I picked up my school bag and popped my skateboard under my arm.

I opened the apartment door and pushed the little button by the deadbolt so that it would stay unlocked. I went into the hallway and pulled the door quietly behind me. I became lighter with each step I took, as though ropes that had held me loosened and frayed and snapped off the farther I got from that door. I jogged down the three flights, jumped the last few steps, holding the railing and swooping down, like I've always done, since I was a little kid. I was weightless.

My breath was short, my heart fluttering when I burst from the service entry into the sunny morning. They—my stepbrother, Layla, my stepmother—were still asleep, I knew, but nevertheless I felt pursued, a fugitive. I dropped my board and stepped on it. Other folks were just starting to emerge into the day, the dog walkers and deliverymen hustling around. I put on my headphones, holding the bright-yellow Walkman in my hand as I kicked off to the opening notes of the Pixies' "Where Is My Mind?"

I thought more about that bird as I skated the three blocks over to the playground to meet my friend Lizette once last time.

I was getting gone too.

CHAPTER 2

I was never going back there. *Never going back.* The words repeated in my head to the rhythm of the board over the lines that divided up the sidewalk squares, *never going back, never going back.* And then I crossed the street and the rhythm shifted and the words changed. *Gotta find her. Gotta find her. Gotta find Mom.*

I was a little bit less of a wreck when I got to the playground. I sat on my swing and tried to get ahold of my breathing. I wondered if other people had to work so hard to try to seem normal all the time.

Me and Lizette met at the swings every morning before school, eating breakfast—usually one of those individually wrapped doughnuts or coffee cakes from the bodega—and steeling ourselves for the day to come. Tenth grade wasn't a pleasant place for either us: I was skinny and weird and the teachers thought I was stupid. Lizette was fat and weird and the teachers thought she was stupid. Needless to say, it wasn't like we had a big social group or anything like that.

Sitting there, I considered for a moment just leaving without seeing Lizette. But no, she was my girl, my best friend. I had to see her. And I didn't want to have her going over to the apartment looking for me when I didn't show up at school.

As I waited, I thought of my stepbrother, and I thought of when he'd pushed me and I'd hit my head, hard, on the dresser. I thought of him saying to me, "*You should be thanking me. You're so ugly, no one else is gonna want to touch that.*"

And then there was Lizette, skating right up to the swings, a little awkward on her board, scowling and talking even before stepping off.

"—get those glasses, too," she was saying, starting right in the middle, her speech fast and clipped, but she stopped abruptly and sucked in her breath. She pulled a face, like something smelled bad. "Your stepmother do that to your eye?"

I shrugged and tried to smile.

"Here," she sighed, taking the big old movie star shades perched on the top of her head. "You wear my sunglasses." She clucked her tongue and then asked, "You bring anything for breakfast? And can you stop looking so ... I don't know ... *creepy* for, like, one second please?"

Lizette's default attitude was exasperated. Sometimes she was even exasperated about having to be so exasperated all the time.

I pretended to laugh, snorting a little, and handed her a packet of Pop-Tarts. She took the gum out of her mouth and stuck it under her swing. That swing, the one Lizette always sat on, was probably a couple of inches thicker than any other swing in the world 'cause of all the gum she'd parked down there.

The playground was empty except for the skinny dude who played handball all by himself every morning. The slap and pop of the ball was like our background music, our soundtrack.

"Lizette," I started. I waited while Lizette tore open the foil packet and took a bite.

"Mmmph—I hate strawberry," she said with her mouth full. She was quiet for a moment, chewing, and she gazed off past the basketball courts.

I started again. "You know, sometimes I think about trying to find my mother. You know?"

Lizette waited for me to go on.

When I didn't, she swallowed and asked, "When was the last time you saw her?"

I shrugged. "I don't know. She left for real when I was a kid, but sometimes she would come back ..."

Lizette faced me and got right down to business. "Okay, so where do you think she is?"

I shrugged again. I wanted to tell Lizette, but I didn't have the words. "I think she's ... around."

I didn't tell Lizette that I had once seen my mother outside of my junior high school. That when I saw her, I'd turned away and gone back into the school.

My mother had looked like a crazy person. She had looked homeless, all skinny and strung out. I was afraid of her. And, even more shameful, I was embarrassed by her.

Another time, she had turned up at the apartment. My stepmother threatened to call the cops. My father told her to get her junkie ass back to the park.

The park.

But I didn't tell Lizette all that, and Lizette, for once in her life, seemed to not know what to say. I looked at her and she looked back, confused, but her face was also softer, more open than usual.

"What are you gonna do, Iff?"

I shrugged.

She stared at me. Then she said, sharper than I usually gave her credit for, "You know you can just stay with me and my mom if things are bad."

But we both knew that wasn't really true. Two nights, maybe three tops, before Lizette's mom would start frowning, sighing. Four nights max and she would say outright it was time for me to go.

I looked into the distance and nodded. "I know, Zette. Thanks."

A part of me wished that Lizette would press me, ask me more questions. Demand that I tell her what I was thinking of doing. But she didn't. Because, in the end, neither of us was any good at talking for real. Lizette made up for it by chattering all the time; I made up for it by just staying quiet. On the one hand, sometimes it seemed as though we already knew all the important stuff, we didn't need to speak it out loud. I knew her mother's boyfriend beat her mother up. I knew that when Lizette showed up tired and cranky and she said, "Yeah, David showed up at like three a.m.," that she had had a bad night at home. I didn't have to make her say it.

But on the other hand, maybe if we had tried a little harder, we could have taught each other how to talk about that stuff. Maybe it would have helped.

That day, though, we sat for a moment and then Lizette informed me, like I should care, that *Beverly Hills, 90210* was going to be on at a different time. "You should come over and watch it with me because it's so dumb, I love it, and don't worry, I'll fill you in on everything." And then she checked her watch and announced, "We gotta get going," so I got off the hook for having to lie about why a *90210* TV night wasn't going to happen.

We were almost always a little late to school; that was another thing we had never said out loud, but rolling in at the very last minute freed us from having to wait for the bell in the cafeteria, where it was like a whole other version of lunch hell, complete with a hierarchy of tables segregated by race, coolness, and clique. We didn't have a "table"—I wasn't Irish or Italian enough for the girls who organized themselves that way; the black and Spanish girls wanted nothing to do with us either. Lizette didn't fit in anywhere either. A lot of people, cruelly, called her "the Missing Link." I wasn't even completely sure what that meant, but it seemed a dis that Lizette didn't know who or what her father was. How the kids at our school knew this about Lizette, I could only guess.

That we both got into skateboarding probably made it even worse, maybe making us not really true girls, even. Sometimes we saw them, our classmates, watching us out of the corners of their eyes. Sometimes they looked at us fully, but then it was always with contempt, disgust.

So, if we came in at the last possible minute, rushing to grab our seats in our homerooms, maybe they wouldn't even notice us at all.

We got up from the swings, grabbed our backpacks from the pavement.

Then I said, "Uh, oh. Shoot. I gotta go back home. Forgot my history book."

Lizette frowned, dropped her head in annoyance and disbelief. "Iffy. Really?"

We looked at each other. *Ask me*, I thought, but I didn't have any idea what I'd tell her.

"You gonna show up later?"

I got busy with my knapsack and shrugged.

"All right," she sighed, put out, then scolded, "You know you can't miss any more."

"Yeah," I agreed. If she only knew. I was failing every single one of my classes. But it didn't matter—I was never going back anyway.

"All right," she said again, disappointed. I went to take the sunglasses off and hand them to her, but she waved them away. "Just borrow them." I smiled to say a silent apology for knowing she'd probably never get them back.

"Zette ... don't come over this weekend or anything. I mean, if I don't make it to school today. My stepmother's in a mood is all."

Lizette pulled her lips to one side and raised her eyebrows. "Okay."

I stepped on my board and she got on hers and we both started off in opposite directions.

I'd covered half the playground when she hollered, "I'm serious! You better come to school later!"

I turned around, waving and nodding.

"Stay sweet, Lizzie," I called.

"Stay sweet, Iffy," she yelled back, like we do.

And as I left her behind, I imagined telling Lizette what I had done, what I was doing. How I had saved all the money from my job walking some neighbor kids home from school and how over the last couple of months I had stolen five bucks here, ten bucks there from my father's and stepmother's wallets. How I had sat in the library, reading black-and-white paperback manuals on "outdoorsmanship." I had taken notes and made lists, stashing my work behind a book about bird-watching in the stacks.

I checked my watch. How long did I have before Layla and Marco got out of bed? I was counting on them sleeping in, or, if they got up, hanging around the apartment, playing *Mortal Kombat*. It was time. Before my next stop at the Army Navy Store, I was gonna call Oscar, Layla's boyfriend. It was an added bonus that she happened to be in the apartment the day I'd picked to run.

Everyone knew Oscar. Even kids like me who weren't in gangs or didn't get involved with all the drug stuff. We knew he was not a person to mess around with.

Oscar lived a block away from my apartment, on 84th street. He always sat on the stoop of his building, doing all his business there, showing everyone that he didn't give a damn about the cops: he couldn't be bothered to be discreet. One time I was walking home from school and I saw some commotion. I was gonna take the twins the long way around, but I couldn't help myself. I walked in closer and I saw a crowd circled around, watching Oscar beat some guy with a big, heavy chain, right in the middle of the street. The guy was squirming on his belly, trying to crawl away, and Oscar walked slowly behind him, swinging the chain high over his head and then whipping it down hard.

Thinking about Oscar beating that guy made my heart beat a little faster. I pulled the crumpled paper out of my pocket which had the number I'd got from calling 411 last week. I took a deep breath and put the coin in the slot and dialed.

It rang once. Twice. My hand began to move of its own accord to hang up when I heard a hissed, "What?"

I sucked in a breath.

"What?" he asked again, irritated. "This better be fucking good."

"Layla," I squeaked.

"*What?*"

"3730 83rd Street. 3C," I breathed into the phone.

"Who the fuck is this?" My mind raced. Would Oscar take the bait? He couldn't know it was me, could he? Maybe he already knew that Layla ran around on him; maybe he even knew that she cheated on him with my stepbrother. Maybe he didn't care. No, even if he didn't care about her, he would definitely care about that.

It was my stepbrother's own damn fault if Oscar killed him, I reasoned. I almost felt bad for Layla, but honestly, she was bad news too. Once, I was sitting on the couch, a.k.a. my bed, and on her way out the door she flicked a lit cigarette at my head. It grazed my shoulder and I winced and jumped, shaking my arm like I was on fire. She laughed. My stepbrother laughed too, before barking at me to pick the smoking butt off the floor. I did, quickly, like the mouse I was, my eyes on the ground, as they laughed themselves out the door.

That was the kind of person Layla was.

"Who the fuck is this?" Oscar barked again.

"3730 83rd Street. 3C," I barked back. "Door's unlocked." Then I hung up.

I was almost hyperventilating, I was breathing so hard. Blindly, I broke away from the phone, got on my skateboard, and rattled away as fast as I could. *Next stop, Army Navy Store.*

Nine a.m. on the dot, a really old black guy showed up.

"Morning," he said, his eyes fixed on his keys as he flipped through them one by one.

I clicked off my Walkman and nodded, giving a quick, tight smile.

The metal security gate, covered in purple indecipherable graffiti, thundered up under his hand. "Gimme a minute," he said, entering the store. I waited, leaning against the glass, thinking and listening. My body felt too light, shaky, and I wondered how conspicuous I looked standing outside of the store. What if Marco came looking for me? What if Oscar did?

I wondered if my stepbrother was getting his ass kicked at that very moment.

I jumped when the man knocked on the window and waved me inside.

The store smelled like canvas and dust and firewood. I took a deep breath to steady myself and then I went right on down my list: tent, sleeping gear, a cook set, pepper spray, a Swiss Army knife, trowel, a lantern, a big backpack ...

"You gonna put it all in now?" the man asked as I started packing on the floor next to the counter as he rang up each item.

The old guy was wearing a green army tee and camo pants and a tool-belt fanny pack with all sorts of gadgets and hardware peeking out of pockets and from under straps. I kind of appreciated how he apparently lived his inventory.

Looking up at him, I shrugged, noncommittal.

"Where you going?"

"Camping." I avoided his eyes, my face almost all the way in the bag.

"Upstate?"

I just nodded into the bag again. When I stood up to pay he looked at me hard and frowned deeply and then handed me my change in silence.

As I skated down the block to the Met Supermarket I wondered if the Army Navy guy knew I was up to something. I started imagining him calling the police, saying a girl had come in and it looked like she was running away from home.

What would the police say? Nothing, probably. They'd say, *sorry, old man, but teenage girls buying sleeping bags isn't high on our list of priorities.* I sort of imagined the old man feeling sad, wishing he'd said more to me, asked me more about where I was going. Maybe even following me out of the store.

I actually looked back behind me to make sure he wasn't there.

Pathetic. Totally pathetic. What, did I want to be adopted by some weird old Army Navy dude? No, thank you. *Probably a perv,* I thought to myself. *Probably, or probably he didn't even notice you at all, Iffy.*

At the supermarket, I bought more supplies and only a few things that weren't already my list: granola bars and peanut butter and apples and Doritos. Triple-A batteries and toilet paper and maxi pads. Cans of beans and lentils and more, stuff that didn't need a fridge.

I left the supermarket with my backpacks and shopping bags and skated to the subway station, where I jumped on the 7 train, which took me to the E. From the E train, I skated, awkwardly balanced with all my bags, to the park. The stop I got off at was pretty far from that park entrance, and I coulda taken another train or a bus, but I didn't want to leave too much of a trail.

I probably didn't need to worry so much. There are some girls that nobody looks for. Turns out, I was one of those girls.

Just like my mother.

CHAPTER 3

The first night went on and on.

I lay in my tent, my stepbrother's voice in my head so clear that it was hard for me to believe I was actually alone. I sucked the tip of my thumb and tried to distract myself, to listen to the noises beyond my nylon shell. There were sounds I had never noticed while sleeping on 83rd Street: the early spring crickets, the rustle of the wind through the trees, the soft hooting of what I guessed was an owl. And beneath that were the sounds beyond the park: the ever-present hum of the traffic on the expressway, a woman's laughing scream, the brief pounding bass from a passing car's radio.

And then there would be his voice in my head again.

"You should be thanking me."

I snatched my finger from my mouth and shut my eyes against the memory. I imagined a movie shot panning out from a close-up: there I am, little me, in a tiny tent, in a huge park, in a huge city, the lights just dots from outer space, and then not even that anymore. Gone. Anonymous.

And then the camera rushes back to my face and I am so

obvious, my breathing loud, my every move echoing in the tent. Exposed.

How could I have been so naive, so stupid, so ... optimistic? Almost sixteen, skinny, shy, and stupid. And now here I was, alone, in the dark, in the woods, in a park in the middle of Queens.

What made me think I could do this? It was cold in the park. It was dangerous. I was alone.

I shuddered.

And yet, I reminded myself, *I had been pretty alone at home too.*

My dad was never home. He worked a lot, always picking up extra shifts, or at least that's what he said he was doing. It wasn't strange for me to go weeks without having to slide past him on my way out of the bathroom or to nod at him as I went to put a glass in the kitchen sink. And even when he was home, sometimes he still didn't acknowledge me at all.

Of course, two other people lived in the apartment.

Although I wasn't completely sure that my stepbrother really *was* a person. In my experience, he was actually a monster.

My stepmother, too. She was even monstrous-looking, with her scary-skinny arms and her weird, bloated belly, her violent red lipstick and her cheap wigs. She was always angry and usually her anger was directed at me. She'd stopped short of kicking me out, but the possibility was always there—the looming threat that if I complained, if I made too much noise, if I ate too many of her Pop-Tarts or drank her SlimFast shakes, that I would no longer be welcome in my father's apartment. Well, it might have been his place initially, but it was her apartment now, and we all knew it. She always gave me the sense that I was an unwelcome freeloader, that I'd stayed long past what was acceptable, that her patience with my face was wearing thin. I imagined that she would probably be pretty pleased when she realized I was gone for real. I wondered if she would bother mentioning it to my father at all.

While living with them had been, quite simply, the everyday normal of my life, I knew that it wasn't really normal. I knew that this wasn't how families acted. I knew this because I had once had a mother.

Snap.

A branch cracked and I sat bolt upright.

The panic flashed into my head: *He's here. He's found me.*

I felt my eyes widening, as though looking hard at the tent walls would help me hear better in the dark. I didn't dare turn on my flashlight for fear of drawing attention to myself. And yet I yearned for the light.

My heart was pounding so loudly in my ears that I couldn't hear over it. I couldn't be sure there wasn't someone there, right outside my tent. Just waiting for me to lie back down.

A moment passed and then another moment and still I didn't hear anything. No one crashed into the tent, no one slowly unzipped the arched entry.

But I stayed cowering in the dark for long after. I was the kid who just knows there's something in that closet, but who can't bring herself to fling open the door and confront it and instead just postpones the inevitable. Because you have to fall asleep eventually. And then it crept out: there was a whimper in my throat and I surprised myself when it worked its way out and I heard it in my ears. God, I was so scared. I sat there, then, succumbing to the fears I had promised myself not to indulge in—*I would not think of* Silence of the Lambs, *and I would not think of psycho killers, and I would not worry about the devil worshippers everyone said hung out in the park.*

More time passed.

Eventually, slowly, I lay back down.

I tried to distract myself, thinking about people who might miss me, or at least notice I was gone. It was a short list. Lizette. Maybe some of the skater dudes, or at least Jorge and Jess. My English teacher, Mrs. Cacciola.

Mrs. Cacciola had once stopped me after class. She was short and shaped like a bowling pin and she always wore reading glasses on a string around her neck. She had many different pairs, and I imagined she thought several of them were "funky."

The ones around her neck that day had cat-eyed purple frames.

"Iphigenia?" She was one of the few teachers who had actually learned how to pronounce my name. "Iphigenia, what's going on with you?" She had smiled vaguely and tried to look me in the eye.

I shrugged, focusing on those dumb glasses, and then looking past her, at the blackboard behind her. Someone had written "Kill Me" on the board and Mrs. C. had erased it at the beginning of class, but it was still there, just smeared.

"Is something going on at home?"

I'd brought my eyes to hers and kept them blank.

She'd gestured toward my face; I had had a split lip. I'd shrugged again, my signature move, and held up my skateboard. "I fell," I'd said.

She'd smiled again, but in a sad way.

"Can I go?" I'd said, and she nodded and sighed and turned to her desk and I escaped.

I had thought of that day many times since.

I thought of it again now.

I started to relax a little. What was the worst thing that could happen?

Someone might murder me.

I mentally shrugged.

As long as it wasn't my stepbrother. And he wasn't in the park.

No, I told myself. *He isn't here. At least not yet.* Because I knew that the choice to call Oscar had probably put me in serious danger. Because my stepbrother was the kind of person who would search, who would make it his business to find me. I had to never forget that, to not ever get sloppy. He would show up, eventually, of that I was sure.

But before that happened, I had to find *her.*

I allowed myself to turn on the flashlight and check my watch. It was 3 a.m. I didn't think I'd ever sleep.

I closed my eyes again, thought about the parakeet I'd put out the window. Wondered if he was okay. Was he cowering somewhere, alone and scared, but maybe also happy to be away from that awful apartment? I thought again of Mrs. C. I thought of Lizette. How much she loved that guy on *90210* ... Dylan. He was cute, I had to admit. I'd only seen the show once, over at Lizette's, and now I thought about California and the palm trees and a boy on a motorcycle who would come and rescue me, and I felt myself begin to float.

But then, I heard the sound of the front door opening. The light from the hallway spilled into the living room where I lay on the couch pretending to be asleep. His face above mine. *"You should be thanking me."*

I sat up in the dark, gasping for breath, filled with a very precise terror.

My heart beating in my head, my hands shaking so hard that clasping them only made my elbows jerk around, I thought, *I'm not there anymore, I'm not there.*

No, I was in a park, a public park in the city. And as scary as that was, a wave of relief washed over me. My lungs seemed to loosen as I exhaled.

I had escaped. I had escaped them all. For now.

I lay back down, surprised at my own relief. Surprised that I could feel safer out here in the dark than I did at home on the sofa.

I thought about my mother.

My father, my stepmother, my stepbrother—they had words for my mother. *Crazy. Slut. Junkie.*

But I had words too. *Beautiful. Gentle.*

Mommy.

I remembered being little and standing on the floor in the back seat of someone's car. She was in the front and she had draped her long black hair over the seat and I combed my fingers through it. It was silky and smelled sweet and I remember taking strands and running them over my lips. It felt so good and made me want to fall asleep.

I remembered trying on her shoes. Green leather platform sandals. Trying to walk around the apartment and her laughing at me. I wanted to look just like her. Of course I did. She was the most beautiful woman in the world.

I remembered coming to a park—this park, I thought—sitting on a bench, eating the most delicious animal crackers out of a red cardboard box that looked like a train car. There were never enough cookies in the box, so I ate them slowly, biting off one leg, one tail, one trunk at a time and waiting for her to come back from wherever it was she had gone. I thought of myself like Hansel and Gretel, except that I didn't have to leave a trail because I never doubted that she would return to get me.

I remembered riding on the subway, sucking my thumb and leaning against my sleeping mother. One of those times, a stranger, holding on to the pole above our heads, had leaned down and asked me if I was okay. I had hidden my face under my mother's arm.

I finally fell asleep in my tent.

I only know that I fell asleep because I became conscious of a wet spot of drool next to my mouth, and when I opened my eyes, it wasn't as dark outside anymore. Although it wasn't yet dawn, the tent was illuminated with a dim glow and I could see the green nylon walls around me, the little hanging pocket with my extra flashlight. I unzipped my window and my spirits lightened with the sky: I had never known the birds woke up so early, singing and chirping, making a real racket while it was still dark out, as if they just couldn't wait to see the sun.

Something in me responded to that singing. I had made it. I had made it through the first night. I was alive. I hadn't been murdered or gotten so scared that I ran home or to Lizette's or even to the nearest subway station.

And so now I had to do it. I had to find my mother.

CHAPTER 4

Each night got a little easier.

It was chilly on the second night, so I was glad to be in the tent, snug in my sleeping bag, my nose cold but my body warm. *I'm getting used to it already*, I thought. It's funny how quickly something can begin to seem normal. Even if it's not. Even if it's the least normal thing in the world.

That night, I'd had a bit of an ache lurking behind my eyes. It was my nose. It'd been broken a couple of times, I knew, although I'd never seen a doctor about it. It was flat where it should be ridged, crooked where it should be straight. And I knew that was why I always got headaches before the rain. I didn't want to waste the Advil I'd brought, so I pinched my nose between my thumb and forefinger, massaged my temples.

On the third night it was raining so hard and the ground was so damp that I didn't bother with the tent. I walked over to an old railroad bridge I had noted, but when I got there I saw other people—other homeless—taking shelter beneath it. They squatted on their heels; one of them had a little fire going.

Without thinking, I turned away, startled at myself because I was afraid of them. I didn't even want them to see me. I tried to put it out of my mind as I walked, forlorn, for a long time in the cold rain, before coming upon a big evergreen, Christmas-type tree. I peeked through the branches and was astounded to find a completely dry bed of pine needles underneath. It was a small space and the branches scratched and poked me as I climbed inside, but it was almost magically dry. I stayed there that night and the next.

It was on the fifth night that I awoke to the noise of scratching and a distinctly animal chirp. My heart began racing.

I took a deep breath and sat up.

It was almost dawn, already a little light within the tent. I coughed—a deep, manly-sounding cough, I hoped, thinking it might scare away whatever it was. I grabbed my flashlight and mace and unzipped the tent—it seemed like the loudest noise in the world—just enough to see out.

There were three of them—a big one and two smaller ones—huddled in a circle. They'd taken the food that I'd hung in a plastic bag from a tree branch. One held an open bag of Doritos.

The raccoons turned to look at me, not dropping the food. For a moment it looked to me like a commercial, the kind of dumb ad they show during football games, "Wild for Doritos?" or something. Then the big one bared its teeth and made a terrible, guttural, noise.

I pulled my head back in the tent and zipped it up and sat, cross-legged and terrified. I was sitting up straighter than I ever had before in my life, at complete attention. I didn't move, not even to scratch my nose, for what seemed like hours. I tried to breathe deeply, to tell myself that those raccoons weren't going to bother me, that they just wanted my food, but I was practically hyperventilating, I was so scared.

Sitting there, unmoving, I imagined telling Lizette about the raccoons. She would hoot and swear, talk about how crazy I was, how dumb it was of me to be living in a park. *"But, like, for real?"* she would say. *"There is something wrong with your brain."*

I smiled thinking of Lizette, and it was strange, because I couldn't remember the last time I'd smiled. But it was also strange because, even though I hadn't been smiling, I also hadn't been sad. And then, pretty sure that the raccoons were gone, but not ready to go out yet, I thought about what I'd done and I was, honestly, a little amazed.

I was okay. I'd made a plan and then I'd acted on it and I'd survived. It seemed to me that that first week in the park, even when I was in the middle of it, I knew I was doing something right and important.

There was more to come. I had to take my next steps carefully. But I did take a moment to marvel, that morning, in the dawn, in my tent in the park.

PART II:
ANGEL

CHAPTER 5

I folded up the tent and covered it with leaves before tramping over to one of my holes to dig up a little store of food. What I'd been doing was burying stuff in various spots around the park. I had also stowed some stuff under that big old pine tree I'd slept under a couple of times. All this squirreling away of food and gear meant I could travel around and outside of the park without making it completely obvious I was homeless, showing up at the library pushing a shopping cart full of everything I owned. Or getting ripped off of all my worldly possessions.

And all that work of digging and marking and moving and digging again had kept me real busy that first week. So, it wasn't until around the second week that I started thinking seriously about how to find my mother.

She had been gone for almost seven years. What made me think she was here, in Queens, in this park?

There had been evidence, I thought.

Clue number one: Forest Park was one of the places she'd taken me when I was small.

She had grown up not far from here. We would come and

she would meet up, secretly, with her cousin. She'd never said it, but I knew that her family did not like my father and that my father did not like her family. And that was why the meetings were a secret, why, when we went back to the apartment, I couldn't tell my father where we'd been.

There had been a fight with the cousin—a girl I could barely remember—but me and my mother still came to the park sometimes. We'd walk the trails and look at the turtles in the pond. I'd loved coming to the park with my mother. She loved this place more than anywhere else.

But that wasn't the only reason I thought she was here.

Clue number two: Something my father had said to her when she showed up at the apartment that one time. *"Get your junkie ass back to the park."* And then later that night, fighting with my stepmother in their bedroom, I'd heard him yell, *"I can't help it if that bitch gets out of the hospital,"* and then she said something I couldn't hear, but it ended with *"... living in the park."*

It seemed like some sort of hidden but acknowledged truth, something we all knew without saying it, the way you know that no matter how many times the exterminator comes, the roaches will always live in the walls, the way you know that the water that comes out of the faucet has traveled through hidden pipes, inside the walls and under the streets, all the way from some upstate Eden: we all knew that I had a mother, that she was probably homeless, that she probably lived in a park—Forest Park.

And then, clue number three: Just a few weeks before I left, as though he was giving me a sign, as though he was giving me permission, even my stepbrother had brought it up. Buried in an otherwise unextraordinary barrage of insults was this: *"Everybody already knows that you're crazy like your crazy homeless slut*

mother." He had laughed humorlessly and kept talking, although
he had turned away from me and was looking at his Game Boy.
"Runs in the family and all," he'd muttered. But then he looked up
sharply. *"For real though. My mother should kick you the fuck out.
And then you could go live with your mother in Forest Park. Mother-
and-daughter bag ladies, yo. Put that on* Jerry Springer!*"* And then
he'd belted his affected laugh, *"Hah hah!"* like he thought he was
on MTV or something.

Despite his obnoxiousness, despite his silly, nasty laugh, I
suddenly felt the way I did when I was younger and my father
would make me go to church with him and they rang the bells to
let you know that something important was happening. It was
like that: it was like bells started ringing in my head because
even though he was trying to hurt me, he was saying something
crucial. Something I needed to hear.

I knew it then in my bones.

And once I'd come to live in the park, I could sense her all
around.

Sometimes, walking the trails, I imagined her walking them
once upon a time, maybe years before, maybe the week before.
I did so much walking in the park that I thought that the odds
were, at least some of the time, I was walking on spots where
she had once walked.

A few days before, as I was sitting on a bench on the side of a
trail, I saw woman coming toward me. She had long dark hair in
a side ponytail and long tan legs. She was holding a man's hand.
My heart began to race because I thought, I really thought, *it's
her, this has been so much easier than I ever imagined,* and I rose
from the bench I was sitting on and I walked straight to them
but then just when they registered me, looking at me like,

watch out this homeless girl is going to ask us for money, I realized the woman was young, maybe even still a teenager and that of course it wasn't her, wasn't anything like her after all.

A part of me actually believed that, that we could actually run into each other. Or that some unseen irresistible umbilical cord would lead me right to her.

But, of course I knew better. I knew that even if I looked for her day and night, I might never find her. She might not be there to be found. So, for what felt like a long time but was only a couple of weeks, I did nothing, in a standoff with myself, telling myself I was waiting-and-seeing but knowing that, really, I was unable to start.

As a half measure, I forced myself to do surveillance on the other homeless people in the park. I'd already encountered some of them. More than once, napping on a bench in the daytime, I'd woken up blinking in the afternoon sun to see someone sleeping on the other end of my bench. If the person was awake, we'd nod at each other, maybe say hello, and then I'd scoot out of there.

I was afraid of them, even though I knew I was technically one of them. They all seemed to already know each other, and when they saw me watching they eyed me suspiciously. But I knew I needed to talk to them eventually. I just had to figure out what to say.

What a joke. I didn't even know how to talk to people I *knew.* I didn't even talk to Lizette—what made me think I was all of a sudden going to be able to go up to some homeless strangers?

"*I'm not ready,*" I'd say to myself, setting up the tent. *Just not ready yet,* I'd think, walking a path. Instead of approaching anyone, I spent time wandering in the woods.

When it was sunny and I felt safe, I'd put on my Walkman

and listen to the tape I'd made off the radio. I'd just walk around or I'd watch ants climbing over each other to collect some crumbs or a piece of chip I'd put down. Setting their little ant lives to music changed everything: if it was the Ramones or the Violent Femmes they seemed angry and frantic and if it was Morrissey or the Cure they seemed romantic and epic. Sometimes I watched bees. Headphones on, I'd try to follow one, to see where it was going. I couldn't ever keep track of them, follow them all the way back to their hidden home. I watched birds too, choosing one to keep an eye on as it hopped and fluttered from bench to grass to branch. Once I saw a flash of color in the trees and I thought it must have been the parakeet. I tried to follow it, but it was too far away and it flitted off. I lost it in the high branches.

Watching, I would let my mind wander and I would lose myself, thinking about my mother. I'd think about what I'd say when I found her. In my fantasy, she would be so proud of me for what I'd done. She'd be amazed that I'd figured out how to live in the park. She would think I was very brave. And we'd talk about how it was when I was still little and she lived with us. And we'd talk about what we would do next. She might have to go to rehab or something; I knew that. I knew she'd probably be pretty messed up. I wasn't kidding myself. But maybe, who knew? Maybe she could get custody of me. I wouldn't even mind living in a shelter if I could be with her. As long as we were together.

Once the batteries in my Walkman ran out I could still do it, just lose myself in thinking about her, spinning out elaborate stories. In one of my admittedly more ridiculous daydreams we bought a restaurant—in my imagination it looked a lot like the bar in *Cheers*—where I cooked and mom waitressed. I imagined telling off a customer that gave her a hard time and her being so grateful. I imagined us sitting at the empty bar, having our dinner after a long day's work. A couple of times, I caught myself moving my lips, like I was really saying the things I was thinking about saying. Of course no one was around, but I felt embarrassed anyway.

Sometimes it didn't work; I couldn't get into the story 'cause I was feeling too nervous or sick or distracted. So, I'd try to read. I'd checked out—indefinitely—a bunch of books from the library, including a book from the "recommended" shelf, *Anne of Green Gables*, a weird book called *The Hitchhikers Guide to the Galaxy* that the skateboarding guys were always talking about, and *Alice's Adventures in Wonderland*.

I was sucking the tip of my thumb and reading *Alice* the day I met Angel.

Summer was pouring in, and each day was just a little fuller with sunlight. I was sitting on a bench set along one of the trails deep in the park. It was one of those quiet, eternal spring evenings, full of birds singing and the far-off noises of kids in a playground.

I was reading the words, "*A mouse—of a mouse—to a mouse—a mouse—O mouse!*" when all of a sudden, a big black dog flew right by me. I had to wonder if I was hallucinating. It seemed almost magical, like a reverse-white rabbit had leapt right out of the book or something. I stood up, my book in one hand and my reading glasses in the other, and looked after it, but it was gone as quickly as it had appeared. I called "Here, boy!" weakly into the trees, almost embarrassed, feeling that if someone was watching me they'd think I was crazy.

I really thought it was possible I had fallen asleep reading and dreamed it. But we must've both been circulating around the same territory, because a few days later I was moving my camp and I came across the same dog eating somebody's garbage out of a Styrofoam container half buried in leaves. A mangy-looking, dirty, skinny mutt. I could tell she was a girl. She was tough looking, but she also had this enormous, curly, puffy tail. Like they ran out of tails when they were putting that dog together and so they went ahead and slapped on whatever was lying around. Just the silliest tail you ever saw.

I'd never had a dog. I had a kitten for a little while once.

"Hey," I called. The dog raised her boxy head and looked at me warily, warningly, and then stuck her snout back in the food.

Seeing that ugly dog made something inside me ache. I wanted her to look at me, to come over to me. I hadn't paid much attention to dogs before, but this felt different.

God, I was lonely.

I squatted down and watched the dog out of the corner of my eye. I didn't want her to think I was after her food. I got some jerky from my pocket and slowly held it out, still not looking straight at her.

The dog ignored me. She finished what she was eating and then started licking the Styrofoam so hard the whole container would turn over, and then she would have to paw it right side up again, and only when that was spotless did she finally deign to notice me again. She approached slowly, sniffing at the air.

Her hair was sticking up all down her spine, and I started getting scared. I was excited she was coming over, but I kind of wished I had kept on walking too.

So, there we were, facing each other among the trees, neither of us moving any closer.

Squatting started to hurt my legs, but I didn't want to stand up and startle her, and I didn't want to sit down because then I wouldn't be able to run if the dog attacked me. So, I stayed awkwardly in a crouch, more and more uncomfortable and miserable by the minute.

And then the dog got closer and took the jerky real gently with her front teeth before trotting a few yards away, looking up at me with sad eyes as she tossed her head back two or three times, gulping down the meat.

I smiled and sat down on my butt. If she was gonna bite me, I figured she would have done it already. I held out more jerky and the dog was more confident the second time—she came over, took it, and trotted away. I fed her about three strips before putting what was left back in my pack. I wasn't even sure if dogs should eat jerky, although I figured it was just as good, or as bad, as anything else she might find to eat in the park.

Then the dog approached, sniffing.

My heart was beating hard, but in a good way.

I tried to keep playing it cool. I slowly held out an empty hand. She paused and then approached again, her snout aimed at my hand. I tried to touch her when she got close, but she pulled back and out of reach again.

And then we looked at each other, into each other's eyes. Her eyes were brown, flecked with green. They were familiar, a lot like human eyes. It was, I thought, maybe like falling in love.

The two of us, black-haired and skinny and lonely. And scared. Like, maybe we were supposed to find each other.

"I'm not gonna hurt you," I murmured, holding out my hand again.

She looked at me as though she understood. She didn't, like, jump into my lap or anything. But she started to gradually inch closer and closer, sniffing at the air and then my outstretched fingers until, finally, she bumped her wet nose against my palm, pushing my hand up so that it would fall gently on her head.

"Hey," I said, softly. "Hey there."

We regarded each other. "What's your story?" I asked, my voice choking in my throat. "Why are you all alone? Huh?" I wanted to draw the dog to my chest, but I knew that wouldn't be wise.

Instead, I shifted to reach in my bag and the dog startled, backed away. I took out my water, poured some in a cooking pot. "Here you go ... That jerky always makes *me* thirsty."

She watched and waited, then eventually, slowly, came over and tentatively drank, looking up at me after every other slurp.

"Well. You want to stick with me?"

She slurped, looked, slurped.

And then something wonderful happened. That big, mismatched, fluffy tail started to wag.

CHAPTER 6

I was pretty sure that the dog was lurking in the deep bushes somewhere behind me as I sat on the park bench, regarding a group clustered around a picnic table. She'd been following me around, only coming close when I had food out and ready to share with her, but always nearby for the past few days. *She's smart to stay hidden*, I thought. *I wish I could.*

It was my third week in the park when I forced myself to linger near two men and a woman and a telltale shopping cart full of crap. The woman sat on a picnic table and the men on its bench. I sat at a nearby table, pretending to pick at something on the top of my hand, building up courage, going over what I would say. I was so nervous; my heart was pounding in my temples and my breath felt shallow. I didn't know why I was so worked up. I told myself that they weren't monsters. They were just people.

I rubbed my eye and looked at my hand. There was an eyelash there. I blew it away and made a wish: *I want to find my mother.*

It wasn't like I really thought that if I found her, everything would magically be fine, like suddenly my life would be awesome. Or, okay ... maybe I did think that a little bit. It was just that that without her all these years I had been lost, unanchored. I'd been waiting. Because she might come back. She might come and rescue me.

Now, I thought, I might rescue *her*. And finding her, saving her, might mean saving myself.

Finally, I took a deep breath and rose and approached their table tentatively, thinking I might hang back a bit until someone noticed me. But they had seen me looking at them and they watched me as I walked over.

"What's up, mami?" one of the guys called.

I shrugged, kicked at the dirt. "Looking for someone."

"Come on over a little closer," the same guy said. "We don't bite. At least, most of us don't."

They all sort of chuckled. The white lady spit. I took a few steps closer.

"You got any cigarettes?" the other guy, a small man with a shaved head, asked. I looked at him. He was the kind of gross-looking, grayish, crazy-eyed man that you instinctively don't sit next to on the subway.

"Nah," I said, looking back at the ground.

"It's a good idea to have some," the first guy offered. He was olive-skinned, probably Spanish. Young. Twenties, maybe. "You know, if you're looking for favors or whatever."

"I'm just," I began again, taking a step closer, "I'm looking for someone."

"Yeah, you mentioned that," the first guy said.

I drew a photo from my pocket and held it out. "You ever seen this lady?"

It was a picture of my mom, sitting on the floor next to a

small Christmas tree, all lit up and decorated. She was smiling: big red lips, long black hair. She was wearing a tight red leotard and jeans and a Santa hat.

The first guy took the photo and looked at it, hard. He grunted appreciation and then raised an eyebrow. "You're looking for Mrs. Claus?" he joked. His friends looked over at the picture in his hand and snorted. "No, really, who is she?"

"My sister," I lied.

He looked at the photo again. "Yeah, I see the resemblance. What are you? You Spanish?"

"No," I shook my head. "Just Italian and Irish and some other stuff."

"Oh yeah? What's the other stuff?" he asked.

"I don't know, like Hungarian or something," I answered. I shook my head again, trying to clear away the distractions. "But have you seen her?" I pressed.

The woman reached out for the photo. I watched her look at the picture and unconsciously run her tongue over a sore on her upper lip. She caught me looking and narrowed her eyes at me. She handed the photo back to the first guy, who looked at it again. "Nah, but I know the people to ask. How long you been looking for her?"

"Just a little while," I said. "But I haven't seen her in a long time," I corrected. The photo was passed to the gray man who looked at it and then looked at me and smiled an awful, ugly grin before holding the picture out to me.

When I reached to take the photo, he pulled it back.

"Hey!"

"Something for something. You want something, you gotta give me something," he said, and actually licked his lips.

I looked around. The woman snorted herself into a coughing fit and the first guy looked off into the distance, like he was bored.

"Give it back," I squeaked. My throat and lungs were filled with tears, but I wouldn't let them out.

"And what are you gonna give me?" the creepy gray man said, smiling even more broadly.

"Chill, man," the first guy said, still looking into the distance. "Give the kid her picture."

The gray man cut his eyes at the first man. "I was just playing." He held the picture between two fingers before releasing it, watching it swoop down, gliding onto the dusty ground. I stooped and snatched it up, never taking my eyes off the gray man.

"Listen," the first guy said, "don't pay him no mind. I'm Danny," he said. "What's your name, mami?"

I just stared for a minute, ready to bolt, but unsure of myself. I didn't know how to answer.

"Brenda," I spluttered. *Brenda*? What was wrong with me? Why had I named myself after the girl on *90210*?

"Brenda, you know what your sister would be calling herself? Like, what name she'd be going by? 'Cause I can ask around. You know?"

"I don't know," I told him. It hadn't occurred to me that she wouldn't use her real name. "Um ... Cristina is her name. So, I guess ..." I trailed off.

"Well, if I come up with anything, where'm I gonna find you?"

"I'll be around." I started to back away. "Thanks."

"So long, Brenda," Danny called. When I felt I had gotten far enough away, I started to run.

I knew the dog had waited, because I heard her running behind me as I moved through the woods.

CHAPTER 7

"You should be thanking me. You're so ugly. You should be thanking me."

The way that man had looked at me, it brought it back in a way that left me unsteady. I felt nauseous and light-headed. Those picnic table people had smelled. The one had looked at me like he wanted to hurt me. They had laughed at me.

Of course they didn't recognize the picture. Had I really thought it was going to be that easy?

I got a small campfire going. Maybe my stomach was upset 'cause I hadn't eaten enough. But I wasn't hungry, exactly. Actually, I was always hungry in a low, humming way ever since I got to the park, but I'd also been feeling a little sick in a way that was starting to make me nervous. Maybe I was about to start my period—it was supposed to be any time now.

I'd make myself a hot meal. It would smell good, I decided, and then I'd want to eat it. I put a pot of beans close to the flames.

I stared into the fire, watching those beans cook and sizzle and bubble and thinking about my stepbrother. I hadn't let myself think about him, not really, not straight on, since I'd left. *"What are you going to do about it?"* he'd sneer at me. *"Yo, you should be* thanking *me."*

I thought about my stepmother. Sucking her lips at me, telling me she'd be happy to throw my skanky ass out on the street. Blaming me, looking at me. *"You stay outta his room,"* she'd said to me, her lips twisted in contempt.

Like I wanted to go in there.

I thought about my father. Turning away from me. "Shut the fuck up," my father said—to everyone, all the time. To the guy on the news, to my stepmother, to me, even if I wasn't trying to say anything at all. "Shut the fuck up."

My father was a doorman in the city. For hours on hours he tilted his head, smiled, and said, "Welcome home, sir," and "Good to see you, ma'am." And then he came back to the apartment and said, "Shut the fuck up."

I felt my face frowning as I stared into the fire.

I heard a branch snap, like in the movies or something, and I sensed that someone was there, just behind me and to the right. Then there was a guy, straight up *leering* at me.

It was the same small bald gray man from the picnic table.

"Found you!" he kind of chirped, his lips pulling back so he was baring his small gray teeth.

I had been going over scenarios in my head for so long, about what I would do when someone tried to bother me. *Scream. Run. Punch them in the neck.* But it didn't help, all that thinking. It might've even made things worse. I was totally paralyzed, except for dropping the stick I was poking the fire with into the embers.

"Dinner?" said the guy. I suddenly realized that he was holding a mean-looking knife at his side, pointed at the ground. It flashed into my head that I had seen knives like that in the Army Navy Store, knives for gutting fish, but I hadn't bought one.

It also flashed into my head that my mace, which I actually did buy at the Army Navy Store, was in my backpack, on the other side of the fire.

I reached out slowly to grab the pot of beans, which were getting too hot and making popping noises.

I felt myself nodding, like I was agreeing to something.

I should run, I thought. I stared into the fire and imagined myself, as though I was watching the scene in a movie: a skinny, dark-haired girl, alone in the woods in the park. He would touch me, he would grab me with those small, cruel hands. His breath would be rotten. And that knife. That knife that was made for slicing things open.

I needed to do something, to jump up, yell for help, anything. I needed to wake myself up, get up some courage, and fast. But the best I could muster was to mumble, "Leave me alone," into the fire.

And in that moment, as though from a distance, I saw it all as so terribly unfair. *Why?* I couldn't help but wonder. *Why me? Why won't they all just leave me alone?*

He took a step closer.

"You just relax," he said low, smiling. "We're gonna have us a good time," and he took another step and he brought up the knife and he reached out and grabbed me by the hair.

He yanked me up and, as he did so, I finally broke out of my daze. I was still holding the pot of beans and, as I rose, I pulled my arm back and whaled the side of his head with it. The pot clanked and fell to the ground; he made a weird, strangled noise and released me.

I ducked away and looked at him. His face was covered in the hot beans; he had dropped the knife so he could frantically wipe at his eyes. I could tell it hurt, but it was also clear that he was surprised and maybe even a little embarrassed.

But that didn't stop him from lunging at me again. Just as he was about to make contact, though, my black dog came flying out from the trees. Literally flying. She launched at him, snarling and ripping at his shoulder. It was like nothing I'd ever seen. I just stood there, stunned.

The man let out a high-pitched scream. The dog growled from where she landed in a crouch at the edge of the fire. The man flailed and kicked his leg out at her. She barked at him, her body inching forward with each bark.

Quickly, I scooted over to the other side of the fire, closer to my backpack.

"What the—? Get that dog away from me!" He was scared now. Angry, but scared. It was like she pinned him with her gaze, and he couldn't take his eyes off her.

Suddenly, I imagined a different ending to this scenario.

Emboldened, I crouched down and grabbed my backpack. "You shoulda left us alone," I growled.

It all happened so fast. The guy was there, clutching his arm, looking, frankly, shocked. His shirt was ripped, but I didn't see any blood, so I wasn't sure if she had bitten him or what. I saw him look to his knife, nearby on the ground.

In what felt like one motion I unzipped my bag, reached in, and grabbed the pepper spray. From where I was squatting I aimed the pepper spray through the flames and up at the man, so that when I pressed down, the spray created a brief, huge fireball that leapt up and engulfed the guy. His mouth was an O; his face, lit and surrounded, looked like something out of a horror movie. He jumped backward, screaming, the front of his shirt on fire. He hit the ground and started flailing and rolling.

I think he actually screamed something like, "Why are you doing this to me?"

I took two paces around the fire and then I hit him with the pepper spray itself—no fire this time. I sprayed him, hard and long, in his bean-covered face. He had rolled onto his side into a fetal position, with his hands over his face, but I crouched down and sprayed him again anyway. His face, from what I could see through his fingers, was puckered against my rage.

I kicked him, feeling his torso both soft and solid through my sneaker. Whatever, I wasn't even that strong. But it felt good to kick him, to kick this creep, this would-be rapist, this terrible man.

I had had enough. I had just had enough. So, after I sprayed him good, good enough that he had to stop screaming and close his mouth shut, I kicked him, all right. More than once.

And then I picked up his terrible knife, stuffed my loose gear into a black garbage bag and grabbed my backpack, fortunately with my tent still packed in it, and said, "Come on, dog," and we crashed off into the woods.

CHAPTER 8

I could hear the dog as I ran. It sounded like she was running circles around me.

"You're my guardian angel," I panted as we ran. "That's what I'm gonna call you," I said, "*Angel*."

I had never been so scared in my life. I was almost high, dizzy, but I also felt very clear and like I could go on running forever. And I started laughing too. Not to be too callous, but I kept thinking about the beans and the fireball and the dog and it was all just so crazy it made me laugh.

I was laughing so hard that I had to stop running and then—bending over, my hands on my knees, somehow, I don't know how or when—I was crying.

My chest was heaving and I lost my breath and I doubled over completely. It was almost like throwing up, I was crying so hard, and it was just pouring out of me, I was heaving on the ground and I was actually scared of myself, for myself.

I didn't even know if the dog was nearby anymore. I was only aware, really, of myself, of the animal noises I was making, the grunting and howling and screaming.

In my life before, I had cried—on the couch, in the shower, in a bathroom stall at school—but it had always been stifled and quiet, my eyes squeezed shut and my hands in fists.

This was something else entirely. It was completely beyond my own control. I surrendered.

When it subsided, I found myself lying on my side on the ground.

The dog nosed me, as though to check if I was alive.

I was exhausted.

I lifted my arm and she put her neck beneath it. She let herself be pulled toward me.

My eyes were suddenly so heavy. But my stomach growled, this discomfort keeping me alert.

We stayed like that for a while, on the ground together. When I finally sat up, the leaves were plastered to my face and I noticed for the first time how bad I smelled. I didn't mind, really, I almost sort of liked the smell. I'd been washing up in the park bathrooms, but they all have those faucets that only stay on for ten seconds after you push the button. Probably to discourage people like me from using those sinks as their primary means of bathing.

But with all the crying and the sweating and the leaves … it was time, I thought, for a shower. I didn't know, exactly, where I was in the park, but I started walking again, and the dog followed. When I got my bearings, I picked up my stuff and headed toward a playground.

Angel walked alongside me and she did this thing where she jumped up at me playfully and then just kept walking along like nothing had happened—like a friendly push. It was as though she was trying to cheer me up or something. It was pretty cute.

There were teenagers smoking on the monkey bars when we got to the playground, so me and the dog hung back in the trees, waiting for them to disperse. I sat on the ground and she let me pet her. I started getting sleepy, so I put my head on the backpack and kept one hand on the dog and closed my eyes. I dozed a bit, I guess, and when I woke up the teenagers were gone. Angel was sleeping, but she opened one eye when I sat up and started to dig around in the pack for the soap.

I went over to the big frog statues that served as sprinklers. It was the kind that you have to push a button and then it only stays on for a minute or two. I put my head right up to the frog's mouth to get my hair wet, to splash my face. The dog trotted over to see what I was doing and take a few licks at a puddle, but she kept her distance from the sprinklers.

Even though the night was humid, the cold water gave me a chill and I worked fast, lathering up my hair, my face, my armpits. I kept my clothes on—even though no one was around, I was not about to get naked—but I thought I did a pretty good job cleaning up. I only wished I had a towel. As we walked through the park on the way back to my tent, the wet clothes were cool and nice on my skin. Angel kept darting over to lick the water as it dripped down my leg, tickling me, making me laugh.

As we walked to where I had some food stowed, I began to consider that Angel would be a mixed blessing. Having her with me would complicate things, that was for sure. I had thought that if it ever got bad enough, I could go to a shelter or even turn myself in. But now that was out of the question. I had to worry about what would happen to her if something happened to me. If I got beat up or died or something, she wouldn't understand;

she'd be confused, like I had abandoned her. I couldn't even think about that, about letting her down like that.

I packed away the creepy guy's ugly knife. I didn't know if I would ever use it, but at least he didn't have it anymore.

Angel and I shared a can of cold lentils.

Before I knew it, the birds started their racket.

And then it was dawn.

CHAPTER 9

Days later, I spoke soothingly as I tied the cord around Angel's neck. "Listen," I said, gazing into her eyes. "It's just for walking outside of the park. So you don't get hit by a car or scare anybody or anything. You know, so people know we're together." I smiled and she wagged her tail.

She seemed accustomed to walking on a leash, confirming for me that she had been somebody's dog once upon a time. She trotted along next to me as I led her out of the park to a pay phone I had spotted several weeks back—one that actually worked.

I had had what I thought was an inspired plan the night before, lying on the ground next to Angel. I was determined to execute it as soon as possible.

"I'm continuing my campaign to ruin his life," I told Angel. "If it isn't ruined already."

I held on to the cord with one hand while I picked up the receiver and dialed the number from the flyers I had seen all over the park: 1-800-577-TIPS.

It rang twice and then I had to go through one of those

menus: hang up and dial 911 if this is an emergency, that sort of thing. The waiting made me nervous; I was ready to just forget the whole thing.

I made myself remember. *"You should be thanking me,"* he had said. *"You're so ugly, you should be thanking me."*

I held on.

Finally, I got an operator.

"Crime Stoppers," a woman answered. "Do you have any information about a crime that you'd like to report?"

"Hi," I said. "Hi," I repeated, unsure. "Um, yes. Yes, I do."

"Would you like to give me your name and contact information or would you like to remain anonymous?" The woman on the other end sounded tired, disinterested, far away. In my mind I saw her as the stereotype of the bored receptionist, cradling the phone on her shoulder while she filed her nails. And I also saw me as someone else: a character in a movie, someone bolder than me, someone older and smarter and less afraid. I hadn't even intended to do it, but pretending I was someone else for those few minutes allowed the words to come easily, to spill out of me and into the receiver and into the ear of a woman sitting, I imagined, at a metal desk in room dimly lit and smelling of burnt coffee.

"I'd rather not say," I said, breathily, conspiratorially. "He's dangerous."

"Go on," she drawled.

I gave the address of the apartment. "That's where he lives. He deals drugs. All kinds: heroin, crack, coke, pot."

"And how do you have this information, ma'am?"

"I've been there. It's all in his room. There's stuff out in the open but he also hides it, like, in his bedposts. Like, they're hollow. The tops screw off. Does that make sense?"

"Yes, ma'am, I understand."

"And under the bed too. And there's other, like, criminal paraphernalia in there. Weapons and other stuff."

"And you've witnessed this activity, ma'am?"

"Uh, yeah."

"And when did you witness this activity?"

I actually laughed. "Like, every day." I cleared my throat, turned serious again. "And there's more." Here is where I had hoped to seal the deal. "He looks like that guy on all the posters. The one who shot that lady? You know, the one they say to call about if you have any tips?"

"Are you referring to the shooting that took place in Brooklyn on March twenty-seventh?"

"Yeah, that's the one."

"And you're telling me the individual at this apartment resembles the shooter whose image has been released?"

"Yeah, I think it might be him."

"You realize that in order to get the reward—"

"I don't care about the reward," I interrupted. "Look, I gotta go now," I glanced around, suddenly aware of the amount of time I had spent on the phone, out in the open. "But he's usually there until around noon, I'd say. So. You know." And I hung up.

My stepbrother didn't really look like the black-and-white sketch of the guy on the poster hanging up around the park, its edges curling up. When I saw it I'd thought, *Someday that'll probably be my stepbrother.* And then later, I thought, *Well, maybe I could say it was him.* Why not? My stepbrother had done terrible things. He might even have shot somebody once. He wasn't, like, an upstanding citizen or anything.

I took a deep breath and looked around again, afraid they'd

tracked the call or something, maybe sent a squad car right over to pick me up. But no, as conspicuous as I felt, nobody seemed to see anything unusual about me, about a scared-looking girl using a pay phone. The cars and buses kept racing down Woodhaven Boulevard, the shop owners kept rolling up their gates, the old men sitting on benches kept feeding their pigeons. *Don't worry, Iffy,* I told myself. *You're still invisible.*

CHAPTER 10

I used a ballpoint pen to write "Hugnry Please Help" on a piece of scavenged cardboard, tracing over the letters again and again to make them legible. I set it against a tree and took a step back to see if I could read it. I smiled a little. I had spelled hungry wrong on purpose; the sign looked perfectly pathetic.

"Okay, Ang," I called, and she bounded over and I put the cord I was using as a leash around her neck and the two of us trudged over to one of the main paths to set up shop.

I was worried, after that guy tried to bother me, about running into him again. I was worried he would try to take revenge or something like that. But a full week had passed and I hadn't seen him anywhere, and I needed money. Not desperately, but I was planning on picking up some supplies later in the week and I worried about spending money without having a little coming in. So, I needed to go out begging.

That first time, I just sat cross-legged on the ground, holding my sign while Angel snoozed next to me, lazily lifting her head and letting out a low growl if she thought somebody was getting too close. I'd pat her and say, "It's okay, girl," and she'd rest her head, sometimes letting out a little contented whimper.

I was playing it cool, but my insides were churning, my heart like a bird trying to break out of my chest. I was afraid someone would recognize me or someone would try to steal from me or the cops would hassle me.

None of that stuff happened, at least not that first day.

The first person to give me money was one of those ladies who collects cans to turn them in for the deposit. That was a surprise to me. She was walking by, pushing her stolen Waldbaum's shopping cart, bags of bottles and cans piled impossibly high, and she came creaking over and parked the cart. Angel growled and I told her it was okay, and when the lady saw Angel wasn't gonna attack she reached into her fanny pack and handed me a handful of crumpled bills. She said, "God bless you," with an accent I didn't know.

I looked up, into her eyes, and I whispered, "Thank you."

When she started to walk away, my throat began to swell. But I swallowed hard and called after her, "Hey!" I stood and jogged up to her, Angel trailing behind me. I dug the photo out of my jeans.

She turned and stopped. "You seen her?" I nodded at the picture.

The woman didn't take the photo, just looked at it as I held it out.

"No," she said, gently, shaking her head. She touched my forehead. "God bless," she said and turned to go.

Her touch surprised me, but I hadn't flinched. Instead, I stayed, as though she'd frozen me to the spot, still feeling the place where her warm fingertips had been.

I watched her walk away and I felt a sharp longing. I almost wished for a moment that I was one of her stupid cans, that she would pick me up and put me in her shopping cart and take me along to wherever she was going next.

Angel tried to sniff at something just beyond the reach of the leash and her tugging snapped me out of my daze. I walked back and sat down on the low curb that lined the walking path.

I looked into the photo.

I squeezed my eyes shut, but too late—big tears pushed their way out.

I wiped them away with my fists.

I had found that Christmas photo between the pages of an anthropology textbook. My hair dryer had blown out one day and, rather than dare to touch my stepmother's, I went digging for an old one that I thought might have been stowed in the back of a cavernous hallway closet. I came across a box of books. This itself was a big surprise. We didn't have a lot of books around the apartment, generally.

Sitting on the floor of the hall, I took the books out one at a time. An old printout fell from one of the book's pages like a feather to the floor. I picked it up and looked at the blue '80s font on yellowing paper for a long time, nervous at having discovered something illicit, the knowledge slowly dawning on me that this was a remnant from a time when one of them—either my mom or my dad—went to college for a semester. The schedule listed "Comp 102, 3 cred. Art 101, 2 cred. Bio 101, 4 cred." That one of them, my mother or my father, had saved these books—*An Introduction to Anthropology, Figure Drawing, An Introduction to Biology, The Collected Works of Aeschylus*—demonstrated a kind of heartbreaking optimism, a promise to themselves that someday they were gonna read the books, like they were gonna go back to school and really do it next time.

When the photo fell out of *Introduction to Anthropology*, a shiver went up my spine. She had put it there just for me. A ghost of her past self had interceded and wanted me to find it. It later occurred to me that maybe *Introduction to Anthropology* had been my father's book, and I felt confused and upset by that. Had he once loved her enough to keep her photo in a textbook? That didn't seem anything like the man I knew as my father.

There was a second photo, too, an even earlier one that I don't remember ever acquiring; I'd just always had it. It was my mom and me on a beach. I liked to think it was Rockaway, just like the Ramones sing about, but I couldn't be sure, not without asking my dad. And I knew what he would say if I asked, and it went something like, "*Shut the fuck up*," maybe punctuated with a slap.

But in the photo she looked amazing, just the way I remembered her: tan skin and long black hair, wearing a tiny pink bikini and sunglasses, smiling up at the photographer. And me, a chubby toddler, sitting next to her, in my matching pink bikini.

I had one other photo, and I knew that was the one I should have been showing around, but I couldn't bring myself to do it. It was taken later, maybe even right before she left for real. In that photo, which I kept stowed, buried with my reserve cash, she was sitting on the green couch and she was skinny and haggard, her hair cut short and bushed out, and her eyes dark and ringed with circles. She looked unwell. She looked unhappy.

I preferred the Christmas photo, so that's the one I'd used.

No one else gave me money for a while, although plenty of people looked at us sideways as they passed, walking their dogs and pushing their baby carriages. Later, I realized that I should've had a hat or a cup out. I don't think people like to get too close or want to risk touching.

About an hour in, it started to get real sticky and hot. Angel sat in a patch of shade, panting, and I had given up on trying to wipe the sweat away. I just let it collect, drops rolling down my face. I thought, *isn't this what people go to saunas for? Might even be good for me or something.*

I noticed a guy after he walked past us several times. Eventually, he sauntered near and then stopped and stood a little distance away and waved at me to get my attention.

"Hey, sweetie," he called. He was a white guy with a round face and a superskinny body. Probably in his twenties. "Mind if I come over and talk to you?"

I just shrugged and looked at him with my best, blank stare. A voice in my head was screaming, though at a distance: *Wake up, Iffy! When are you gonna learn? Just get out of here!*

But there were tons of people around. I didn't really feel in immediate danger. Plus, he wasn't threatening. Just the opposite—he was working real hard to *not* seem threatening. But still. Something was not quite right. What did he want with me?

He walked over and Angel rose. Her tail was down and she looked nervous. I patted her.

"Your dog friendly?" he asked, putting out a hand toward her.

"No."

"Okay," he said, again, trying to keep things calm, keep things smooth. He walked around us, to avoid Angel, and squatted nearby.

"I just seen your sign and all. Pretty girl like you ... it's just so sad to see a pretty girl like you living on the streets."

I was skeptical. I might be a lot of things, but pretty probably wasn't one of them.

He was wearing those guido parachute pants and a white T-shirt that looked like it had been ironed. He talked like he was trying to sound like a black person or Southern or something.

He caught and held my eye. He wasn't terrible looking, but I noticed that he had bad skin, bumpy and blotchy and irritated.

"Can I take you out, get you a bite to eat?" He took a buzzing beeper from his waistband and looked at it. I was happy to have broken eye contact, to go back to looking at my raggedy Converse sneakers.

"No thanks."

"Aww, come on," he said, pulling his eyes away from the beeper and then placing it carefully back in his waistband. He pointed at the little curb I was sitting on. "May I?" I shrugged again.

Angel came around and tried to sniff him; he made that novice mistake of trying to pet her right on the top of her head and she pulled away, moved to my other side and watched him.

"Aww, now doggie, don't be scared," he cooed.

His beeper went off again and again he took it out, looked at it and put it back.

"Sorry about that," he said, not really apologizing. "Business." He nodded and I don't know why, I nodded back. "So, honey," he began again, the tenderness returned to his voice. He was unhurried, talking slowly, almost like a singsong. He leaned toward me, as though he was going to nudge me. "I just think that you and I could help each other. I could take care of you, you know, be your boyfriend. I can tell you don't got a boyfriend, 'cause there is no way you'd be sitting out here hungry if you did. But I could be your boyfriend, you know? I got plenty of money." And here he reached into his pocket and took out a wallet and then, slowly, opened the wallet and took out two tens. He held them in the air and then offered them to me. When I didn't take them right away, he kind of shook them at me, thrust them a little closer. "Go ahead. This is for you," he said softly. "No strings attached. Just don't want a pretty girl to go hungry." I wanted to tell him that twenty bucks didn't impress me, but the reality is that I wanted that money. So, I reached out, shyly, only looking out of the corners of my eyes, and took the bills. I held them, looking and not looking, like the way you would after the teacher puts a test with a bad grade on your desk in front of you.

"There you go. And I got a real nice car too, you know. I'd love to drive you around in that car. And I got a nice big place, not far from here. Why don't you let me show you? I'd really like to show you."

I was lulled by his voice. It made me feel sleepy ... almost.

He drawled on. "I got this big old king-size bed and, you know what I'd like? I'd like to put you up in that bed and turn up the AC and bundle you up in blankets. That's what I'd like to do, just tuck you right in. Feed you some french fries and a milkshake." He laughed, delighted by his own image. "Wouldn't you like that, too?"

I was aware of the sweat beading on my forehead and I felt ashamed, because a part of me couldn't help but imagine it: a cool room, a soft bed. Pillows. French fries dusted with salt.

I stared at my dirty shoelaces, just listening. But then he reached out and gently took hold of my arm and I startled.

I whipped my arm away and he let go. Angel growled.

I stood up, quickly. "No thanks." I shook my head, trying to get whatever had been loose in there back into the right place.

I was about to walk away, but I forced myself to stop, to hold out the photo still clutched in my hand.

"I'm looking for her," I said, thrusting it forward. "Have you seen this lady?"

He rose and took the photo and looked at it. Angel growled at my side.

"Your mom?"

I just stared at him. How did he know?

"Maybe," he said, smiling. "This an old picture?"

My stomach fluttered. "Sort of."

He looked again at the picture and then handed it back to me. "She looks familiar, but I meet a lot of people," he shrugged. "Can't really help you, though."

"Thanks," I said, absurdly. I started to back away, Angel at my heels.

"Talk to Dougie."

I stopped. His eyes flicked past me, to the distance and then he looked me in the face. The kindness was gone now, although he didn't seem angry or upset. Mostly he seemed chillingly indifferent.

"Mean dude, hangs out around here. He might know something. Yeah," he said, wiping his hands on his pants as though he'd touched something filthy. "Now I think about it, I mighta even seen them together."

I was frozen, unsure of the abrupt turnaround. Was this a ploy, a trick?

I forced myself to speak. "Really?" I squeaked. "Dougie?"

He laughed, a full, deep laugh and his face changed again. "Shit, no, I'm just messing with you. Never seen her before." He looked me up and down. "Now I see you standing up, you too skinny anyway." He wrinkled his nose. "And you need a bath too."

He turned and limped away, an affected gangsta walk.

I stood, watching, still stunned. Why would he make something like that up? Just to be a jerk? Or had he recognized her, but then changed his mind about helping me?

I wanted to stop him, to shout for him to come back, but I was stuck in my spot.

It wouldn't have mattered anyway, I told myself. *Something-for-something.* He wasn't going to give me any more for free.

The exchange left me dizzy, the way he changed from being one thing to another thing without warning. Or maybe I'd stood up too fast in the heat.

A bird shrieked in the trees above me. I wished I'd checked that bird-watching book out, instead of just hiding stuff behind it back when I was making my plans in the library. Maybe then I'd know what kind of bird that was, calling out a warning so loud.

Angel and I started walking. I wanted to tell that bird I didn't need its warning. I knew what he'd been offering. I knew that if I had called "Wait!" or if I'd smiled, he wouldn't have thought I was too skinny after all.

There was too much in my mind. I walked, trying to figure out what to feel first. Gratitude that Angel had been with me, that her reliance on me had made it not a question, made it impossible for me to have gone with him. And fear of him and of myself and of what could be or what could have been. And uncertainty of whether or not he was telling the truth, and a longing that he was. And that other longing that was always there, underneath it all, just as there is always the hot core of the earth under our feet, under rugs and floors and leaves and dirt and rock. A longing for her was always there, the pull so constant as to be unnoticeable, like gravity, keeping me from spinning off, keeping me on the earth.

PART III:
CORINNE

CHAPTER 11

A few days later, I was begging at the off-ramp of the Interboro, a highway that ran next to and in some places cut through the park. Watching from the woods, I had seen another girl doing it: she held a sign and when the cars stopped at the light, she'd walk up to each driver's window, peering in. Some of them rolled down their window and gave her money.

At first I couldn't bring myself to approach the cars. I just waited at the light and every so often a window would roll down, a hand would wave me over. I always could tell right away who was going to cough up some cash. Some people were working so hard not to make eye contact, staring at their radio dials or out the passenger window, I'd almost bust out laughing. They'd see me and then look immediately, totally conspicuously, down, to check that the door was locked. Like I was gonna try and jump in their car or something. They were so scared of little old me.

Then there were people who you'd see right away look to the seat next to them or the cup holder, and others who'd look for their wallets or purses—they were the ones who usually came up with something. A buck. Sometimes only a quarter.

"Thanks," I'd say. Sometimes, "God bless," 'cause that's what I'd heard other panhandlers say and it seemed to make people happy.

Women gave more than men, at least to me. And men, well, sometimes they were fine. Some said things like, "You okay?" or, "Take care of yourself." More than one asked me if I needed a ride anywhere, more than one asked how much for a blow job. When they said stuff like that, I'd just walk away, not even touch the money.

Times like that made me feel glad to have Angel, too. Maybe it didn't make a difference, but she made me feel safer, less alone.

That cloudy day, though, I was there at the off-ramp and a police cruiser came along and they were just looking at me, the way cops can—completely frankly. I saw them staring at me, talking out the sides of their lips at each other, so I tucked up my sign and started moving along, crossed the street to get back to the park. And then they hit the lights and made a left and pulled over, right alongside me. "Hold on there," a female voice called over the loudspeaker. "*Espera*," she added flatly, a word she'd learned but couldn't be bothered to pronounce correctly.

I stood, frozen. Angel looked at me, looked at the car, and let out a low growl. I didn't know what to do. Take off, run into the woods? Would they chase me? Would that just make things worse?

I didn't have time to even decide. They were out of the car, their belts all loaded down and jingling and squeaking as they sauntered, the male cop walking around the side, the female getting out and crouching down, her hand out to Angel.

"I love a pit," she said.

I didn't say anything.

"What'cha doing?" the male cop said, resting his hands on

his heavy belt, on which hung a walkie-talkie. Static and voices burst out.

I looked at him.

"You speak English?"

I nodded. The radio in their squad car crackled, a woman's voice called out numbers. I looked past them, seeing the people driving by turning their heads, watching us on the sidewalk. *People in cars think you can't see them back,* I realized. I had always almost-known that, but it was so obvious suddenly. *They think they can just watch you and not be seen.* A blond woman in red shades gaped out the passenger window of a Jeep. I scowled back at her and she looked away.

"I asked you what you were doing," the male cop said again, this time a little more severely. Angel had tentatively approached the other cop and sniffed her fingers.

The female cop was almost a girl cop, she looked so young. She was dark-skinned and lean and probably just a few years out of high school, if I had to guess. I wondered if her partner felt lucky to be paired with her. He was almost-cute too: a kind-of-stocky, pale-skinned dude. It made me feel like I was on a hidden camera show or something.

"We're not trying to jam you up." She said it like she was talking to Angel, not to me. "Just wanna make sure you're okay."

I looked at her, then at the guy. He was frowning.

"I was just, you know, trying to get some cash," I spit out. I was working real hard not to cry for some reason. My throat was tight and my face hot. I needed to hold it together.

My mind was racing. I was scared and cornered and I just wanted to get out of there, but they also seemed not completely unkind. But then again, on the other hand, it was like, *are you kidding me, you can't trust the cops even if they aren't gonna mess with you—you know what their first call will be? Social services, social services, social services. And what about Angel? The kill shelter for sure. And big black pit mixes do great at the pound. Probably about as good as small fifteen-year-old girls in group homes.*

"You homeless?" the male cop cut to the chase.

"No," I said quickly. "I was just looking to get some cash. Go to McDonald's or something."

"That is neither safe nor legal. You on drugs?"

"No, sir—"

"You working for someone?" he followed up, interrupting me.

"No, sir," I said, looking him in the eye so he would know I was telling the truth.

"If you're hungry," the woman said, now scratching Angel's ears, still talking to the dog's face, "we can help you out, you know, get you somewhere safe." I wondered if she expected Angel to answer her.

"No, I'm fine. We're fine. I'm just gonna go home now. Thanks. Or sorry. Or whatever. Can I go now?"

The cops looked at each other; the woman stood. Angel put her paw on the cop's foot. The woman smiled at her.

"You can go," the man said. He turned away and spoke into the walkie-talkie before turning back and saying, "You can go, but I don't want to see you hanging out over there again. Or else we'll pick you up. Find out who you are." He looked right at me, and I dropped my eyes and looked at the ground.

It was like he had punched me in the stomach. "Okay," I said into the ground. "Okay." And I started to back away, pulling Angel along with me. She wanted to stay, get some more scratches behind her floppy ears. "Come on," I said softly to her.

I turned to go and I heard the guy cop say under his breath something and then *"garbage"* and then the lady cop made a sound like *"awww,"* but also almost laughing too, like when a boy makes a mean joke or a racist joke and the girls around him want him to know they think it's funny but that they're too nice to make jokes like that themselves.

Awww, she'd said.

My heart was racing.

Garbage, he'd said.

I went along the perimeter of the park before, suddenly, without warning Angel, I turned and dove into the trees. The cops weren't still watching me, I didn't think, but even if they were, I didn't care. What did they even stop me for anyway? Just to put on a show for the people driving by?

I recognized my own ambivalence, my own desire to escape notice and be left alone at the same time that I was perpetually awed by the fact that no one, no one at all, seemed to care that I was technically a child, living alone, in a city park. Was I lucky or unlucky? I wasn't even sure.

I jogged a little way, Angel behind me, before I slowed to walking. We walked and walked through the woods. I needed to get my head clear.

Near one of the big trails I saw a mound of clothes. I knew it was a person and I thought of the cop's word, *"garbage."* It did look like garbage. Is that how I looked too?

I started to cut left, to give a wide berth, but the mound sat up. "Hey, mami," it called.

I was about to start running, but when I looked over I realized it was Danny, the guy who'd been hanging around with that creep with the knife.

I stayed where I was, not running away, but not coming closer either.

Danny pulled himself up and wiped a dirty hand over his face. "Just sleeping," he explained. He squeezed his eyes shut and then opened them. "You find your lady yet?"

I took a step closer, Angel at my side still.

"No."

Danny smiled, suddenly remembering something. "I heard you had a run-in with Ian," he said. "Don't worry, I ain't like him. You can come over here."

He reached out and picked up a bottle from under a towel near his feet and took a swig. I took a moment to survey his squalid camp, clothes and towels like a dirty little nest. Scattered around were beer bottles and green plastic soda bottles, cigarette butts, a broken umbrella perched like a shelter. I was repulsed and afraid. *Garbage*, I thought again.

I took one more step closer. I didn't trust Danny, but I wasn't afraid of him either. In the shady daylight I realized he looked a lot worse than when I'd first met him a few weeks before. Now he looked pale and sick. He didn't look like he'd be strong enough to try and grab me, to chase me.

"Ian. Is that that pervert you hang out with?"

"He's not that bad," Danny chuckled. Then, "Well, actually, he is. Good for you. He totally deserved it."

"He still in the park?"

"Nah. He got picked up for smoking dope and I don't think he'll be back soon. He said there was some warrant out for him in Pennsylvania, so you're safe for now. From him, at least." He took another drink from the bottle. "You don't have no cigarettes, do you?"

I shook my head, no.

"You don't learn, do you? Listen, I was thinking. You know, give me that photo. I'll show it to the people I know. And next time you see me, you better have a pack of cigarettes for me. I prefer Newports, menthols, but whatever, I'll take anything."

I considered him for a minute. I hated to part with one of my only pictures. But it seemed possible that this person might actually be able to help me, might actually be true to his word.

"Why are you helping me?" I asked, trying to sound tough.

Danny smiled. "'Cause you're sexy."

I guess my face must have turned ashen. I was about to walk away when he said, more gently, "Hey, girl, I didn't mean that. I didn't mean to scare you. I was just kidding around."

His face looked earnest, apologetic.

He held out his hand. "Gimme the photo. Don't sweat it. I'm just a nice guy is all."

I deliberated a moment and then took the picture out of my back pocket and approached him. "You sick?" I asked, as I put the photo in his hand.

He answered with a phlegmy cough and spat on the ground. "Believe me, I been worse."

I couldn't help but look at the yellow mucus in the dirt. My stomach churned and I thought I might throw up.

I turned to go. "Thanks," I choked out.

"Don't forget the Newports," he called after me.

I'd wanted to bring up Dougie, the guy the pimp had told me about, but I couldn't look at Danny for a moment longer.

Back at my campsite, I got out some baby wipes and started scrubbing my hands. It was because I just didn't want to get sick, I assured myself, as I almost frantically rubbed. Getting sick, that could be game over.

CHAPTER 12

I had been only vaguely aware of the date. But that night people all over the park were setting off fireworks like crazy—more than the sporadic fireworks that happened on the nights leading up to it—so it must have been the Fourth of July. Independence Day.

At Victory Field, a big track near Woodhaven Boulevard, I sat on a bench—with Angel cowering underneath—and watched. When I was little, I loved fireworks. Now, I felt more like Angel. They had me skittish, uneasy.

But we stayed up late anyway, waiting until some of the noise died down and the people had left. Then, like the most bold squirrels, we crept toward the overflowing trash cans and picked out what, for us, was the least offensive: a full bag of potato chips, a hot dog for Angel, and a turkey sandwich, still wrapped up but with one bite taken out of it, for me.

Then we walked back to my site, set up the tent, and climbed in. My stomach felt sick and I regretted the turkey sandwich. After a while I felt okay enough to lie down on my side on the mat in my sleeping bag, one arm out and wrapped around Angel, who was also on her side. It was warm and nice, actually. But whenever

I started to drift off, a pop or screech or rat-tat-tat would explode too close, and both Angel and I would sit up. When I put my hand on her chest, I could feel her heart racing. Mine was too.

I guess they must have stopped at some point, because I dreamed that my mother found me, came into my tent, and lay down beside me. When I reached out to her, the walls of the tent receded and she was terrifyingly, urgently, painfully, beyond my reach. I woke up with my heart still pounding and tears in my eyes.

I heard the crickets and felt Angel. Even though it wasn't a good dream, I wanted to get back to it and I kept chasing it in my mind.

I was aware of myself, of my loneliness.

But it wasn't so bad, I thought. *It wasn't as bad as being at home.*

Sure, most of the time I was hungry, and I was itchy and I was scared. But that wasn't so different from the way things were back when I lived in the apartment, except for the itchy part. Most of the time in the park I felt okay, and for real, that was a change from how I used to be. In the park, I went to sleep at night, Angel against my back or curled up in the curve of my bent legs, and I wasn't afraid anymore—I wasn't afraid of snakes or raccoons or even knife-wielding psychos. Angel wouldn't let anybody get too close to me.

And I didn't have to dread going to school and having someone make fun of me, sticking their half-eaten hamburger in my back-pack when I wasn't looking as a joke about charity or how trashy I looked or whatever it was they were trying to prove. Or snickering when I came in late to class, or when I wore the same old ratty T-shirt day after day, or when I got called on and it was as though someone had dumped cold water on my head, 'cause I never knew the answer and most of the time I was unsure of the question. And, in the park, I wasn't afraid of my stepmother getting pissed and kicking my ass 'cause I made too much noise coming in after school and woke her up or I left some of my hair in the shower drain. Or of being hungry 'cause I ran out of money and the only food in the kitchen belonged to her and she didn't want anybody else eating it. And, for once in a long time, I wasn't afraid of the front door opening, the light from the hallway falling on my face, and then my stepbrother sitting on edge of the couch. *"Wake up. Come here, I need to talk to you in my room."*

So, there were bad things in the park, but I didn't have to be afraid of any of those other things anymore.

And I was proud, too, about what I had accomplished. I had made it work, and I was getting better at it every day.

I wasn't garbage. I was just in the park temporarily ... until I found my mother.

I knew, from television, from health class, from just not being a complete moron, that it would probably have been a good idea for me to talk to someone. To tell someone about the things that had happened to me, what my stepbrother had done. But who? I didn't know how to begin. I didn't have the words. Or I did have the words, but I didn't know how to use them.

And who would I tell anyway? I was alone, for real. Just me and Angel. I was a little worried that I might be getting weirder and weirder. Too much like myself, too little like other people— to the point that I'd never be able to, like, rejoin society again.

But that wasn't even the biggest thing. The biggest thing was that I knew it couldn't last forever. That there was a clock, maybe more than one clock, and those clocks were ticking. If it took too long to find her, I would run out of time. Fourth of July. Independence Day. Had I really been in the park for over a month? There was something nibbling at the corner of my mind, but I couldn't look at it straight on yet.

And what if my stepbrother showed up after all? I kept telling myself I hadn't left a trail, that he wouldn't even think of Forest Park. But for a stupid guy, he could be pretty smart, pretty resourceful. I didn't doubt that if he wanted to, he'd hunt me down. I had to just hope that Oscar had taken care of him or that the police had, that he was either too messed up or too incarcerated to come after me. I just had to hope.

If I could stay alive, stay away from the rapists and weirdos and assholes for just a little bit longer, maybe it would all be okay.

But just when I'd reassure myself, there was that worry again, the worry I was trying not to acknowledge, like when you're on the train and some pervert is staring at you and you keep your eyes down and figure if you just ignore him maybe he'll go away, but then he takes a seat even closer, and you know he's there and in your periphery; you can see him staring at you. You know not looking doesn't make him go away, maybe even makes it worse. You know this, but still.

Maybe if I found my mother she could help. I just had to focus on finding her and then I could worry about the other stuff.

The next day, early, me and Angel were sitting in a little clearing, listening to classic rock on a handheld transistor radio I'd found and bought new batteries for. The trees around us were lush and green, the park alive with birds singing and the breeze in the leaves and the insects humming.

I didn't know the song that was playing and I'd thought to myself that I had to remember to pay attention, to hear who it was, when there was a break between songs. I'm always meaning to do that and I always miss it, my attention wanders, and I never find out who was singing.

So, the singer was singing and I was waiting. I slapped a mosquito on my forearm; I mused whether the smeared blood was my own or its last victim's. Then all of a sudden, this guy came up to us, through the woods. It wasn't so strange to see a person—we were hanging near one of the hiking trails and people walked or jogged by occasionally—but this guy was walking directly toward us. It was almost like he knew us or was looking for us. But we didn't know him.

I picked up the radio, called Angel to my side.

"Hey," he said, smiling.

I stood up and sort of smiled back, for some stupid reason. I hadn't gotten politeness out of my system yet, I guess.

"What kind of dog is that?" he asked. He was a white guy, blondish hair. He was wearing a wifebeater and his arms were muscular and covered with ugly, smeared tats.

"Mutt," I said to the ground.

"Cool." He took another step closer. "Stupid tail, though."

I didn't say anything.

"Cut that tail off," he said, to no one in particular.

"What?"

"Yeah, gimme your dog," he said, now holding out his hand, like I was gonna give him the leash or something.

"What?"

"I said I want that dog." I looked away, but he didn't. He took another step toward us.

"Leave us alone." I started to back away. I could feel my pulse pounding in my head, the way it did when I bashed the beans at that guy's head. Angel was standing next to me, kinda crouched. She knew something was wrong too; she let out a low growl.

"Come here, doggie," he said.

"My dog will bite you if you touch her," I warned.

"I'll have to beat that out of her," he said, taking long, fast strides toward us, reaching one hand toward Angel's neck.

She didn't bite him, but instead feinted slightly and then dodged. He made to kick her and she dodged again, just avoiding his foot, and he lost his balance. It was almost comical, the way he swiveled and fell right down on his backside.

"Angel!" I shouted and took off running, only looking behind me to make sure she was coming too. She was. She was doing laps around me. We just ran and ran, blindly, 'til we got to a big, populated trail. I knew it was a risk to be on the main path, that we might run into the guy again, but I figured he might not try anything with other people around.

Later, after I met Corinne, I told her that story and she said, "Ohjesuschrist it was him."

"Who?"

"What'd he look like?"

"The guy who tried to take Angel?"

"Yeah, yeah, what did he look like?" she asked again, waving her hand impatiently.

"I dunno. White guy, blond hair. Kinda built. Ugly tats."

"It *was* him."

"Who? Not ...?"

"Yeah. Looking for me, I bet. Great. So, he knows I'm in the park."

"We don't know for sure it was him."

"Yes, we do. Why would he want Angel? But that's just exactly something he would do, though. And then brag about it later. Stealing some kid's dog."

"Bad dude," I said.

"You got that right."

CHAPTER 13

Corinne.

It was July 6th that I met her. It was drizzly and gray and Angel and I had taken shelter under one of the unused railroad bridges.

We had just arrived at the bridge and I figured maybe I'd pick up a bit, seeing as we might be spending some time there. That's what I did sometimes, trying to do my part to keep the park clean and all. I'd found some great stuff that way too, like a ring with a pearl on it and a pocketbook, which was probably ripped off and then dumped—there was no cash, but it had a comb and a lipstick and a roll of mints. I liked having those things for some reason, so I kept them stowed. I found a plastic lawn chair that I kept covered with branches in one of my spots and took out only now and then, a dog collar I used for Angel, and the cord that served as her leash.

I had also found more than one gun, which was pretty nuts. The first one scared me. I was walking along, looking at the ground and the sun glinted off something under a bush, catching my eye. I stopped and bent down to investigate. At first I thought it was a toy pistol but its weight in my hand told me otherwise. I got nervous and put it right back down again. I just kept moving, thinking someone was watching me or would come back for it and would track me down. Later, I thought maybe I should have put it on the main path because it might have been used in a crime and the cops should have it. But then I was afraid some kid would come across it and get hurt. Or that if I moved it, I'd leave fingerprints, implicating myself in a murder or something.

The second gun I found, well, that one scared me too, but it was after that thing with the creep and the knife, so I took it and buried it in a special spot, because by then I was thinking that you never know when you might need a gun. I wasn't about to tote it around with me—way too risky if I got picked up by the cops or if someone harassed me and got it away from me. But I figured it was better for me to know where it was than to just leave it lying around.

So, that was just my way: I would poke around, pick up, check things out. That day, under the bridge, I was collecting beer bottles, thinking about getting the deposit for them later, feeling all authentically homeless, when I saw a red backpack sitting on top of a pile of leaves just beyond the bridge. It was left unzipped, so it kind of gaped at me. I imagined that was what Alice must've felt like when the cake said "Eat Me."

"Hmmm," I said aloud. Angel, of course, bounded over, happy and curious, and stuck her nose in the bag.

I walked over and gave her a gentle shove with my knee and peeked inside. In a glance, I could tell it was a get-gone bag, run-away-in-a-hurry stuff: a bottle of Coke and what looked like some clothes—underpants, socks, a T-shirt. Wrapped in the T-shirt was a big, serious-looking kitchen knife. I crouched down and unzipped the front pocket. There was a toothbrush and toothpaste, a bottle of Advil, and two other label-less prescription drug bottles, a tube of some cosmetic cream, a pack of cigarettes and a lighter, and, in an even smaller inner pocket, some smashed bills.

Whoever'd left it hadn't gone far.

I stood up and looked around, but I didn't see anybody. I totally wanted to take it. My first thought was, like, *what a great find.* But I didn't really need any of that stuff, except for maybe the money, and there was a part of me that would feel like crap for ripping off somebody who might actually need it.

"What are you, the Parks Department?"

I spun, startled. Angel, who had lost interest as soon as she determined there was nothing edible in the bag, had been off sniffing around under the bridge. She looked up and barked once sharply. But she wasn't afraid. She came leaping over to my side and barked again, but the hair on her spine didn't shoot up, and she didn't growl.

"Sorry. Didn't mean to scare you." It was a girl, tall and skinny, and a little older than me. She was still about twenty feet away and had her eyebrows up, as if to ask if it would be okay to come closer. "You made a good choice, there," she said. "I didn't want to have to kick your ass."

I just stared at her.

She approached and Angel went tentatively toward her and they met around halfway. The girl was good with dogs: she bent down and let Angel sniff the back of her hand.

"Hey, doggie ..." She slowly reached to pet Angel on the side of her neck. "Hey, doggie," she said again.

She was a white girl, super pale. One side of her face was covered by her dirty blond hair, which was in what looked like braids but were now becoming dreads. I generally hate white girls who have dreadlocks. But I felt myself leaning toward her. I was drawn to her. Her hair seemed to suit her somehow. And she knew how to act around a dog.

I also noticed, right away, that she looked freshly beaten up. She had a black eye and a bruised and swollen cheek. One side of her face was so swollen, in fact, that it didn't look real, all pink and blue and shiny. It looked like movie makeup or something. And there was another bruise peeking out from under the big scarf she was wearing. The scarf itself was a little strange for the weather, but then she was dressed dramatically: short shorts and a tiny tank, platform sneakers and the big scarf.

"Great dog," she said, looking up at me.

I nodded and walked over to them.

"I'm Corinne."

I smiled at her.

"So ...?" she asked, looking at me, kind of laughing. "Do you talk or ...?"

"Oh," I croaked. "Sorry. I'm ... Brenda." I tried to smile again. My voice sounded strange to me.

"Relax," Corinne said, standing up. "I'm not, like, a narc or anything. You live over here?"

I shook my head no. "I move around." I didn't get out much more than a whisper.

"What?"

"I move around," I said, a little more loudly.

"Oh. Me too." She nodded to where her backpack sat on the pile of leaves. "That's my stuff."

"I know." I added quickly, "I wasn't gonna take it."

"I know." She shrugged. "I was watching you. I heard you coming and hid. I was cursing myself for not grabbing the bag. But why wouldn't you just take it?"

I thought for a minute. "What do I need someone else's underpants for?"

"Ha," she said. "You never know. Sell them?"

I made a face.

"Sometimes you gotta hustle in this world, sister."

That made me laugh a little. "I guess."

"For real, though," she said. Her voice was low and gravelly. She had a way of talking that made everything funny, or almost funny. Like if she wasn't completely joking, she was almost joking. "There must be something wrong with you. Why didn't you just take it and look inside later?"

"I don't need to steal from anybody." I was maybe a little too emphatic. I wondered for a moment if I had forgotten how to act around other people. Everything I said was coming out too soft or too loud, too fierce or too timid. I was out of practice.

"Okay, there, calm it down. Just asking."

"I just meant, you know, I'm doing okay is all."

"Oh yeah?" She snorted. "Then you're doing better than I am."

Despite the bruises, she was really pretty. Beautiful, even. Thinking back, I know that one of the things that made Corinne so attractive was that she always seemed like someone who was exactly in the right place, wherever she was. She was always where she belonged. The way she dressed, the way she moved, the way she talked. She seemed completely at ease.

"What happened to you?" I ventured.

Before answering, she reached into her back pocket and

took out a crumpled pack of cigarettes, gingerly sliding one out. Then she took a few steps over to her backpack and picked out the lighter, dropping it back into the bag's gaping mouth after she lit the cigarette.

She inhaled and looked me in the face. "Got my ass kicked. Got my ass kicked and took off." She winced as she blew smoke out of the side of her mouth.

"Why? In the park? Who kicked your ass?"

She shook her head and smiled. "No, not in the park. At home." She exhaled and added dryly, "He just really loves me."

"Ouch." I looked at the ground.

"Ouch is right." She smirked. "What's your excuse?"

"Me?" I looked up and grinned back. "Nobody loves me. So, I'm doing okay."

"You look a little worn out, if you ask me."

"You shoulda seen me before." She smiled at that. Her teeth were big and dazzling.

I smiled back, but with my mouth closed. The girl seemed okay. Actually, to be honest, I was more comfortable than I'd been in a long time. Like, my time in the park had left me feeling, I don't know, maybe less scared in general. Or maybe it was just that I hadn't had a real conversation since the last time I saw Lizette. Maybe I missed people more than I realized. Whatever it was, I found myself laughing with this funny girl with her dumb hair and talking more than I had in a long time.

I slid down to sit with my back against the base of the bridge. Angel trotted over and nudged me, looking for some scratches. I let her knock my elbow up so that she could sit with my arm around her, scratching her chest.

Corinne came over and sat with us. She smoked with one

hand, used the other to pick up leaves, crumple them and flick them away.

"So, you're into the Ramones?" She nodded at my T-shirt.

I nodded to confirm this. "Do you like them too?"

"I don't think I ever heard them."

I wanted to say, "Of course you have," and to sing to her, "*Rock-rock Rockaway Beach ...*" or "*I wanna be sedated ...*" but I didn't.

"So ...?" she drawled. "Like, what are you? New wave or gutter punk or what?"

I shrugged, but she waited for me to answer. "I guess I'm a skater?"

"No way." She looked pleasantly surprised. "That's cool. Can you actually skate or do you just like the fashion?"

It was my turn to make a face. "Of course I can. My board is just stowed right now."

"Yeah, I guess it would be hard to skate around here," Corinne said, surveying the muddy paths.

I nodded.

"So, what, you're like, urban camping?"

I smiled. I liked that one. I nodded.

"So, you're an urban-camping, skater-slash-gutter-punk, like, anarchist-type?"

"What's a gutter punk?"

"Oh, you know. A tourist. Homeless for the weekend, then back to dad's split-level in Jersey. In it for the story, that kind of thing."

"Huh. I don't think I know any of those."

"Sure you do. Shoot—" Corinne took a drag on the cigarette. "I'm not so far off that myself. Want a cigarette?"

"No thanks. You know, those things are really bad for you."

She made a face of mock horror. "Really? I'd been doing this for my health." She flicked some ash, got back to business. "So, why'd you run away?"

I shrugged.

"That bad?" she asked, watching me.

I looked at her.

"What—a stepfather?"

A chill ran down my spine. Who was this girl, who seemed to know so much so fast?

"Brother," I said, quietly, looking at my hands, one on each knee. "A stepbrother."

"Yikes."

I didn't say anything.

"Yeah." Corinne sighed, took a deep drag of her cigarette. "Yeah." We sat there for a minute. Then I leaned down and kissed Angel on the snout, started nuzzling her and petting her. "I've got a mom," Corinne said after a while. "She's cool. I can go back to her. And I will. But not yet. *He* knows where she lives. He'd find me there."

"Where's your mom live?"

"Jersey. Split-level. Ha. But it's not really like that. She's got money, she's got boyfriends, she's got cars, she's got problems. You know? *Problems.*" She rolled her eyes. "But I could call her, I guess. She might come pick me up." She dragged on the little stub of cigarette. "She'd be pissed, though. There's a whole lot of ... you know ..." She made a little propeller motion with her hand in the air. "She doesn't ... *approve.*" She looked off, into the distance, as though imagining the reunion and then her shoulders visibly dropped and she sighed and said, quietly, "Fuck."

I sat and waited.

"It's nothing," she sighed again, looking a little hopeless and a lot tired.

"How long you been in the park?"

"Since Saturday night. Or really early in the morning Sunday. So, just since yesterday," she added, when it was clear I had no idea what day of the week it was. "How about you?"

I smiled to myself. "A long time."

She widened her eyes. That seemed to confirm it for her: I was, clearly, insane. "What? Like since 1989 or something?"

"No, no, just, a month or so. Since May thirty-first."

"So, what've you been doing for money since May?"

"I brought a lot of gear with me," I explained. Corinne lit a third cigarette; she was lighting each off the one that came before, like it was somehow important to keep each ember alive, like getting through that pack was a chore she had to complete before we could move on. "And I do a little begging when I need to."

"Bet the dog helps out a lot."

"I guess. I don't know."

"For real, though. People will give you more money if you have a cute dog. Although that dog," she scrunched up her face and pointed the cigarette at Angel, who was snoozing at my side, breathing heavily but with one eye open, "isn't exactly what I'd call cute. No offense or anything. I mean, she's ... appealing somehow. And she's tough looking. That tail, though." Corinne grimaced.

"I think she's cute." I patted Angel's side. "I think you're cute," I reassured her.

"Well, she is your dog," Corinne said. "Face only a mother could love and all that. You bring her with you?"

"No. We sorta found each other in the park." I patted her

even more vigorously, which she took to be a sign that it was time to play. She stood up, licked my face, put her paw on my thigh.

"That's cool." For the second time, I saw her drift away, her face almost going slack as she thought about something, somewhere, else. "I have a dog too."

"Oh yeah?" I pushed Angel's paw off my leg and pushed on her butt to get her to sit. "Relax," I told her. She sat, put her paw back on my thigh, stood up again. I surrendered and she maneuvered her way in so that she was standing with her front legs inside my crossed legs, breathing right in my face. "Ugh," I complained, but I put an arm around her.

"I left him behind, though. I guess I shoulda taken him with me. Then we could both have dogs." She gave Angel a half-hearted pat. "I'm kinda worried about him. The dog, I mean. Prince. He's named after the singer. You know?"

I did, vaguely, so I nodded. "What are you worried about?"

"My boyfriend. Ex-boyfriend. He's the kind of jerk who, you know, would take it out on the dog. You know, to get to me? He's *that* kind of bad news."

"That sucks," I said a little lamely, a pit in my stomach. I did know that kind of bad news; she didn't have to tell me.

"Yeah. Or ... I don't know. That's the worst-case scenario. I guess best-case scenario is that he just neglects him. And that's no good either."

"Can you go back and get him?"

She snorted. "I don't know. No." She waved a hand over her face, as if to say, *do you have eyes?* She let out a sigh. "I mean," she said, dragging on the cigarette and then looking up and blowing the smoke into the sky. "You see, if I go back there, one of two things are gonna happen."

I waited.

"He'd kill me. Like, literally murder me. Or," she continued to look up and away, brought the cigarette to her lips, inhaled and then blew three smoke rings, slowly, casually, before continuing, "or, he'd be really sorry and we'd get back together. And then he might change. For real, really change. Maybe we could work things out and all that. And then maybe things would be better for a couple of weeks or months or whatever. And *then* he'd kill me." She finally brought her eyes back down. They were filled with tears, but she didn't cry. I had never met someone who was so honest, just like that, right out the gate. I wasn't even sure how to respond.

"I guess you can't go back there then," I said finally.

"I guess not."

She rubbed her hand over her face and eyes, crying "argh!" and laughing. "Drama, drama, drama! I'm okay. For real, I'm okay. Whatever, you know." She forced a laugh. "But listen girl—Brenda—if that's your real name," and she laughed again, a throaty chuckle and I wondered how she knew it wasn't, "you don't have anything to eat, do you? Because I am star-ar-arving. Since you're like, a veteran homeless person and all. You got anything? Anything at all?"

"Not here. All I have on me is water. But come with me. I have food stashed. And you stay with me tonight, in my tent," I added, impulsively. "It's small, but you can stay with me."

"Really?" Corinne abandoned any attempt at remaining cool, her eyes lit with excitement—and maybe hunger. "Camping out in Forest Park!" she declared. "What a crazy world. I am so lucky I ran into you, aren't I?" She ground out the cigarette and flicked it off, away into the bushes.

Standing up, brushing the damp leaves from my butt, I wondered if I had made a mistake. What was I doing, bringing this girl back to my camp? She might rip me off or who knows, she might be a crazy park serial killer.

But, to be honest, I think those weeks alone taught me just how hard it is to be person-less. Don't get me wrong, Angel was the best. She was good company, for real. But it's different when someone talks back.

And I knew something that day, talking to Corinne. I knew that even though I thought I could do it alone, I needed somebody else. I knew I needed her.

CHAPTER 14

The rain had stopped while Corinne and I were talking and we headed over to my camp. Hiking through the woods, she told me stories: about Prince and how she bought him at a pet store even though you're not supposed to do that, but how it was just so sad and pathetic she couldn't leave him there, and about Henry, her ex-boyfriend and how it was love at first sight but now he was deadly, "literally deadly, girl," she said, and about her mother, who sometimes "got religion" and started speaking in tongues, which Corinne loudly imitated, her voice ricocheting through the woods. I nodded and laughed at the right times, marveling all the while at this girl's ease, at how easy she made talking seem, at how easy she made it to be with her.

When we got to my spot, we sat on a log while she scarfed down a can of cold lentil soup. When she finished she was suddenly quiet and looked at me expectantly, like it was my turn to tell her something. I knew that this was how it worked with friends, especially girlfriends. I thought: *What can I tell her?*

There was something—something I was ashamed of, but which I knew I should probably get out in the open.

"Um," I began.

She waited, her face serious and alert.

"So, like, at night I sometimes chew my thumb?"

She paused. "Do you mean you suck your thumb?" she asked, not able to restrain her smirk.

"I mean, it's just the edge ..." I began, my face getting hot.

"Whatever," she laughed. "That's cute."

I shut my eyes. Why couldn't I be a normal person?

"Honestly, I really don't care. So, tell me," she said, mercifully changing the subject, "anybody give you a hard time out here all on your own?"

I told her about the time the guy with the knife tried to grab me and how I threw the beans at him and all that. When I was done, she looked at me like I was crazy and then she started laughing. "Well, check out skinny little you! I bet *he* was surprised! How sneaky with the pepper spray. Saint Sneak, that's what I'll call you. Patron saint of the gutter punks."

I laughed.

"I wish I had been there!" She jumped up and bent both arms, like bodybuilders do when they want to show off their muscles. "We woulda showed that guy. Me and Saint Sneak," she kissed each bicep in turn, "we'd be like superheroes."

"Well," I said, feeling good, feeling, I don't know, like I could be funny too. "You know, not to brag or anything, but I kinda did. Show him. You know, by myself."

"Oh yeah?" she laughed, sitting back down. "Is that right?" she said, all sass, to Angel. The dog, loving the attention, danced around her and then lunged forward to lick Corinne's face.

"Ouch," Corinne winced, and protected her face with her

forearm. "And, gross, dog!" she complained, pushing Angel off her, but Angel kept jumping back, wanting to play more.

"I'm sorry." I got up and grabbed Angel around the neck.

"It's okay," Corinne said, wiping at her face and fixing her scarf. "Just, you know, still a little sore is all."

I hugged Angel into submission, whispering a scolding into her ear. She kept twisting around to lick me.

"Anybody else give you problems?" Corinne asked.

I shrugged, releasing a calmed-down Angel to sniff around Corinne in a more civilized manner. Corinne put out a hand to tickle Angel's ear and I knew all was forgiven.

"There's a couple other homeless. They sleep on the benches around the perimeter mostly, though. They don't bother me. But if I leave stuff out or like, not hidden, even for a minute, it's usually gone when I turn around."

"So, then, like, what's the long-term plan? What are you gonna do?"

"What do you mean?"

"I *mean*, dummy," she said, shaking her head, rising to dig out her cigarettes, "so, you get assaulted by like, a rapist child molester monster or something. And then you're like, okay, that's cool. Night-night?"

"Well, I was pretty scared."

"Exactly."

"But where am I supposed to go?"

"Uh, I don't know. How about anywhere besides Forest Park?"

I kind of laughed. She was right, of course. "I don't know. I can't go home. And I've got Angel now, so you know, I can't go to a shelter or anything."

"Okaaaay," she drawled the word out, rolling her eyes.

I wasn't ready to tell her the rest, to tell her about my mother, to tell her I couldn't leave until I found her or until I knew for sure she wasn't in the park anymore. I knew it would sound too crazy. "Where else is there?"

Corinne was serious. "I don't know. I really don't." She picked a leaf and stripped it down with her fingers, the shreds falling. "It might be better to like, live in the subway. Or, really, I mean, home can't be all *that* bad, can it?"

"I think I like the monsters here better than the ones at home."

She smirked. "I hear you."

"Come on," I changed the subject. "We've got to set up camp." I crawled a few feet to a spot I had marked with a rock and then I brushed away the leaves to reveal the tarp that covered my gear.

"What's that?"

"A tent and sleeping stuff." I pulled back the tarp. "And some more food." I handed the tent to her. "Go ahead and unpack that." She put her cigarette out against the tree carefully and stuck the unsmoked half, unlit now, deeply into her hair.

"All the comforts of home," she said, wonderingly.

"It's not much. But it's not too bad, either."

She slid the tent out and stood there waiting for me to start the assembly.

I spread the tent out on the ground and started expertly popping the poles together.

"So, Brenda, I have something I think I have to tell you ..." My stomach dropped a little, like, the way she said it, whatever it was, it wasn't gonna be good news. I looked at her.

"If it's not cool with you, that's fine." Corinne fished the cigarette out of her hair. "I can just, you know, move along." She was pretending to be casual, but I could tell by the pitch of her voice that she was nervous.

I waited.

She tugged at her earlobe, lit the cigarette carefully because it was so short. "So, I guess, you know, you've been real nice to me and all so I want to tell you something. It doesn't matter, really, but ..." She exhaled and looked off into the trees. "It's just that I am not, like, one hundred percent biologically, a girl. I mean, I am a girl, but, you know?"

It took me a minute to understand what she was saying. Then I looked at her again—I couldn't help myself—in a new way, noticing her skinniness, her small chest, her big hands.

"Okay," I said uncertainly.

"Okay? So, that's okay with you?"

"Okay," I shrugged. I felt like staring, but I knew that would be rude, so I continued sliding the poles in, making the tent take shape.

I won't lie. It was weird to me. I never knew anyone like that before. There were people like that on Roosevelt Avenue, under the overhead train tracks, but you only saw them very early in the morning or very late at night. They were prostitutes and they made me a little nervous, the way they slunk around and then smirked at you if they caught you staring. And I felt a little scared for them, too, perched on perilous heels, getting into cars with strangers.

But I wasn't like, disgusted or anything. It was just strange. And with Corinne, I suppose the fact that we had talked, that I already liked her, made a difference. Maybe otherwise I would have judged or been uptight about it.

"Um, do you, like, have any questions?" Corinne's voice was

mocking, teacherly, but I could tell she was also sincere.

I shook my head. "I don't know. I guess it's not that big a deal. It's none of my business, really. So, whatever." I shrugged. "You seem cool to me."

"All right then!" Corinne laughed and came over, put an arm around me. "You, my friend, are pretty cool too. The cool and quiet type."

I smiled.

"I guess I do have a question."

"Gimme." She released me, but kept a hand on my shoulder, looking me in the face.

"Your boyfriend."

"Ex-boyfriend."

"Is he ...?"

"He is biologically male. Hetero. Straight as the day is long." I looked at her.

"It's complicated," she said, patting my shoulder. "But not very." I nodded.

"Now, I've told you a secret. So, it's your turn."

Secrets. Sure, I had some. They were buried so deep, though, I didn't know if I'd even be able to find them anymore myself.

Corinne dropped her chin. "What's your real name anyway?"

I laughed, relieved. "How do you know Brenda's not my real name?" I turned to unzip the tent and knelt down to unroll the mat and put it in the sleeping bag.

"It's the way you say it. Like you got marbles in your mouth. 'Hi, I'm ... Brenda!'" she mimicked, completely absurdly. "Like even *you* don't believe it's your name."

I smiled. Kept at my business organizing the tent and didn't say anything for a minute. There was only so much organizing to do. I crawled back out. "My real name is Iffy," I said finally.

"Iffy? What? What kind of name is that?"

"Iphigenia. Iphigenia Murphy."

"Well," huffed Corinne. "I think I might have just gone with Murph, myself." She paused and let out a quick laugh. "That is some name."

"It's Greek." In my head, I heard the explanation: *My mom did a year of college. She read it in a play and she thought, "that's what I'm gonna name my daughter." Of course, the character gets killed in a sacrifice. So, that's not very cool. But when she told my father that's what she wanted to name me, he thought it was pretty. Didn't know about the sacrificing part. Probably still doesn't.* But I didn't say all that. Instead, I said, "My mom's idea. Maybe not her best one?"

Corinne laughed. "Our moms should get together sometime. Mine named me Corey T. Wales."

"What's the T for?"

"That's just it: nothing. My mom just thought it would look nice. Like, distinguished."

"That's so funny."

"She's a funny lady," Corinne said dryly.

"My mom left when I was eight," I blurted out.

Corinne looked surprised, probably by my delivery. "That sucks."

I shook my head in assent. Silently I filled a bowl with water for Angel.

"Where'd she go?"

I almost laughed. "I'm not sure."

"Wow. You ever think about trying to find her?"

"All the time."

CHAPTER 15

The days passed quickly with Corinne. We hung out, Corinne talking endlessly and me contributing only when I had to. We walked around the park, looked at the turtles in the pond, listened to the radio. We made tiny fires to heat up lentils and guarded each other when we took showers at the sprinklers. At night, when I woke up gasping, she'd pat my arm, tell me it was all right, go back to sleep.

Money started to get tight. We had to get more gear, more food, more cigarettes for Corinne. I still had a little cash and so did she, but I started panhandling more and, since Corinne was around to take care of Angel, I also started leaving the park more. I would go to the Kmart or a pizza place or the public library to "take a bath" in the sink, brush my teeth, pick up supplies. It was weird to be in the world again, to feel at once so conspicuous and so irrelevant. I didn't like it.

But Corinne was pretty nervous about being seen by someone she knew. Her ex-boyfriend's place was right off the park, which is how she wound up at the bridge that day in the first place. She had waited until he fell asleep, drunk, and then sneaked out and ran into the park, into the trees, as fast as she could. She said she hadn't thought much beyond getting out of the apartment and away from him.

And I had run into Henry, the ex, the day before Corinne and I met—that was when he tried to take Angel away from me. We didn't know each other, of course, but the meeting seemed ominous, a close call. It meant he was or had been in the park, and it also meant that he was looking for Corinne.

But then about a week into what Corinne called our "cohabitation," she started making noises about going back.

She'd been talking about Prince a lot, like whenever Angel did something sweet or cute or even naughty, she would say, "What a good doggie! You're just like my Prince," and then she'd launch into a story about when Prince ate a whole bag of Hershey's kisses, or the time he jumped out the car window when they were stuck in traffic on the LIE. "And then, the little so-and-so, jumps *in* the window of the car behind us! The poor driver almost had a heart attack!" The car one was funny, but in general, I'd say, other people's dog stories aren't all that interesting. I'd listen, maybe with half an ear, and smile or laugh at the right times.

But so, after she'd tell her story she'd get sad, wondering if Prince was okay, chewing her lip and saying we ought to go back and get him. I usually didn't say anything. Just sat there, waiting. She'd conclude regretfully that it wasn't a good idea, but maybe soon ... and then we'd get on to something else. But one morning, as we ate our granola bars, she announced with a new determination, "Iffy, we have to go get Prince."

I looked at her, cocked my head. Waited to hear more.

"We can't leave him there with Henry." She looked at my

face and added, "You don't get it, Iffy. Could you just leave Angel with some jerk? He's probably totally neglected. Pooping in the house and all that stuff."

I grimaced.

"Or worse. God knows what's going on there. My poor Princie," she continued, a little whine in her voice making her sound just a bit like a lonely dog herself. "He might be hurt. And if he's hurt … he's probably wondering where I am, why I haven't come back for him."

It got to me. She could see it getting to me. That's the thing about animals: you can't explain things to them like you can to a human. If you could just tell them, "Don't worry, I'll be back in a little bit, I still love you," it would be that much easier. But you can't.

I looked at Corinne again, but softened my stare. "I had a kitten once."

I watched Corinne as what I was saying registered.

"Oh." She put an arm on my shoulder. "Never got to be a cat?"

"Yeah." That's how it was with Corinne. I didn't have to spell it out; she just got it. I *had* a kitten *once*.

"So, you hear me." She went into planning mode. "We'll go to the apartment when Henry's at work. He works nights at the restaurant. We'll go to the apartment and see if there are any lights on. If there aren't, I'll just run in, grab a couple of things—I've got to get my medicine and I might be able to dig up some more cash—and we'll snatch Prince and we'll get right out of there."

"Okay, Corinne. We'll go get him. But you do know this is totally nuts?"

"It will be fine."

"What about Angel?"

"She can come with." She patted Angel's rump. Angel looked from Corinne to me and back again, like, telling us she was in, she was excited about the mission. "She and Princie are gonna love each other," Corinne kind of squealed. "It'll be good for her too, Iffy. Angel needs more dog companionship. Don't you, girl?"

Angel barked once, making us laugh.

"Yes. All right." I had my reservations; I straight-up knew it wasn't a good idea.

I shuddered, images of a kitten I'd called Oreo swimming in front of my eyes. I saw his quick little tongue lapping up milk and felt his tight tummy against my hand.

I heard the sound Oreo made when my stepbrother threw him against a wall.

I squeezed my eyes shut tight and when I opened them I saw Corinne frowning. "Let me tell you about the time Prince ate my wallet," she began. She launched into a disgusting and improbable story and I forced myself to listen, happy to have Corinne's voice to carry me away and calm me down.

That night around ten o'clock we set out.

I retrieved my skateboard, excited to get on it. Outside the park, going down the sidewalks, I'd alternate between riding along real slow next to Corinne and then going on ahead and circling back. It was good to ride. It was extra good to have Angel trotting next to me. I hadn't been sure if she'd be cool about it or if she'd be too skittish to walk alongside the board, but she seemed to like it, jogging right there with me and looking up with that big, goofy smile.

It wasn't much of a trip though, because, as Corinne had said, the apartment was only a little ways from the park. When we got to the corner, Corinne told me the address. "It's the second-floor apartment. You can tell from the street if there are any lights on."

I handed her Angel's leash and the two of them waited under the awning of the corner store. The subway rumbled overhead.

I skated down. The block was lined with attached houses, all the same style, painted different colors, all fading to the same ghostly pastel. The apartment was in a three-story house, a yellowish building with a peeling red fire escape on the front. Five steps up to the glass front door, seven doorbells. Second floor, all dark. I skated back to Corinne and nodded. I put the board under my arm and we approached the front door.

I was more nervous than I thought I'd be. There's something about going into someone else's home when they're not there; it's almost like when you're a kid, playing hide-and-seek, the way it's inevitable, even in the best hiding spot, that you'll be found, that you'll be made it eventually. But this wasn't a game. This was for real and, from what Corinne had told me, Henry was not a guy we wanted to be messing with.

I must've looked pretty freaked out, because Corinne looked at me and frowned. "It's my place too, Iffy. Don't look so guilty."

Then, as Corinne placed a foot on the first step, the door flung open and a woman emerged. We both jumped and Angel, who must've sensed our alarm, barked once at the woman, who glared and hurried off.

Corinne exhaled loudly and murmured a sarcastic, "Hello, neighbor," and continued up the stairs. She handed me Angel's leash, unlocked the front door, and swung it open, holding it until Angel and I had passed through. We waited in the vestibule as she opened the next set of doors. "We'll be fast. Stop looking so worried!"

Even though it was an apartment building and it wouldn't be suspicious to make normal noise, I still tread extra quietly and carefully as we jogged up the stairs. *This is a bad idea,* I thought to myself. *What am I doing here? If anything, Corinne should've come alone. If we get busted, it will be all over for me. They'll send me to jail. Or to foster care. Or home.* I almost turned around and walked right back out, but then Corinne had the apartment door open and she was gesturing me inside.

As I came in behind her, she flicked on the light and groaned. "He woulda barked, if he was here. He's not here, Iffy."

I looked around, Angel sniffing the air, the carpet, the sofa arm.

It felt strange, as though I had walked in and got a glimpse of someone naked, like I was seeing something I wasn't meant to see. The air was warm and stale, the inside of a closed car in the summertime, and the living room was a mess: pizza boxes and beer cans, overflowing ashtrays and clothes and boots and shoes. Henry clearly undressed as soon as he came in the house, threw whatever he was wearing right there on the floor in the entryway. You could probably excavate the layers to see what he had worn each day that week.

There were some nice things, too. My eyes kept returning to a framed print that said "MOMA" down one side. It was a picture of a woman's brown face and she had the most wonderful unibrow I had ever seen and a little bit of a mustache too. It was hard to take my eyes off the picture, but I had a look around. There were bold-patterned curtains, a worn, vintage-y couch with what looked like velvet cushions and one of those round seventies chairs. The chair faced the television, which sat on a low table and was hooked up to a game system. The cords were strewn everywhere, like intestines spilled on the floor.

Corinne closed the door behind me and walked into another room. Me and Angel just stood there. My heart thumped in my chest. A fan spun slowly overhead, doing little to cool the hot, closed apartment.

I noticed another framed picture, hung high up on the wall: a black-and-white picture of Corinne and Henry, smiling broadly. Corinne didn't have the braids; her hair was long and blond, and she looked beautiful.

"Don't be totally horrified—it's not usually this messy," Corinne called from the other room. "He's just a total slob." She returned with a full duffel bag. "Lemme just check something else before we go," she mumbled and disappeared into the kitchen, where I heard her opening and slamming drawers. "Let's go." She stepped back into the living room, scanning the floor, like she was trying to see if there was anything else she should take.

We caught each other's eyes and her face relaxed and she laughed. "Oh my god, you should see yourself. You look like you're going to have a heart attack."

"I might," I said tightly.

"You want to take a shower or anything while we're here?"

"Please, Corinne, can we just go?"

She slung the bag onto her shoulder. "I think I should like, take a poop on the bed or something first."

I started toward the door and opened it.

"I'm just kidding," she said, following me. "I bought those sheets anyway."

I practically ran down the stairs, shoving open the doors and pulling Angel out after me. I was sweating, my shirt soaked through, and my head was pounding as we stepped from the hot building into the cool night air.

But before we reached the bottom of the steps, behind me, Corinne cursed under her breath.

"What is it?" I looked up, and there he was, just up the street. He strode quickly, too quickly, toward us.

"What the fuck is this?" he yelled.

We stood there, frozen on the steps. "Should we run?" I said, but Corinne was panic-stricken. She clutched the duffel.

But there was no time to run—suddenly he was there, screaming and pointing in her face while she kept repeating weakly, "I just needed some of my stuff," her voice shaking. He backed Corinne into the step behind her and she almost fell down. He kept pointing his finger in her face and calling her all sorts of names. I stood, breathing out of my mouth, my eyes unfocused, my feet stuck.

"And who the fuck are you?" Henry turned his rage at me.

"Leave her alone!" Corinne's voice was a little stronger this time. "Listen, I just needed a few of my things. I didn't touch anything of yours."

"You better not have—"

"But where's Prince?" she put in, her voice high and pleading. "I want Prince back."

"Get in the apartment," Henry ordered.

"No!" Corinne tried to go past him and he kept stepping in front of her, blocking her from leaving.

"Get in the fucking apartment," he yelled into her face, the way drill sergeants do in movies about marines.

People walking down the street were crossing to the other side to avoid us. Someone yelled a profanity out the window.

Henry grabbed Corinne's arm. "*Get inside,*" he hissed.

She looked at me and then Henry did too.

"Don't I know you?" He looked back at Corinne. "Who is she?"

"Nobody," Corinne said. "Please, let me go. We're just gonna go." She was crying.

She turned away from him and he grabbed her by her hair.

I knew what this was. Just like when the creep tried to bother me at the campfire, I could imagine what was coming, what would happen next. He would drag her into the apartment. And then. And then. And then.

"Help," I screamed. "Somebody call the police!"

"You shut up, you stay out of this," Henry screamed at me. He hit me, hard, a backhand across the face. I dropped my board and fell to the ground. I was on my hands and knees, Angel's leash under my left palm. She was crouched near the gutter, straining to get away, but also turning back to growl and snap at Henry.

I looked up. My skateboard was upside down, a few inches from my right hand. I left Angel's leash, picked up the board and sprang into the air, using both hands to whale him with the board, wheels right in the crotch.

The board flew from my hands, skittering down the street. I bent down and grabbed Angel's leash and ran.

I didn't look at him, I didn't see his face or see whether or not he let go of Corinne, I just took off and Angel did too.

After a moment I was aware that Corinne was behind me and we ran, crossing streets wildly. After a block or two I looked back and I didn't see him, but still, we kept running. Crossing one tricky intersection, I grabbed for Corinne's free hand and we ran like that, me now holding Angel's leash in one hand and Corinne with the other, until we were back in the park. Once we were in the woods, we slowed down, walking more carefully, watching for rocks and downed branches. My chest heaved, my lungs burned, and I wasn't even a smoker.

Back at our camp, Corinne dropped the duffel bag and embraced me. She was crying, but she was laughing too. We just stayed like that for a while, not saying anything at all.

Then she pulled away and looked at me, her hands on my shoulders. "You lost your board," she said.

I shrugged.

She hugged me again. "I'll get you a new one someday."

I didn't say anything. She added, whispering into my ear, "That single hit to the nuts was something else, Iphigenia Murphy."

I couldn't help but smile.

CHAPTER 16

"Cut it out," I objected, waving her hand away. "It's not the first black eye I ever had. And it's definitely not the worst."

Corinne frowned. "That makes me feel even sadder, Iff."

I *tsked* and rolled my eyes. "I'll be fine." I clicked the compact closed and handed it back to Corinne. It probably looked worse than it was. I didn't tell Corinne, but what really hurt was my neck. It was sore from how it snapped back when he hit me. I had to move carefully, like my head was a glass of milk I was balancing. *I'm trying not to spill myself*, I thought.

It was morning and the crickets and the birds were all screaming, as though they could sense that the day would only get hotter and they'd better use up all their noise now. There was a low mist, making the whole park seem like some exotic place, like a rain forest or an enchanted fairy-tale land.

The mist will burn off soon though, I thought. *It'll be a good day to stay in the shade, take it easy and recuperate.*

I sat on a tree stump. Corinne moved around.

"I'm really so sorry." She was beginning to sound like a broken record.

"Please stop saying that. It's not a big deal."

"It's a little bit of a big deal."

"I mean, sure. But whatever. I'm not upset."

"You're not?"

"No."

"You look upset."

I paused, thought. "Yup. He's a jerk. You were right about that. He's pretty scary."

Corinne stopped pacing and nodded. "Yeah."

"But I don't know. I guess it was kind of … exciting?"

Corinne smiled widely. "It was, wasn't it?"

I laughed a little.

"You were amazing," she went on for the hundredth time. "Shoot. You are great in a pinch, huh? You are really are Saint Sneak—patron saint of the sneak attack. I am so glad you are on *my* side."

I had been going over it again and again in my mind. How the skateboard felt in my hand, the noise he made when I made contact, my heart pounding in my ears as we ran. The whole thing had been terrifying, but also intense in an almost pleasurable way. And the best part was having someone who had been there, someone to talk about it with.

"I just wish I had seen his face."

Corinne hooted. "He looked like his eyes were about to pop right out of his head!" She did an impression, grabbing her crotch and falling to the ground.

"Oh my god," I laughed.

"I hope someone had, like, a camcorder and sends it to *America's Funniest Home Videos* or something. They love those ball shots."

I laughed. "It *was* a low blow. Literally."

Corinne smirked but cycled back into concerned mode. "Your eye ..." she began.

"I'm fine," I groaned.

"Should we try to get some ice or something?"

"*Puh-lease!*" I took a swig of water.

She made a face, lit a cigarette. "Oh, Iffy."

Angel, who had been sniffing around, returned, panting, and put her head in my lap. She looked up at me with those sweet, pretty eyes. "Hey, Ang," I said, stroking her neck. "You're hot. I know."

"Iffy," Corinne started. "I just want to say to you ... you are like my best friend, you know that?"

I smiled at her.

"I mean it when I say I'm glad you're on my side. You are so fly."

"Cut it out."

"I just ... you know," she looked down and then back at me. "I appreciate it, is all I'm saying. You know, you just taking me for who I am and being my bud but also, you know, going to bat for me. Or should I say, going to board."

"Of course," I said.

"You know I love you, right?"

I kind of laughed and looked at the ground. "Me too."

She had to make a joke, of course, a "no funny business now" joke, before she embraced me.

I thought about how strange it was to be touched. I almost even enjoyed the hug. Most of the time I shrank back when somebody tried to touch me and I had at first, too, with Corinne, but I'd had to get used to it: she was always hugging and patting and reaching and grabbing. She was a toucher, all right. And while I found it surprising and a little embarrassing at first, I had almost started to like it, to consider using it myself, this communication through hands. Because it was different when Corinne touched me, it was always playful or kind or affectionate. It was never nasty or pissed off. She never touched me like they used to touch me: the way you touch something that is in your way, something that irritates you, that is large and heavy but also useless, disposable, disgusting.

When she let me go, she turned me by my shoulders to face her. "You know you can talk about it if you want."

I played dumb. "What?"

"Anything."

I thought for a minute. I looked at the ground. "I guess there is something," I mumbled.

Corinne waited.

"You know how I told you about my mom?"

She nodded.

"I think she might be here. Like, I'm sort of looking for her."

Corinne considered. "Living *here*? In the park?" she clarified.

I nodded.

"Holy shit, Iffy. We have to find her."

CHAPTER 17

It was mosquito time when we set out—just dusk, when they descended in full force, unavoidable, relentless, bloodthirsty. They weren't as bad outside the park, at the gas station where we bought Newports, but they were waiting for us once we reentered. Swatting and complaining, we stomped through the woods to where I had last seen Danny. He wasn't there anymore. All that was left were some empty bottles and half-buried rags that had once been clothes. I wanted my photo back, if nothing else.

The place was still repellent. It was as though someone had died there and nobody had bothered to clean it up. Leaves had blown over the spot but didn't cover the smell and the rot. Even Angel seemed uneasy, ready to look elsewhere.

Pursued by the mosquitoes, we went next to the park benches where I had first seen him, but the benches were lonely in the heat.

Corinne had an idea of another spot. "Let's try over by Strack Pond." We took swigs from our water bottles and set off again. I imagined the mosquitoes like a parade following behind us. Hansel and Gretel's trail of mosquitoes.

I immediately forgot about the bugs, forgot to be annoyed by them, when I saw Danny on a bench by the pond. There were four or five homeless people with him. My first, terrible thought was that they were like pigeons perched on the park benches. They roused as we approached, alarmed and fluttering, and then they settled back down when they saw we held something for them.

"You got an extra smoke?" a guy, a kid really, asked.

I nodded and Corinne took one out of a pack. Suddenly, all of their hands were extended.

I stopped in front of Danny while Corinne distributed cigarettes. Red-eyed and bleary, Danny's vague gaze finally met mine.

"Hey, yeah, I know you," he choked and then cleared his throat and said more clearly, "What's up, girl? Find your sister?" He glanced at Corinne.

"No. I was hoping maybe you knew something."

"You got my cigarettes?"

I held out a full pack of Newports and he smiled at me and took them and I tried to smile back.

"What happened to you, mami?" He was immediately packing the box against his thigh.

I shrugged, "Whatever."

Danny laughed in an almost-admiring way and fumbled trying to unwrap the cellophane off the cigarettes.

"You don't look it, but you're a fighter. Yo, so yeah. I do have something for you. A girl over on Woodhaven Boulevard. A working girl? She thought she recognized the picture."

My heart pounded in my ears and my vision swam for a moment. I shook my head to clear it. "*Really*?"

"Yeah," Danny looked at me strangely. "Why you so surprised?"

"I ... I'm not," I stammered. "What did she say?"

"My girl, Monique, said she thought your sister looked familiar. I told her you'd be looking her up."

"Well, where is she? What does she look like?"

"I know who Monique is," Corinne interrupted.

Danny looked Corinne up and down. "Oh you do, do you?"

I looked at Corinne too.

She cut him a side-eye and turned to me. "Come on, we can go over there now. It'll be dark soon."

"Okay," I was feeling excited and sick at the same time. "Thanks, Danny. Thanks so much."

He tossed his head. "No thing."

I was going to ask for the photo back, but he beat me to it. "I'll keep the photo," he said. "Case I run into anyone else."

"Okay," I relented. My fingers itched for the photo, but I made fists with my hands. My breath was shallow and I felt myself blinking, hard, and I realized everybody was looking at me.

"Let's go," Corinne took charge, looking at me like, *what are you waiting for?*

We walked away from the pond in silence, and she touched my elbow to steer me back to the main path. I waited for her to say something, but she didn't. We passed a playground and the sounds of the swings, their heaving chains, and a faint and familiar childhood chant drifted through the trees. Waiting, listening, I heard the birds, too, and then looked up to see a little speck of an airplane cutting across the darkening sky at an impossible angle.

Corinne cleared her throat.

"You know, Iff, I'm not as innocent as I seem," she tried to joke, but her laugh was weak and weird. She took out her cigarettes.

I realized that she was embarrassed. I was so busy thinking about my mother that I hadn't noticed. I didn't think I'd ever seen her embarrassed before. I wasn't sure what we were talking about.

"So, whatever," she rattled on. "A girl's gotta do what a girl's gotta do ... You know what I mean, Iff?"

I didn't, so I didn't say anything.

"I'm just saying I know some of the working girls is all. I just didn't want you to be ... surprised."

And then I knew what she meant. I was so sad for her then, because I hadn't known before. Not really.

"It's okay with me, Corinne," I said, but she looked at me sharply, hearing something else in my voice.

"I don't give a shit if it's okay with you."

I was stunned. She had never spoken to me like that before. I went into my default mode: I shut up.

"I'm doing you a favor, remember?" she snapped.

I looked at the ground.

My nonresponsiveness only seemed to make her angrier.

"I don't even know why I would help you," she spat at me. She started to walk away from me, into the woods.

There was a lump in my throat as I stood, watching her walk away from me. I had to say something, I had to stop her.

I forced myself to speak.

"Please don't go, Corinne," I said, my voice just a little squeak. I looked back at the ground. "I'm sorry. I didn't mean anything."

She glanced back but kept walking.

"My mom ..." I called to the ground. I couldn't get anything else out.

I could hear that Corinne had stopped walking, and when I looked up I saw the anger fading from her face.

"Yeah," she said, with attitude still, but not with the rage that I had seen building. It was like watching a wave recede, watching her go from hot back to cool again. And it was like a wave, too, in the way I had felt helpless, unable to control it or to stop it, like I was just being tumbled around in it. It was scary. My skin prickled. My nose itched, but I didn't lift a finger to scratch it.

She flicked the lit cigarette off into the leaves, a habit of hers that I hated. "Shit. Stop looking at me like a lost puppy." She set off walking again, looking back to suggest that I better hurry up. I scrambled to keep up with those long legs.

Corinne was silent all the way, a long walk, out of the trees and over to the boulevard that sliced the park in half. I still felt tense, nervous, and, if I was being honest, a little afraid of her. The traffic and noise were almost overwhelming. I was tired and hungry. We had been walking all day, but I didn't dare say I needed to stop, take a break. I didn't dare say anything at all.

But Corinne was suddenly herself again as we approached a girl in short shorts and high boots standing in a bus shelter. "Hey," she called out brightly. "What's up? You know if Monique's around?"

The girl in the bus shelter half turned to look at Corinne. "You know Monique?"

"Yeah. She's a friend of mine," Corinne returned, pursing her lips and then smiling at the girl. The girl was distracted by a car that slowed down and then sped up again. She turned back to Corinne. "She just went over to the deli. She'll be over on that side of the street anyway." The girl regarded me. "What you looking at?"

I looked at the ground.

"She a lesbian?"

Corinne laughed. "Nah, she's just skinny." She grabbed my arm and pulled me into the street. "Thanks," she called back as we skipped across the busy intersection. When we got to the other side she turned to me. "*Are* you a lesbian?"

"I don't think so."

"Interesting answer."

"I mean, no," I protested.

"Humph."

I was relieved that the sarcasm and jokes were back. I knew Corinne liked the excitement, liked being on a mission. I almost did too.

I followed Corinne to a deli. A bell on the door tinkled as a girl walked out, also dressed in tall boots, but in a tiny tube-top dress.

"Hey, girl!" she squealed when she saw Corinne.

"Hey, Monique," Corinne matched Monique's enthusiasm, "Oooo, and red was always your color! So, hey, this is my friend Iff—" She stopped herself. "Brenda."

Monique barely gave me a nod and turned back to Corinne. At first glance, she seemed like a woman. She looked sophisticated, grown-up. But up close I could see she was my age or even younger.

"You're obviously not working," she said to Corinne. She waved a hand up and down the length of Corinne's face and torso. "What is happening here, Corinne?"

I regarded Corinne. It was true, she wasn't looking quite put together. The two of us, I realized suddenly, probably looked like the homeless weirdos we were.

"Long story ..."

"And I do not have the time," Monique's voice was high-pitched and sweet. "I'd love to catch up and all, but Jackson will be all over me in a minute."

"I know." Corinne turned to me. "Give her the picture, Iff," she instructed.

I took the couch picture—the one I didn't like to look at so much—out of my back pocket and handed it to Monique. "She's looking for her mom," Corinne explained. "You told that guy Danny or whatever that you might know her? Like, he showed you a picture?"

Monique nodded. "Oh, yeah, sure." We looked at each other and she said, "Your mom, huh?" and looked at the picture without waiting for an answer.

Monique nodded a little more and then looked at me again. Her face was kind. She frowned as though to say, *I'm sorry.* "Yeah. I think I seen her around."

My stomach fell through to my knees.

She glanced behind her. "I only got a minute, for real, but, yeah. She was working and all, but she was like," she looked at me apologetically, "kind of old? But she got picked up. You know? I think they put her in the hospital, like the crazy-person type hospital."

"When?" Corinne pressed.

Monique sucked her lips, thinking about it. "I don't know. A while ago. Like six months ago maybe?" She looked around nervously again. "Look, I gotta go. But you should talk to Dougie. You know that guy? Crackhead? He was always hanging around with her."

I inhaled sharply, alarms going off in my head. Dougie again.

"Thank you, Monique," I squeaked. "Thank you so much for helping me."

"No big deal. You know. I just like to think ..." She looked out into the cars flowing on the boulevard. She had a sweet voice. "You know, if somebody came looking for me, you know, I would want someone to help them too."

"Like karma," Corinne said.

"Yeah. Sure."

I wanted to grab Monique, to ask her more questions, but my words were dead in my throat and then she was walking away, a different person suddenly, an exaggerated sway in her hips. She called over her shoulder, "Say hi to that cute boyfriend of yours, Corinne!" before a long dark car pulled over, and in a moment she was gone.

PART IV:
SWEET SIXTEEN

CHAPTER 18

We walked around for a while, me breathing short and quick, wanting only to get back into the tent and lie down so I could think. We didn't find Dougie that night, of course. But I don't even know what would have happened if we had. I had gotten information and then I didn't know what to do with it. Was I really surprised that my mother was a crackhead? Or that she was, or had been, a prostitute? What had I expected? That I would discover that she'd been living off wild berries and sparkling pond water in the park?

Maybe I *had* expected that. I don't really know what I had wanted, beyond an impulse, a desire, an undefined longing, a gut-level hope that I would find her and she would be okay. Maybe not perfect, but okay. We would take care of each other. And then we could get better together.

I couldn't sleep that night, chewing on my thumb, my mind churning with Monique's words. I was glad Corinne had been with me, because then I could ask her over and over again to verify what I had heard. That girl had known my mother. She had known my mother and my mother had been living in the park *six months ago*.

Six months ago.

If only I had run away sooner.

The next morning, I woke up with a tugging in my stomach. I brought some toilet paper and a maxi pad with me when I went to pee, but there was nothing on the paper. I had been pretty studiously not counting, but it was becoming impossible to ignore.

I thought it might be malnutrition. Once, in gym, when we had to sit on the bleachers and watch the teacher demonstrate how to serve a volleyball (supposedly before having to perform this feat ourselves), I overheard the two girls in front of me talking. "*I haven't had my period in like, two months,*" the blond one said. "*It's 'cause you're so anorexic,*" her friend said. "*I know!*" the blond returned. "*I love it!*"

I went back to camp and sat down on the ground next to Corinne. I wasn't going to think about it. I couldn't.

Corinne handed me a granola bar. "What? What's wrong?"

"Nothing." I stuck the granola bar in my mouth so I wouldn't have to talk. It was too dry and I reached out and Corinne handed me the bottle of water.

"Don't be upset. We'll find her. We gotta find that guy Dougie."

I nodded as though it was no big deal and I hoped that she wouldn't notice my lack of talk.

"Today, though, we need some supplies. We're running low on food. So, one of us should beg and the other one should go buy stuff."

I nodded again, patted Angel.

"I'll go," Corinne declared. "I'll get some soups and beans and chips and jerky? Right? And cigarettes. Sorry. But I'm in a bit of crisis. They're a necessity." She looked expectantly at me. I shrugged.

"You want me to stop at the library too, you know, and check what's on the sale shelf in the lobby? I know you've been wanting to."

Now I knew for sure that she could tell something was wrong and she was trying to cheer me up.

I swallowed hard. The lump was still there, but I managed a weak, "Great."

"Okay," Corinne pursed her lips doubtfully. Then she added, "I'm gonna get us some good *row-mances*."

I rolled my eyes.

"You're a snob, Iffy. Everybody likes a good *row-mance*."

"Get some, like, *literary*-type books," I insisted, rousing a little, a reluctant smile on my lips.

"Watch out," Corinne warned, giving me a gentle shove. "Next thing I know you'll be starting a lending library of your own. Why not? You've got everything else here." I rose to start repacking our food to hang in the tree. "Why don't we just get a refrigerator for that stuff?"

I really smiled this time. "Might as well. Actually, I was thinking of building a tree house."

She grinned. "You are not serious."

"I mean, yes and no. Just need a hammer and nails, some boards ... I was thinking the trees would be a good place to sleep. And definitely not a bad place to hide."

"You are insane."

"I just can't figure out the best way to get Angel up there."

"Don't even humor her, Angel," she ordered the dog. "Don't even." Corinne looked around, making sure she had collected what she needed. "All right, I'm gonna get going." But she hesitated. "Look, Iff. Sorry about yesterday. Getting so mad and all."

I shrugged as if to say, *it's nothing.*

"Are you still mad?"

"No. I wasn't ever mad."

She narrowed her eyes. "I don't know," she said. "But that was about me. Not you. I know that much. Okay?"

"It's okay," I pretended it was nothing, but I was glad she said that. It was amazing to me, the way she just dealt with the awkward stuff head-on, like she dealt with everything.

She grabbed me and hugged me. At first I just stood there and then I hugged back. "You forgive me?" she said into my shoulder.

I don't think anyone had ever asked for my forgiveness before in my life.

"Of course." My throat closed again and my eyes got wet. I blinked, tried to pretend everything was okay.

Corinne saw that and maybe she didn't want to make me feel even weirder, so she looked into the distance and smoothed her hair. "Okay, so where you gonna be?"

I hadn't decided. "I guess over by the statue. It's pretty high-traffic."

She raised her eyebrows. "I'll see you later at the bridge, then."

"All right. Be careful and all."

"You too."

She gave me a quick smile and set off for the outside world.

When I couldn't hear her crashing through the woods anymore, I rubbed my eyes, took a breath. Time for me to get going too.

We'd slept out, not bothering with the tent the night before, so I finished bundling up our stuff pretty quickly, putting the big garbage bag in the shallow hole and then covering it with leaves.

"Okay, puppy," I called to Angel. She leapt up, ready to go.

Walking over to the big path I worried, a little abstractly, about getting sloppy, staying too many nights in one place, not cleaning up after ourselves like we should have. Henry hadn't been able to find us, but still. There were the police to worry about. And the other homeless. And god knows who else.

We came to the path I was looking for and I found a good spot in the sun. I took off my backpack, propping my "Hugnry Please Help" sign against it. I put my finders-keepers Mets cap on the ground upside down and popped in two singles. Nobody likes to be the first, I'd learned, and it helped to have a suggested donation amount.

So, me and Angel sat, watching the joggers and the dog walkers and the baby-carriage pushers passing by.

After a little while a woman who was jogging past turned her head to look, I thought, at my sign. She kept going along the path, toward where it curved out of sight, but then she looked back again. She slowed down, staring over her shoulder, frowning, glancing forward now and then, but returning her gaze over to us. Was she thinking of giving me money?

Something seemed off.

For a moment, I weighed the possibility of running, worried that she recognized me, like maybe she had seen us that night outside Henry's apartment or maybe she was a friend of his or something. But I just sat there, pretending not to notice her.

Then, like in a nightmare, the lady did a slow, wide U-turn and jogged back. I stared into the distance, watching her out of the side of my eye. Framed by the big trees that met in the middle and formed a canopy, she ran smack down the middle of the path, all the other folks parting and streaming past her on either side.

She was an olive-skinned white lady with cropped gray hair. She was old looking, but muscled and wiry the way exercise fanatics are. She was wearing baggy green shorts and a white 5K T-shirt.

When she got closer, I saw that she was actually staring at Angel. Still, I sat there like a fool, my eyes focused on a point just beyond her shoulder.

And then Angel started wagging her tail.

"Hey," said the woman, her voice deep and breathless. She was suddenly smiling, slowing to a trot and then a walk. She pointed at Angel. "Hey, I'm sorry. It's just that ... I think that's ... Hey, Lola!" She looked at me, excited. "I think this is my dog!"

She started to swoop down toward Angel who—traitor!— jumped up to meet her. I jumped up too, yanking Angel back and away from the lady. I grabbed Angel's leash high, up by the neck, to keep her behind my thigh.

"This isn't your dog, lady."

The woman stopped smiling. She was pink-cheeked and breathing hard in the heat. "Hey," she frowned and then kind of smiled again, nodding her head, seemingly unable to make up her mind about how this conversation was going to go. "No, I think it is. Lola ran away, like, three months ago. We've been looking for her. Did you find her in the park?"

"*I said* this isn't your dog. This is *my* dog. This is Angel."

The woman was apparently stumped. She looked at me and looked at Angel and then looked back at me. I focused on the lady's torso, her face a peripheral blur, and I busied myself trying to control Angel, who was doing these little hops on her back legs, whining and squirming.

Other people were looking at us now, too. An elderly man and woman, both wearing unnecessary raincoats, had stopped and were staring at us. I felt self-conscious, obvious, criminal somehow. *What, was this old lady gonna accuse me of stealing her dog? Would anyone even believe me if I said I hadn't?*

"Look ..." The lady was not going to let this go. "Look, I recognize her by her tail. She has that distinctive tail. No other dog has that tail. And see," she said, holding out her hand, palm up, toward Angel, "she knows me."

I started to back away, pulling the struggling Angel with one hand and, with my other, grabbing my backpack and shrugging it on one shoulder and then grabbing my sign and the Mets cap with the money in it.

I looked at Angel's tail. My face felt tight; my throat felt tight. I turned and started walking.

"Wait!" She was sounding a bit desperate.

I turned back to her. "Lady. This is Angel, see. And Angel is all I got. That's it. Me and Angel. That's all we got."

We stared at each other for a minute. Her sweaty face showed no comprehension for a moment. It was flat, blank as a turned-off TV.

I turned again to go.

I started walking away, but I could feel her still behind me, following, but not too close, almost staggering, like there was a string between us that was pulling her along against her will. Meanwhile, I really was pulling Angel, who was being a first-class pain in the neck and wanted to turn back, to go to the lady.

I tried to keep moving, but Angel was strong, so I bent over and put my face down near hers. "What, Ang?" I practically begged, her hot breath in my nose. I spoke softly so that the lady wouldn't hear, but sternly too, because I was getting freaked out. "We don't know her. Just come on."

"Wait!" the lady called again.

Was Angel her dog? I didn't know. But at that moment, for me, it didn't matter.

I spun to face her. She was real close to getting punched. "You better leave us alone," I growled.

CHAPTER 19

The jogger stopped walking.

"Wait. Hold on now. I won't ... fine. She's yours. I won't try to take her back." I nodded like, *you got that right*, and kept moving, not on any path, just straight back into the trees. Not running, just walking, like the lady was a wild dog or a bear or something and I was afraid that running would only tempt her to chase me. And then I could hear her coming up behind me again anyway, but quickly this time.

"Just listen for a minute. Please stop."

She touched my shoulder and I whipped around. Angel started going crazy, jumping up on the lady.

"Leave me alone!" I shouted. I yanked Angel, hard, harder than I meant to. She let out a yelp. I wanted to hold her head, apologize and hug her, but I was so angry and scared, I just locked my eyes on the lady. For her part, the lady looked scared, too, like she was finally getting it that she was pursuing a crazy-looking homeless person into the woods.

"Fine," she said, holding her hands up like, *sorry I touched you* or *I surrender* or whatever. "I'm not gonna try to take her.

Don't cry. Don't cry, honey." She lowered her hands slowly and then put one near the side of my arm, like caressing the air above it. I stepped back. I didn't know why she said that. I wasn't crying. Was I?

"Okay," she still held her hand close to my arm, like, levitating over it. I could feel the warmth on my skin, even though she wasn't touching me. It reminded me of something, but I couldn't think what.

"Just listen for a minute." She started talking quickly, urgently, like she knew I might just run off and this was her only chance. She kept trying to look in my face now, but I kept looking away. "Please, listen. One minute. She just looks like our old dog is all. And I want to make sure that you and the dog ... I mean, you look like you could use a thing or two. Like money. Or food. I just want to make sure the two of you ..." She stopped and started again. "That dog just looks like a dog I used to have. You know? You obviously care about her, you know? So, if you saw a dog that looked like your dog, you'd want to make sure she was taken care of, wouldn't you?"

I wasn't sure what this old lady was getting at. I wasn't gonna give her my dog.

"See," she was gaining speed now and talking even faster, "I want to give you what you need so that your dog is taken care of." She crouched down and I loosened up on Angel's leash a little, not really thinking about it, just acting the way you do when someone normal wants to pet your dog. Well, Angel started going nuts, licking the lady's sweaty face.

"Hey ... doggie," the lady said. I could tell she was holding back from calling her Lola or whatever that stupid name was.

I just kept standing there, struck dumb, I guess. I didn't have any more energy to protest.

"Listen ..." She scratched Angel on the ears and the rump and looked up at me and then back down at Angel and then at me again. She would smile and then frown and then smile again. I thought, *Jesus, make up your mind already.*

"I don't have anything on me now. I don't have pockets." She looked down at herself and kind of laughed like not having pockets was the most ridiculous thing in the world. She kept on playing with Angel's ears and kissed her on the head. "But I could run home real fast and come back. We don't live too far from here."

She must have been able to tell from my face that this was not going to fly.

"Well, is there a place I can find you later? Or better yet, leave you something? Just twenty bucks or something? You know, just so ... it looks like maybe you might ... your sign said ..." She took a breath and tried again. "What do you need?"

Another question I'd never been asked before. It must have been the day for it.

I just stood there, feeling awkward, looking down at her. My stomach was grumbling. We'd been rationing pretty carefully the last few days.

"Sure, we could use twenty bucks," I said, as nonchalantly as I could. My voice was higher than usual, tinny and weird in my ears.

Angel jumped up, put her paws on the women's shoulders, knocking her off balance and to the ground. The lady rolled on her back and Angel nuzzled her and licked her face. Dogs go crazy for that, when you get down on the ground with them. "She's just real friendly," I grumbled, still in my weird voice. "You know, to everyone 'n all."

"She's a nice dog." I thought maybe she was the one who was gonna start crying now. I couldn't handle that.

She sat up and hugged Angel, who kept shoving her snout in the lady's face and neck and armpit, trying to get even more scratches.

The lady looked up at me, kind and serious. "Where can I leave you the money?"

I glanced around. We were off the main path, but not so far that she would get lost if she tried to come back. "You can leave it here, under this rock here." I took a half step away and nudged a convenient and big rock with my foot. Angel, who was acting totally bonkers, stopped bugging the lady for a minute, to playfully snap at the foot I used to kick the rock. Then she leapt back to the lady. A real joyful jump. I felt my mouth start to pull up at the corners, even though I didn't like it one bit. Angel was just so cute sometimes.

"Great! Great—I'm gonna go home right now. I'll be back in just a little bit." She was smiling like crazy.

"That's fine," I said, pulling Angel back and away from her. The lady stood up and started brushing leaves off her body. There was one leaf hanging awkwardly out of her hair; I wanted to reach out and pluck it, but I just stared, watching it flop around.

Angel jumped up, lunging and nipping at the air and trying to get me to play. "Angel! Down girl," I said, working to keep the pressure on her leash steady, wishing she would cut it out. I looked at the lady. She was still all smiles. Just standing there, watching us, smiling. I picked up my backpack and the sign, which I had dropped at some point—of course, Angel was all about knocking my head with her nose—and then we turned to go.

"Okay, then," she said.

"Okay," I said over my shoulder.

"Okay," the lady repeated. "Bye, Angel."

Angel kept turning around, trying to go back, but I didn't.

"Wait! What's your name?"

I didn't stop. "Brenda," I yelled, not looking back.

"Okay, Brenda! Okay," she added weakly, "I'm Ann."

"Don't worry, Ang," I murmured to Angel, putting my forehead to hers once we were out of sight. "Don't worry, girl. Don't worry about that crazy lady."

But Angel didn't seem worried at all. She licked me right on the mouth. I held her mouth closed and kissed her on the top of her snout and we got moving again.

I had absolutely no idea how to feel. Worried, but maybe a little excited too. Sad that that lady might actually be Angel's owner, but angry too. I even forgot about the money.

I just wanted to talk it over with Corinne.

CHAPTER 20

I removed Angel's leash as soon as we were a little deeper in the woods. I really only put her leash on for appearances, around people, so they didn't get afraid of her and so they'd know she was mine. Although so much for that last part. The leash didn't keep that jogger away. As we trudged and crashed toward the bridge to meet Corinne, I thought about how crazy and happy and weird that lady had acted. Ann.

We got there quickly and no Corinne yet, so I settled down with Angel, pouring her a bowl of water and going over in my head what had happened.

I couldn't find anything truly suspicious about what the lady had said or about her offer, but I was jumpy and feeling weird about it anyway. Like, maybe she might come back with the cops. It could be that she wanted the dog, or maybe she was just a busybody, one of those radical animal lovers or something, determined to get Angel into a shelter, and me too, for that matter.

It occurred to me I was mostly nervous because I hadn't interacted with any adults in a while. Corinne was kind of an adult, but not really. The fact was I didn't know if I could trust that old lady. I wanted to, though. And it wasn't even about the money. It was almost like ... *finally.* Finally, somebody noticed. It was embarrassing to admit that to myself. But it was a relief, that feeling of *finally.*

Maybe Angel did look like her dog. Or maybe she really was hers. But what kind of dog owner had she been anyway if her dog had wound up alone in the park? Angel was messed up when we found each other. She was skinny and scared and just messed up. That lady didn't deserve to have a dog if she couldn't keep track of her.

"Ang!" I would call when she got a little too far away and she would come bounding, that's just the right word, bounding, back to me, jumping over downed trees and wagging that ridiculous tail. *Whatever. She's my dog now,* I thought.

I was starting to get worried when we finally heard Corinne's whistle and Angel, who had settled down at last and was lying at my feet, jumped up and bolted through the woods toward Corinne. Corinne was kind of jogging and stumbling, and when I saw her face I could tell that something was wrong.

I rose and rushed toward her. I grabbed her arm. "What is it? What's wrong?"

"He saw me."

"What happened?"

"I don't know," she said. We stood looking at each other and her face was transformed with fear. My friend Corinne was usually smiling, or looking bemused, or at least calm. Now, her jaw was tight, there were lines on her forehead.

"He must've seen me walking. Like, I didn't notice anything. I went and bought the books." She lifted a plastic bag at her side and tossed it over toward where I had my stuff piled near the base of the bridge. "I don't know, he was definitely looking for me. Someone must've seen me ... or I don't know what. I left the library and then I went to the gas station—I knew I shouldn't have gone to that place—and I was buying cigarettes and stuff and then he was right there, like, literally breathing on me and he grabbed my neck."

"Oh my god, Corinne."

She brought her fingertips to her throat where he had left red marks. I imagined him, that ugly man, digging his fingers into my friend's neck. The muscles of my jaw clenched.

"Iffy, I don't know what I'm gonna do," she choked.

"Tell me everything." In the pause I guided her toward the big rock we usually sat on, handed her the bottle of water. She took a long drink and then looked around, as though she didn't know where she was.

"I don't know," she repeated. She took out a cigarette and lit it with trembling fingers. "The guy at the counter—in the gas station—he was like, 'Hey, hey now kids,' and Henry was like, 'We're just playing around,' and he steered me out of the store. By my neck. I thought he was gonna kill me right there. Oh god, Iffy, he knows I'm in the park. He said it. He said, 'So, you're living in the park?' He laughed, like he knew it but couldn't believe it. He said, 'You smell like shit.' And he called me a ... all sorts of things." Corinne began to cry. It had started with just big, plump tears rolling down her pink cheeks, but then her eyes turned into slits and her mouth turned down and she sobbed. "He said he would get me. The things he said, Iffy ... It was ... just ... He said," she gasped out, but softly, quietly, as though she was speaking not to me. Angel, who was lying at her feet, looked up at her and I swear to god that dog looked concerned too, like she was asking, *What's wrong, Corinne?*

"So, how did you get away?"

"Well, the guy from the gas station came out again and he said he had called the cops and that we had to get out of there and Henry was all like, 'That's fine, I'm just leaving now and you're free to go Corinne,' and he kind of threw me, by like my neck. He was doing that weird smile. He said I was pathetic, that I had to come back because I had nowhere else to go. He said that I could die in the park. But then he said I should come back, he wanted me to. But then he just got in his car and left, you know? And I was so scared. I just started running. I just ran back to the park. But what if he followed me? What if he comes looking for me? How long before he comes looking for me, Iffy?"

"He won't be able to find us," I assured her.

"But if he does," she sobbed, "then he'll hurt you too. And Angel. I don't want him to hurt you two."

"He won't hurt us, Corinne."

"Iffy."

"We won't let him."

"He killed Prince. Or, I don't know. He said Princie was 'gone.' I don't even know what that means."

I didn't say anything. But I was thinking. I was thinking about my stepbrother. I was thinking about how, before I left, I got a knife one night. My stepbrother was asleep in his room, drunk and high, and I knew I could kill him. I knew I was capable of sticking that knife into his chest, more than once if necessary, until he died.

I didn't do it. I knew that if I killed him I would go to prison, that even if I ran they would look for me for real and they would find me. So, I didn't do it.

But I knew I could.

"Corinne," I said so calmly and seriously, I knew I meant it, "we'll kill him first."

CHAPTER 21

After she'd calmed down, I told Corinne about the guns.

"You ever shoot a gun, Iffy?" She was impassive, unimpressed.

"No," I confessed, deflating a bit.

"You know how?"

"Sure," I shrugged. "Don't you just pull the trigger?"

"Well, sort of. It's not really as easy as it looks."

"You've shot a gun?"

She nodded. "But not *at* anyone. I'm telling you Iffy," she sighed. "It's not that easy."

"Well, it might not be a bad thing to have anyway," I said. I gnawed on the side of my thumb, thinking.

Corinne worked her way through the cigarettes, and me and Angel sat there, quiet, just keeping her company. She was thinking, every so often mumbling to herself. Sometimes she put her hand up to her head like she was gonna run her fingers through her hair and then her fingers would get caught in what was becoming a knotted and smelly mess. Then she'd scratch at her scalp and run her hand over her face and look at me and look at Angel and get real still. Then the whole routine would start all over again.

She got up and started pacing. "You know, when I first met him, that was it. Like, I looked into his eyes and it was love at first sight."

I had heard this story already. I didn't want to hear it again.

I must've been frowning, because she added, "No, for real. I went with my friend Karen to the Limelight. I was totally trashed at the bar and he was across from me, leaning against a wall and we made eye contact and that was that. I went back to his place that night and, like, I basically never went home again," she exhaled through her nose and smiled a little, but then the smile faded and she rubbed her hand over her eyes. "That's not true. I left him a couple of times. But after that first night, I didn't even bother going back to my mom's to pick up my stuff. I just moved right in with him."

"He's not a good guy, Corinne," I said softly, digging at the dirt under the leaves with the tip of my sneaker. A worm wriggled helplessly. I covered it with leaves again and started digging in a new spot. I thought, vaguely, that we could always eat worms. If it came to that.

It wouldn't come to that.

Would it?

"I know. I know. But god, I love him so much. I mean, loved him so much. I think that's the problem, you know. I've always loved him too much."

"I don't think that's the problem, Corinne."

"No, but it is. Like, he never loved me as much as I loved him. Or at least that's how I always felt. And then I'd act stupid, you know? You don't know, Iffy. I would get so jealous. You know?

Like kind of crazy sometimes. We were once at this party and ..."
She stopped, reconsidered. "I mean," she began again, looking
at me, "so, like, to be honest I guess I kind of used to do a lot of
drugs. Pills, whatever. And he really helped me to stop with all
that, you know? But before, sometimes I would just do stupid
stuff. And then we'd fight ... and Iffy, I can be really mean if I
want to, you know?"

"Corinne, please tell me you made it to at least one 'Abusive
Relationships' assembly in school. I mean, I went to a crappy
school, and even we had special programs on this stuff. You
know better than this."

"Of course I know better," she snapped wearily. "I know all
sorts of things." She tapped a finger to her head. "Here. But that
doesn't make any difference. I don't know it here," she tapped
her heart. "Not yet."

I didn't say anything. She continued. "It was just crazy." Her
voice became kind of a whine, as though she was a child and she
was trying to convince me to let her stay up late. "Like I'm so
angry right now, at the way he talked to me, about the way he
treats me. But at the same time ... I can't forget how it is when
it's good. I mean, I love him so much. So, when he does bad shit,
if he hits me or something," here she began to cry again, "it's
like the worst thing in the world. So, when he's sorry, when he
loves me again ..." She stopped and buried her face in her hands.
I worried that the lit cigarette would set her hair on fire, but
then she moved her hands, looked up, flicked the ashes. "When
he loves me it's the best thing in the world. And it becomes like
this thing, just the two of us, in our own world. We're the only
two who understand. Does that make sense? Like, it's so bad,
but then when we get back together it's that much better, we

need each other that much more? Or something. It's almost like. I don't know. It's like I *need* to get back with him."

"But you don't. You're away from him now. We're doing okay."

She wiped her face, looked at me. She was frowning. I was willing to keep talking about this, all day and all night if we needed to. But it was boring. It was painful and obvious and boring.

I'd known plenty of guys, men, who hit women. My dad hit my stepmom sometimes, although sometimes she'd hit him back. And Lizette's mother's ex-boyfriend used to hit her. And I knew, too, that what happened at home, in your real life, was different from the stories on *Beverly Hills, 90210* or what they talked about in school. Just totally disconnected, like all that stuff they said about domestic violence and molestation and abuse, it was all well and good, but it had nothing to do with what was happening to me, to any of us. You can't just walk out of your own life, like they do on TV.

Except, I guess, that sometimes you can. I did.

Corinne was looking at me.

"I know that you think your ... situation or whatever it is, is, like, different or special or something—" She began to protest. "—And maybe it *is*. It's just ..." I sighed. "Corinne, he's bad. He hurts you. Just promise me you won't go back."

"I won't," she said, wiping her eyes. I was unclear, though, as to what she meant.

"You're not gonna go back," I insisted.

"I know, I know. I'm not going to go back, Iffy."

"I won't let you."

She snorted. "I'm just saying, Iffy. It wasn't all him. You don't know. *I* would've hit me. Like, I have done things I'm not proud of, Iffy. You just don't get it."

"None of that matters," I told her. "What matters now is that you're here and you're not going back." I was surprised at myself, at my calm and how clear this was to me. What Corinne didn't know was that I did get it.

I got it and got it and got it.

CHAPTER 22

Later, I told Corinne about the lady. "She just came up to me and said that Angel was hers."

"What?" Corinne sat up, alarmed, putting the book she'd been flipping through open-faced on the ground.

"No, but it's okay," I reassured her. I instinctively reached out for Angel and patted her head. She was chewing on a stick. I grabbed it, threw it for her. She ran after it, pounced on it like she was a cat. "I was like, 'This isn't your dog,' and then she was all like, 'What can I do to help you guys,' and at first I said, 'Leave us alone,' but then she goes, 'Can't you use twenty bucks or something?' So, I was like, 'Sure.' So, we have to go back to this spot I showed her, see if she left us anything."

"No way! For real? Do you think she'll leave the money?"

"We'll see, I guess. Should we head over there?" I offered, grateful for a distraction, grateful for something potentially good in our lives.

"Yes," she replied, nodding vigorously.

As I led the way back, I was actually pretty excited. It was like looking under your pillow after the tooth fairy visited or something. I wanted to see if she had come, if she had left me anything.

And she had. You could see even from a few feet away, because not everything fit under the rock.

And did she ever come through. There were cans of dog food and a real leash and collar, dog biscuits and a bottle of water, a handful of (melted) chocolate bars and a bunch of bananas. And under the rock there was an envelope with twenty bucks and a note.

Dear Brenda,

I will leave you some supplies every few days if you'll accept them. If there is a better place, let me know. Your dog reminds me of a dog I used to love, and I'd like to think that you're both taken care of.

All the best,
Annie

I looked at Corinne and the two of us just busted out laughing.

"*Annie?*" Corinne asked. "Is she a child?"

"She didn't look like a child," I answered. "She had short gray hair. She was actually more Daddy Warbucks than Annie."

"Ha! Annie grew up to be a lesbian! And Daddy Warbucks was totally bald, by the way."

"I loved that movie when I was a kid," I said.

"Of course you did. Everyone does." She crooned, "*The sun'll come out ...*"

Angel howled along with her, stopping only when I gave her a dog biscuit.

And then I was rolling on the ground with her, wrestling and laughing. It was good—it was good to let some of it out that way, in laughing and playing.

Corinne watched us, her arms folded across her chest. When Angel lay on her side, panting, ready for more, but ready to stop, too, if that's what I wanted, I patted her rump and collected myself. I hastily wrote my own note and left it under the rock. It said "Thanks." I didn't really have anything else to say. Every few days? That seemed like a lot. Why would she do this? Maybe she was just trying to trick me. Maybe she was gonna come back with the cops after all. But those bananas sure tasted good. Just right, just ripe enough. And that twenty bucks looked pretty good too.

CHAPTER 23

We didn't bother to take down the tent the next morning—
we sat outside of it, reading the romance novels Corinne had
gotten at the library. Whenever one of us would come across
a particularly dirty—or particularly silly—passage, we'd read
it aloud.

"... *pushed her against the cliff and, with one hand, ripped the
breeches from her body ...*"

"Yikes," I said.

"It gets better," Corinne raised her eyebrows.

"I'm not sure I want to hear."

Angel leapt up all of a sudden and Corinne froze. I stood up
too. Corinne and I looked at each other, eyes very wide, very
awake.

"What is it, Ang?" I took the pepper spray out of my back
pocket.

"Hey," a male voice called. "Didn't mean to scare you."

A guy stepped into sight, emerging from a thick knot of
trees. He stopped and nodded at us. We all looked at him—me,
Corinne, and Angel, standing in a row. Understated, but cool

looking, in blue jeans and a white tee, a big backpack. Maybe a little older than me. Brown skin and black hair. A small hoop earring in each ear. Kind of cute. Definitely cute.

Angel gave a quick, short bark.

"Your dog friendly?" He sounded somewhat concerned, but like he was trying not to.

I shook my head, no. "Not really." To emphasize this point, I squatted beside her and held her back by her collar.

"All right. Just passing through and I saw your camp. I'll leave you alone." He turned to go.

I looked at Corinne. She shrugged, like, *why not?*

"It's okay," she called, a little invitation in her voice. "You can chill with us if you want."

The guy looked back and hesitated. "I'm not trying to bother you or anything."

"It's no big deal. We're just hanging out."

He approached, slowly. When he got closer, he smiled. He had beautiful teeth. "That's a great-looking dog." Angel, as always, was a conversation starter.

I stroked her back. She had a low growl going, but I think it was mostly for show. I let go of her collar and she stayed next to me, wagging that tail.

"Yeah," I allowed.

"Cool tail."

"You think so?" Corinne piped up, doubtfully.

"Yeah. It's like ... unique."

"It is," I put in. I kind of laughed. When I laughed, Angel relaxed. "Go ahead," I said, patting her. I stood up and she trotted over to sniff our visitor. He crouched down, held out a hand. She sniffed him, then nudged his elbow so that his arm bumped up and over her neck. She was getting real good at that move.

"I'm Anthony," he said, to Angel. "What's your name?"

"That's Angel. I'm Corinne."

"And I'm Brenda," I said, before Corinne could introduce me. I suddenly remembered that I was wearing my reading glasses and my hand flew to my face, touching the lens. I tried to be casual as I took them off, folded them up. But then I was left holding them in my sweaty hand. I made my way over to my backpack, to get out the case.

Corinne made a face at me, laughed, and then nodded at Anthony. "That's us," she said. "Me and Angel and *Brenda*," and she rolled her eyes as she said my fake name.

Anthony looked confused. Corinne added, "Or you can call her Saint Sneak. Saint Sneak of the Burning Heart."

"That would be a great name for a band," he said, laughing a little. "So, you guys got a regular camp going, huh?" He was nodding at our tent.

"Yep," Corinne said. "We're, like, vacationing here."

I put the glasses away and eased back down to sit cross-legged. Corinne lit a cigarette and Anthony stood to take off his backpack and then got back into a squat to give Angel a good rub down. Next thing, she was lying on her back, waiting to have her tummy scratched.

"Gutter punk?" I said to Corinne.

"Nah. Looks too much like a construction worker."

"What's that?" Anthony looked at me and then Corinne and back again.

"Just wondering what you are," Corinne said. "What brings you to our park and all."

"Oh," Anthony said in a way that made me wonder what he wasn't saying. "Just somewhere to stay, I guess. So, for real, you live here?" He looked straight at me.

I looked at the ground. I wanted to answer him, but my voice caught. It was the way I used to feel in class, when I knew the answer, but I just couldn't say.

Corinne waited for me to respond, but I didn't. "Forgive my friend Brenda," she ended the awkward silence. "She's a woman of few words. We're just crashing here too, I guess. Well, she's a runaway." She nodded at me. "I'm a ... what am I, Iff? I mean, Brenda." I scowled at her. "I guess I'm a runaway of sorts too. I don't know. I'm maybe too old to be a runaway? Ugh. That just makes me a plain old boring homeless," she finished, looking back at Anthony, flipping her matted hair charmingly.

"You're from around here?" Anthony asked, again looking at me and then Corinne and then back at me.

I shrugged.

"No. Jersey. What about you?" Corinne asked.

"Monticello." Corinne was asking the questions, but he kept looking at me when he answered. I just watched. Listened.

"That upstate?"

"Yeah."

"Isn't it nice up there?"

"Not really," he said. "I can't stand it, really. It's ... upstate. You know? So, I came down here to crash with my brother. We were going to start a band. But then he got a girlfriend and he kicked me out. So, here I am."

"What was the name of your band?"

Anthony smiled broadly. "The Beat Drums."

"The Beat Drums?" Corinne seemed doubtful.

"Yeah. Know where it's from?"

"No idea."

"It's dumb," Anthony said, but he was still smiling, like he didn't think it was dumb at all. "It's just what Animal from the Muppets always says. You know?" and he made his voice deep and gravelly and he belted, "*Beat drums! Beat drums!*"

Angel leapt up and barked at him.

"You don't know it? Animal from *The Muppet Show*?" Anthony asked, unbelieving, holding his hand out to Angel, to comfort her. I was cracking up, but I shook my head, no.

Corinne nodded and said, unenthusiastically, "Yeah, I think so. Cute name, I guess."

Anthony looked disappointed. He patted Angel, who now stood next to him, looking expectant, like he was gonna do that funny voice again or something, and then she sat down. She licked him, nudged at him for more attention. He put his arm around her and she settled down.

"What kind of music?" Corinne asked.

"I don't know. Like, alternative or lo-fi or whatever."

"That's cool." My voice was a little more than a whisper.

He smiled at me. "Yeah, like sort of, I don't know. You know, like, Pavement, Guided by Voices, stuff like that?"

I didn't know, but I nodded and smiled. Not for the last time, I wished desperately I knew more about music.

"You ever play a show?" Corinne continued her drilling.

"Not one," Anthony conceded.

"And your own brother kicked you out on the street," Corinne added with false sympathy.

"It wasn't as bad as all that. I mean, it's a tiny place. And I guess his girlfriend didn't want me around anymore. And then he was just like, 'Okay, bro, it's getting kind of crowded here.' So, I said I'd take off. You know how it goes. The weather's nice. It's not so bad." He had a nice, deep voice and a quiet way of talking. I wanted to stare at him, to really study what he looked like, but I mostly kept my eyes on the ground.

There was a lull in the conversation and we all just sat, waiting, then Anthony opened his backpack and took out a couple of granola bars. "You guys?" he asked, gesturing toward me with one.

"Sure," Corinne said.

"Thanks," I said.

Anthony threw it over, which of course bounced off my palm and landed in front of me. He held a second up in the air, ready to throw to Corinne, but she walked over to him and took it herself.

"Thanks," she said. She moved over to the rock and half sat on it, putting her cigarette out. "How long you been in the park?"

"Just since Saturday," Anthony said, unwrapping a bar. "I'm not, like, planning on *staying*. Just wanna see some more of the city before I head back upstate."

Corinne teased, "If you want to see more of the city, what are you doing hanging around in a park in Queens?"

Anthony chewed. "My brother's place is just a few blocks away. I figured this might be a good place to stop, take a nap on a bench, that kind of thing. I can always pop into his place for a shower and stuff. And it's a great park. Really great. Don't you think?"

"I do," I said. "My mother—" It just popped out of my mouth. I looked down.

Corinne looked at me, surprised.

"My mother," I started again, "loved this park." Angel came over and sat down next to me. I pulled a silky ear through my fingers. "She used to take me here all the time when I was a kid."

"No way," said Corinne, gently. She caught my eye and gave me a little smile. "That's nice."

Nobody said anything for a minute. Then Corinne asked, "Why here?" I knew she was prodding me, but it was okay.

"She grew up over here. But when she met my dad, most of her family, like, disowned her. But she had this one cousin, I called her my aunt, who still, like, hung out with her in secret. And Mom would bring me over here with her."

Corinne looked surprised, probably because it took me ages to tell her this about my mother, and here I was dishing it to a total stranger, but she was smiling in this way that I knew was meant to be encouraging. She didn't have to worry; it just kept coming out.

"And it was a secret from my dad too. It was, like, our thing. But I forgot about it for a long time after she ... left."

I stopped.

"So, here you are," Corinne said.

"Here I am."

Again, there was a pause and we all just sat there, but it didn't feel weird or anything, it almost felt like the most natural thing in the world. Then, I heard myself continue: "I used to think this park was so huge, like, immense. It doesn't really feel like that anymore. Not really. Now it seems ... small."

I looked at my granola bar before opening it, tearing through the white man with the big hat. I took a bite. Chocolate and oats. Amazing.

"It must seem tiny to you," I said to Anthony when I'd swallowed. The words just kept coming; I was being someone else, someone capable of making conversation. "Is it all country where you live?"

"I guess."

"But isn't it, like, scenic and all?"

"Well," he said, "there are some nice spots. But there's just not a whole lot going on."

"I think I'd like to live in the country." I seriously had no idea where that idea came from.

"You might," Anthony agreed. "But Monticello, I don't know. I don't know how to explain it. Like, we had a Kmart once. It closed."

"Oh."

"No, I mean, it's home." He seemed to feel guilty talking trash about his hometown. "And we have the racetrack. Still. It's not easy. I mean, including my uncle, we're literally the only black people. Which maybe isn't actually as bad as it sounds. Just weird. And, it's one hundred percent boring. I don't know." He shrugged. "I'm looking for something, you know? And I don't think I can find it in Monticello."

"What are you looking for, Anthony?" Corinne asked in her best soap-opera-therapist voice.

"No, not like that," Anthony said, laughing at himself. He waved a hand in the air dismissively. "It's totally cheesy. I just, you know, I wanted something else. I thought maybe I'd find it in the city. But the city is ... well, the city is damn expensive, for one thing." His face flushed and he looked down, embarrassed. I liked that he had said something true, something difficult. I caught his eye and smiled and then looked away quickly.

"You're telling me," Corinne agreed. "But still. It's pretty awesome."

"Yeah," said Anthony. "I just can't get enough of the city, to be honest. I'm that total tourist, bumping into people 'cause I can't stop looking up at the skyscrapers."

"Me too!" said Corinne. "I wish I grew up here." She was pointedly looking at me.

"Whatever," I said. "I grew up in Queens." I rolled my eyes.

"Yeah, but you have the subway. You have Manhattan."

"The only time I ever went to Manhattan was on school trips," I confessed.

"What?" Anthony was surprised.

"Yeah," I could feel my cheeks starting to redden. It was so lame that I didn't ever venture out of my borough. I tried to explain. "Manhattan's like fifteen minutes away, but, I don't know. It's far in other ways, you know?"

"I guess," Corinne countered. "But I grew up in Jersey and I came to the city almost every weekend once I turned thirteen."

I just shrugged. We all sat there for a minute. I could tell Corinne was still kind of gaping at me because of all the stuff I had said. I shot her a look out of the corner of my eye.

"You got some books there?" Anthony nodded at the little pile of books Corinne had bought from the library.

"Yeah," said Corinne. "I was teasing Iffy, I mean my friend here—she's gonna start her own public park public library. You got a membership card?"

He shook his head. "How do I get one?"

"Well, let's see. I guess you have to make a donation. A significant donation."

Anthony looked at me, smiling, and shrugged. "The wallet's a little light today, but I'm good for it."

"I think we can trust him, Corinne," I put in.

Corinne looked skeptical but handed him the stack of books. Most were trash, but she had a couple of good ones, a couple I was interested in. Two Stephen Kings, a book called *Watership Down*, a thriller called *A Good Girl*.

Anthony looked at each one and picked out the thickest paperback, *Watership Down*. Its pages were yellowed and it had a picture of a rabbit on the cover. "Can I borrow this one?"

"Well. I don't know ..." said Corinne, the strict librarian. I think it all seemed a little absurd to all of us; what did borrowing really mean in this life we were in?

Anthony looked at us in earnest. "I'll see you guys again," he protested.

I suppose I continued to look dubious. "Well," he added, kind of shyly. "We could plan to meet up sometime. Where do you guys usually hang out?"

He was looking at me.

I smiled.

CHAPTER 24

"Oh my god, he was totally checking you out," Corinne squealed in my ear as he walked away.

"Shut up," I hissed.

"No, for real! And he's totally hot. You should hook up with him, Iffy."

"Corinne," I said, exasperated. "Shut *up!*"

"What?" She gave me a little push. Angel saw that we were playing and started leaping around, feinting and darting away.

"You two!" I laughed and complained. "Corinne, I have not had a real shower in, god, I don't even know how long."

She wrinkled her nose. "No kidding. I do think this is something you might want to remedy, Iffy."

"Whatever. He's probably just gonna steal our book."

"Maybe. Maybe not. Maybe he'll become a famous musician and he'll take us both away from all this." She pulled a face. "He's looking for something, you know."

"Stop it, Corinne," I groaned. "Don't be mean."

I got up and started putting things away just to have something to do.

"I'm just kidding," she said, rising too. "He's just so ... earnest. I guess that's how they grow them upstate. And you!" she cackled. "With the glasses!" I didn't look at her, feigning ignorance. "And I've never heard you say so much since I met you!"

"That's not true," I protested.

"It is so true!" she laughed. "I just thought you were quiet. Now I find out that you only talk to boys. You were saving all your energy to be a flirt."

"Please, stop." I was trying to frown but smiling all the same.

"Iffy, I think that's awesome," Corinne was suddenly sincere. "I think he's cool." She poked me, and when I looked she was smiling. "Lucky," she said. "Lucky Iffy."

I pretended I didn't want to talk about it anymore, but I could have talked about Anthony—what he looked like, what he said, what he meant when he said whatever he said—I could have talked about those twenty minutes for the next twenty hours. He was just so cute. So cute.

And I didn't have my hopes up or anything, but I felt something when I looked at him and he looked at me. Recognition or something. Whatever, I knew it was crazy. But I had a vague sense that I would now better understand all sorts of lyrics that I used to sing along with but never really got.

Of course I knew there was no way he could actually like me. I was literally a bum. A homeless person. A bag lady.

Corinne mused, "Crazy days, huh? Henry, that lady, now this guy. Who knew we weren't invisible, am I right?"

I smiled.

"Or maybe we're still invisible," she added. "But they can smell us coming?"

"That bad?" I scrunched my nose.

"Not good," she replied. "Why not go over to McDonald's? Stop at that Rockbottom while you're there and buy yourself some cosmetics. You need to clean this up," she said, flapping her hand up and down at my face. "Angel will protect me 'til you get back."

"You sure you're okay?" I suddenly felt guilty. I had completely forgotten about her run-in with Henry.

"I'm fine. Just need to keep my head down is all. Go now, before it gets too late. Tomorrow," she promised me, "tomorrow we'll find that Dougie."

Because we didn't think it was safe for Corinne to show her face, I'd been asking around without her. It had gotten me, predictably, nowhere. Most of the people I approached—homeless, junkies, people sitting on random benches—looked at me like I was crazy and ignored me or told me to get lost when I asked, "Do you know a guy named Dougie? Hangs out in the park?" Others listened and then sneered or acted suspicious or made remarks or jokes, usually at my expense. Without Corinne, people saw me for what I was, a skinny little loser.

I nodded, uncomfortable with the thought of her going around with me tomorrow, but grateful for her offer of help. There just wasn't a way to avoid it. I wasn't getting any info without Corinne.

I packed up, gave Angel a kiss, took the list, and headed out of the park. I wished I still had my board; walking everywhere takes so much longer. Plus, it would have been fun to ride fast, the board making its chug-chug rhythm over the lines on the sidewalks, broken by the high-pitch of the wheels on the asphalt when I crossed the street, and then the chug-chug again. I resolved to get enough money to get a new board soon, and then to get out of the park more, skate again. Maybe clean myself up a bit more.

The bathroom at McDonald's was mercifully empty, although a mom came in with her kid and pulled him close, watching me in the mirror as she stuffed him in a stall. I'd already taken a wet cloth to my face and now I was brushing my teeth.

I stared at myself in the mirror. I couldn't really tell how I looked. Can anybody?

I still had a bit of blue around my right eye, courtesy of Henry. So, that wasn't particularly attractive. I was wearing the same old black Ramones muscle shirt, which was cleaner than the shirt I'd come in with and I actually thought was looking better and better with wear. I was definitely scrawny, but otherwise I thought I was looking okay. Lizette had helped me dye my hair earlier in the year, and it was growing out, so it was a few inches of brown, a few inches of black. I had chopped it too, once I got to the park, and now it was down to my chin. I liked it. I had always had long hair before, and I thought this new length was kind of nice. More mature or something. I had small hoop earrings that I never took out and a tiny nose ring that I had forgotten about too. I thought it looked cool, but I also realized it might have been a little scary to that mother who had hustled out of the bathroom.

I wondered if it looked scary to Anthony.

Suddenly, I was seeing what I might look like through Anthony's eyes, and through that jogger's eyes. Did I look like a weirdo? Did I look desperate?

I didn't think so. Not desperate, at least. There was something different in my face now; a new toughness, a way that my mouth was set that wasn't there before. *Strong*, I thought. *Someone not to be messed with.*

Whatever, though, I told myself. I was totally obsessing about some guy that I had met for like, five minutes. In a park. Because he was *living there. That's pretty bad,* I thought to myself. *Now you want to date homeless guys? Pretty bad.* But still. There was something about him. He seemed really okay. He seemed nice.

He seemed gentle.

I got out of the bathroom before someone alerted the manager that there was a homeless chick cleaning up in the sink. I hadn't been able to resist the smell and I'd already eaten some fries, so I wasn't too hungry before stopping at Waldbaum's to get food for camp. I bought crackers, lentils, apples, some powdered milk, and some soft-baked chocolate-chip cookies. Cigarettes too. I wouldn't waste the money on real cosmetics, but I did buy a cherry Chapstick and baby wipes, and the Oil of Olay hair-removal stuff that Corinne used.

On the way back to the park I stopped at a pay phone outside a gas station. It smelled like gas, which I actually kind of liked.

It was cool in the shadow of the station.

"Who's this?" Lizette answered.

"Hey, Zette, it's Iffy."

"Iffy? What the—? Where are you, girl?"

"Nowhere."

"What do you mean nowhere? Everybody's been so worried about you!" Lizette was shrieking into the phone.

"I had to go, Lizette."

"Why? What are you talking about? Are you talking about your stepmom and all that? You coulda moved in with me and my mom. You coulda just come to my house. Where are you?"

"I couldn't live there anymore, Lizette."

"Are you coming back?"

"No."

"Iffy, what is going *on* with you? Why don't you just come back? Just come back," she repeated. "You can crash with me and my mom. I swear I won't tell anyone."

"Thanks, Lizette."

"I'm serious!"

"I know you are. But you know I can't. Your mom would turn me over to social services in five minutes."

"No, Iffy, she really likes you—"

"I'm not living in some group home."

"What are you even talking about? You need to just come back now, Iffy."

"I'm okay where I am. Really. I just wanted to let you know that."

"Marco was looking for you. He, like, hunted me down and was all like, 'Tell me where Iffy is.'"

"He was? I'm sorry, Zette."

"He's a scary dude, Iffy. You know he got arrested?"

"What happened?" I asked.

"So, I don't know but I guess they like busted down your door or something. So, they got him on like drugs or something."

I felt myself smiling.

"That's good," I said. "I'm glad. But he got out already?"

"Oh, yeah. That's what I mean." Lizette was as serious as I'd ever heard her. "He came over to the playground, he was asking me about you. He thinks you did it, girl. He thinks you turned him in or something."

I snorted. "I did!"

I could almost hear Lizette's eyes widening. "You did? What

are you, crazy? Did you also set him up with Oscar when you left? 'Cause there was a whole thing with that. Your stepbrother got his ass *kicked*, and he thinks you did that too."

I laughed again, out loud. "That's amazing! Tell me more!"

"No, for real, Iffy. Like, broken bones. Like, he walks with a real limp now and all."

"Good."

"You're crazy. I mean, he keeps bothering me. He kind of, like, pushed me and stuff."

"What?"

"He wanted me to tell him where you were."

"Marco pushed you?"

"Like, just up against a fence. But he got all in my face. He's pretty scary, Iffy."

"Yeah?" My heart pounded, but not with fear. With straight-up rage. Poor Lizette. I could just imagine her there, scared, cornered on the empty playground, hoping someone would help her. I hated him for making my friend feel that way.

"You just stay away from him, Lizette," I said harshly, the way a mother would. "You see him, you go the other way. You hear me?"

"Yeah, sure, Iff, but ..." she started. "He's been actually real nice since then. I don't know, he's been coming around the park ..."

"What do you mean, coming around the park?"

"Like, you know, the playground. He apologized for pushing me and he's been coming around and bringing snacks and stuff. I think he might, like, *like* me or something," she added doubtfully, but in a way that let me know she wasn't immune to his snakelike charm.

I was speechless.

"Iff? You there?"

"I'm serious," I said, my voice pinched in my throat. "Don't let him anywhere near you. I'll take care of this. I promise."

"Iffy, what is going on?"

Before I could answer she said, "Hold on," and she shrieked, "*Don't touch that!*" She was back. "Just gimme a minute, Iff." And then, "*I said, put it back. Just go watch your show or I'll turn it off.*" And then, "Sorry. I'm watching these kids for my mother. Shoot, Iffy. I wish you would come home. I miss you so much. I wish you would let me help you."

"How are you doing, Lizette? I only have another minute so I want to hear about you." My heart was still pounding and my breath short, but I tried to act normal, to pretend I wasn't freaking out.

"Fine," she said weakly. "It's been weird without you."

"Yeah."

"I miss you, Iffy."

"I miss you too. But, look, Zette. I gotta go. Remember what I told you, right? You see him coming, you go the other way. Marco isn't nice. He is *not* a nice person."

"Yeah, yeah," she said, her voice plaintive. She had heard me; she was listening.

"I gotta go, Lizette."

"I miss you, Iffy. You come home. Do you understand me?"

"I miss you too." I was trying to keep it together. "Bye, Lizette."

"Stay sweet, Iffy," she said, her voice a bit thin and pleading.

My quarter hadn't run out, but I had to get off the phone. I couldn't concentrate on what Lizette was saying because I was roiling.

Just because I was safe from him didn't mean he wasn't out there. Didn't mean he wouldn't bother someone else.

I wanted to be alone, in the woods. I had to think. I had to figure out what I was going to do. Because I knew I had to do something. Something more.

CHAPTER 25

Getting ready for bed that night, Corinne kept teasing me about Anthony.

"So, you excited for your big date?"

"Corinne," I warned, "he's meeting up with both of us. It's obviously not a date."

"Will you wear your black tank top or ... your black tank top?"

"I think I'll go with the black tank top. And it's not a date."

"If you two get married you could have the wedding right here in the park! And then you could live under the bridge together. Like Smurfs."

I feigned impatience. "I think they lived in mushrooms or something. But," I let out an exasperated sigh, "whatever. Good night."

"Good night. Sleep tight. Don't let the fleas and ticks bite."

"Too late." And that was the truth. All three of us—me, Corinne, and Angel—had flea bites. Angel really was the one who was crawling with them, but we all slept in the tent, so they jumped off her and onto us. Between the mosquitoes and the fleas, I was always scratching somewhere.

It had been a hot day, but the night was cool. Most nights were. There were lots of summer storms—not too much rain, but the bottom of the tent would be wet when we woke, and sometimes it was downright cold. I felt good and safe, lying on my side, breathing that musty tent smell. We never went to sleep right away, even though we always waited until we were both really tired before we climbed in. It was still too much like a sleepover: the minute I zipped that tent up, we had a million things to say, to tell each other.

I was quiet for minute. Then, I turned onto my back. "I called my friend Lizette today." I spoke into the air above my face. "It was nice to talk to her. She told me my stepbrother got arrested."

"Oh yeah?" said Corinne. She had been turned away from me, but now she turned onto her back too. "What'd he do?"

"He was dealing drugs and stuff. But I guess he's out already."

We lay in a silence a little longer. Angel, who had been nestled in the curl of my legs, now tried to work her way in between them. She groaned and settled.

"It was me. Who turned him in," I said at last.

"What do you mean?"

"I called the police one day and told them where to look."

Corinne was quiet for a minute. "Wow, Iffy."

After a while I just said it, out loud, for the first time ever: "He did stuff. To me ..."

Corinne inhaled sharply, but she knew already. She kissed me on the side of the head. "Oh, Iffy ..." She wasn't surprised, but I could hear in her voice that she was upset.

"He said ..."—I told her what I had never told anyone—"that I should thank him. That I was so ugly, that no one else would ever want to ..."

Corinne sucked in her breath again. "God, Iff. That's disgusting. That's so awful."

I listened, hearing her.

After a while, Corinne asked, "What's up with your dad?"

"What do you mean?"

"I mean, what's his deal? Why didn't he, like, do something?"

I lay there, thinking.

"He's just ..." I was at a loss, really. "He's just ... kind of ... I don't know," I said. I almost laughed. "I honestly don't think he cares. He doesn't ... there was this one time. I was just a kid, like twelve or something. My stepbrother had me in his room and my dad came home and my stepbrother was like, threatening me and telling me to get out and all that and I went in the living room and I was crying. And my father looked right in my face. He looked right in my face and he saw me and he turned around and walked into the kitchen."

"Iffy," Corinne whispered. She squeezed my arm.

"And then you know there was my stepmother and she said things, messed-up things. God, I don't even want to repeat it ... about me, like, dressing a certain way or bothering my stepbrother. Like she was always suggesting ... that I *wanted* to go in there or something." A sadness seemed to settle deeply in my stomach. I was saying out loud things I had long seen in the periphery but had never looked at straight on. "They knew, Corinne. Maybe they didn't know everything. But they knew. And they didn't protect me."

I heard Corinne sigh. "Yeah. I think it's like that a lot, Iffy. I think that's how it is a lot."

Again we lay, listening to the crickets, the cicadas screaming in the night. "So, they moved in when I was nine." It looked like

Corinne was going to get the whole story.

"That must've sucked."

"I mean, it did, but it didn't at first," I said. "I was excited at the time. She was really nice to me in the beginning. She actually told me to call her 'Mom.'" I felt an anger rising in me as I told Corinne this. Anger and shame and guilt too: guilt that I so badly wanted to replace my mother that I called another woman "Mom" in exchange for some stuffed animals, some peanut butter cups, a few minutes of pretended interest in my television shows.

"Then she turned on you?"

"I guess. I think it was probably all just a show."

We were quiet for a minute.

"For a long time," I continued, "I did think it was my fault. Like, she found out what I really was and she was so disappointed and that was why she hated me so much."

"Fuck her."

I made a noise like a laugh, even though it wasn't funny.

"But the worst part ... was that I ... oh god, Corinne." My breath caught as the shame came. I didn't think I could say it.

"It's okay, Iff," she said, facing me in the darkness. I couldn't see her features, but I felt her there. She put her hand on my shoulder. "You can tell me."

"My stepbrother, so you know, he's, like, older than me?"

She didn't say anything.

"It's just that ... I remember thinking he was ... Like, I was so excited to have this older, handsome stepbrother." I took a breath and then spit it out, "It was like I had a crush on him."

"It wasn't your fault, Iffy. You were a little kid."

I turned my face away and began to cry.

I hadn't ever really thought about that before, I don't think. It had been there, in my mind, but I hadn't thought about it. In a flash, I remembered the day they came over for the first time. I was playing with my Barbie dolls on the coffee table. My dad brought this woman and her son into the living room. I didn't know then that they were monsters. They were smiling.

I had met her one or two times before that and she had always been nice to me. She introduced her son and I put the dolls under the table, feeling embarrassed, like I was too old to play Barbies. My dad had said we would all be a family now or something like that. I looked at these people, tried to smile. The boy smiled back at me, said, "Hey, little sis." I thought, *everyone will be so jealous that I have this cute stepbrother.*

"You were just a little baby," Corinne kept saying. "None of it was your fault."

She put her arms around me. I was crying, sobbing in the way I had once before, after the guy with the knife, just kind of heaving. It felt terrible and embarrassing, but it was also a relief to cry into my sleeping bag like that, to have someone else there.

There was more, more that I felt like I wanted to get out, but I didn't know how. So, for a while, I just kept crying.

It was a long time, I think. When I finished crying, I sat up, still hiccuping, Angel groaning because I disturbed her. I grabbed a dirty T-shirt to wipe my nose and eyes.

"You okay?"

"I'm okay."

We just lay there together quietly, me hiccuping at odd intervals. Angel settled down and started snoring.

"Smell that?" I asked.

"Yeah," Corinne confirmed. "Skunk. You think it's nearby?"

"Probably not. I think the smell just really carries."

"Yuck."

"I kind of like it."

"You would," Corinne teased, gently.

We lay there longer, smelling and listening.

"Iffy?"

"Yeah?"

"You got a plan?"

"Not really," I paused, "I didn't really think I'd make it this far."

"What do you mean?"

"I guess I figured I'd wind up in jail or in foster care or dead or something," I confessed. "I didn't think that a fifteen-year-old could just start living in a park and no one would notice."

She pressed. "But what's next? You can't stay here. Not in the fall. Not in the winter."

"I'm not sure yet." I hadn't wanted to think about this. "What about you?"

"What about me?"

"Can you go to your mom's?"

"I don't know," she sighed. "There's a lot of history there. She's ... disapproving. Plus, last time ... well, last time was probably the last time, you know? She's pretty fed up. And, like I said. She's got her own ... you know."

"But she might take you back?" I persisted.

"Maybe," Corinne conceded. "It's iffy, Iffy." I heard her smile. I almost smiled too.

CHAPTER 26

Corinne promised me, eventually, that she would try to go to her mother's, but said she wasn't leaving until we found Dougie.

But no one knew Dougie. We even went back to find Corinne's friend Monique, but she wasn't there and none of the other girls wanted to talk to us. And I hadn't been able to find that guy Danny again either. It was hot and quiet every day. It seemed like we had hit a dead end.

One good thing was that there was always more stuff by the rock. Wet wipes, dog treats, cans of fruit cocktail, a carton of six eggs with a note that said "hard-boiled, for humans and dogs," a big, fluffy pillow, ten bucks, twenty bucks.

"We hit the lottery," Corinne said each time we recovered another haul.

We toted stuff for a picnic at a little clearing by the old railroad bridge that day, all three of us, me and Corinne and Angel, in great moods, eating our eggs and our fruit cocktail. Anthony had said he would find us, but he didn't say what time, so I was nervous, always listening, waiting, hoping he was gonna walk up any minute.

Corinne had brought my little radio and she changed the station maniacally, never wanting to hear any commercials.

"Is this your kind of music?" she teased, landing on a song I recognized. It was Bon Jovi.

"I used to kind of like him," I said. When I saw Corinne's face I asked, "Is that embarrass—"

"Yes," she cut me off. "Very. And I'm from New Jersey."

She switched to Hot 97.

"Better," she said.

I wanted to talk more about music, to get more information. The guys I had met when I first started skating made it clear that pop was for losers, so of course I never said anything about the music I liked back then, including poor Bon Jovi. The boys all had Ramones T-shirts; one day Jess gave me a tape. And then I was like, *this makes sense.* It felt, in my ears, the way really good food tastes. I couldn't get enough of it. And then, even better, was that the Ramones were from Queens. They could've been guys I knew; they could've been me, even.

From the Ramones I discovered the Sex Pistols and then I started listening to more old stuff: the Velvet Underground and David Bowie. I don't remember how I found the Pixies, but they made sense to me in the same startling, exciting way that the Ramones had.

Hot 97 went to commercial and Corinne ran a finger over the serrated dial.

I heard a few muffled chords that I recognized. "Wait, the Rolling Stones," I said. "I think?"

Corinne propped the radio on a brick, neatly extinguished the cigarette she was holding and rested it carefully next to the radio.

"Let's dance," she said.

Corinne stepped in front of me as though she was stepping onto a stage and began to sway and move. She had one arm bent at the elbow and held in the air as though she was holding one of those fancy, long cigarettes and the other arm also bent, but held down along her body. One foot was in front of the other and she twisted at the waist as she rocked back and forth. Sometimes she shimmied her shoulders.

She was smiling, but she was completely serious about this dance, so completely unselfconscious, like there was absolutely nothing absurd or insane about it. "Come on," she demanded. "You dance too."

She grabbed my hands and pulled me to stand. I resisted, saying, "I don't really dance."

"Whatever." Corinne let me go, backing away, but still facing me, as though she was taunting me. She started kicking her feet in this really awkward way, not at all in keeping with the song's rhythm.

I laughed—at her dance, at its unexpectedness and silly beauty—and then she was laughing too, although probably not at herself, just laughing because she was the kind of person that laughed when other people laughed. I surrendered and got up there with her and started pumping my hips a little, which is my standard move-a-little-but-not-so-much dance, although it didn't really fit the song. So, I started to try to copy Corinne and we were both moving and jerking and Angel was nipping at our kicking feet and jumping up, like trying to tell us to stop such silly dancing, that we would hurt ourselves with this nonsense. We both kept trying to grab her front paws when she jumped up, tried to make her dance like a human, but then she would dodge and escape and harass the other dancer.

And then I heard the leaves crunching and Angel started barking and I stopped dancing. I saw Anthony through the woods, carrying something big and unwieldy. Angel ran to him, circled him as he approached, nipping at the air around him.

"What is going on here?" Anthony laughed.

"Um, we might ask you the same thing," Corinne said, still dancing.

"Bookshelves," he announced, putting them down. "You know, for the Public Park Public Library. This is my donation."

I broke out in a huge smile. "That's so awesome!"

"Oh lord," Corinne groaned, collapsing dramatically on the ground. "What the—?"

"Where did you get this?"

Anthony turned to me. "I didn't buy it," he explained. "Someone was getting rid of them."

"So, it's trash," Corinne put in.

"Isn't there a saying? One man's trash?"

"Is another woman's lending library?"

"I think that was really nice of you," I said.

"Where should I put it?"

"Um, right here is fine," I said. "Corinne?"

"A little to the left."

"Perfect."

We looked at the shelves, leaning a little against the big oak tree, and the whole clearing suddenly became a little more civilized, a little more homelike.

Anthony took *Watership Down* out of his back pocket; placed it on the middle shelf.

I smiled at him.

"I wish I had a camera." I surveyed our setup. "I like how this looks."

"You finished that book already?" Corinne asked, sitting up. He nodded.

"You must be a fast reader," I said.

"Nah, just broke. Broke, with a lot of time to ride the subway." But he smiled as he said it. I noticed he had a faint laugh line on the right side of his mouth. Someday that little line might be a deep wrinkle. It was the sweetest thing I'd ever seen, I thought. "And it was a great book, actually. Might even be my new favorite book."

"Well, it sounds good," I said stupidly, realizing only after I'd said it that he hadn't told us anything about the book.

"It's about rabbits."

"Rabbits," I echoed. "Yeah, I guess so ..." I picked up the book and looked at the cover. Yes, there were rabbits all right. I put the book back on the shelf.

"But it's good though," he insisted.

"Cool," I said, smiling, wishing I had something else to say.

"*Cool*," Corinne mimicked. "Whatever, you two." She bent down and grabbed handfuls of leaves and tossed them in our direction. Rather than flying, they fell, pathetically, from her hands. "Why don't you just start making out and forget all this talk about books." She stuck her nose in the air and did an exaggerated snooty voice. "Oh yes, and have you read Shakespeare? No, my dear, I was too busy showering at the children's playground!"

I had already shouted, "Shut up, Corinne!" but she just kept going. I picked up a handful of pebbles and sprayed her with them.

"Eek!" she cried. Angel lunged, snapping at the rocks.

Corinne lifted her hands in the air and threw herself at my feet. "I give up," she said dramatically, before Angel leapt on her and started licking her face. "Oh my god, stop! Call off your hounds, Iffy!"

"Angel," I tried to admonish her through my laughter. She jumped up on me, back to Corinne and then back to me again, her tail wagging, her big jaw smiling. She wanted to just keep on playing.

"Hey, good dog," said Anthony, holding out his hand to pet her. She obliged, hitting at his palm with her big skull, resting a paw on his foot. "So, hey," he said suddenly. "What did she just call you anyway?"

"What?"

"Just now. 'Iffy'?"

"Oh. Yeah. That's a nickname."

"It's cute," said Anthony.

Corinne groaned; I smiled.

Angel, feeling neglected, jumped up on Anthony, sticking her face in his face. He rubbed her neck.

"How long have you had her?" he asked.

"Couple of months, I guess," I said.

"Found her in the park?"

"Yeah," I admitted, trying not to think about Ann.

"How long you been living here?"

"She was born here, right under that bridge," Corinne said. "She owns the joint. In fact, the city is gonna change the name. Gonna call it 'Iffy Park.' Sorry. Make that 'Brenda Park.'"

"The Park of Saint Sneak?" I offered.

Corinne's face lit up. "Good one, Iff! I mean, Bren."

"You are just something else today, Corinne," I said, laughing, but screwing up my lips at her.

She flipped her hair. "Must be because there's a gentleman around."

"Where?" Anthony joked, looking over his shoulder. I grinned.

"Sorry," I said. "I've been here since the end of May."

"Whoa!"

"Yes," said Corinne. "I tell her she's veteran homeless now. An expert. A pro—professional, that is. Do not get the wrong idea."

"I *am* a gentleman," Anthony insisted. "I would never."

"A professional bag lady," I said. "I prefer pro-hobo."

Corinne laughed at that one.

"I read about these people," said Anthony, "who plant vegetables on public property. I think it's called guerrilla farming or something. You should totally do that."

"Not a bad idea," I said, lifting my eyebrows.

"Oh, yes it is," said Corinne. "It's hard enough to convince her she's gonna have to leave this park someday as it is. Don't get her starting a garden."

"Well, I suppose it's too late in the season anyway," I said. "Gonna be fall soon."

"There's always next year," Corinne said sarcastically.

"What are you gonna do for the winter?" Anthony asked.

"We were just talking about that," Corinne said.

"Don't know," I said. "I've got the dog." I looked at Angel, who had thrown herself to the ground and seemed, amazingly, to be already asleep. "I guess we're just gonna have to bundle up and all. You know?"

Corinne rolled her eyes. "Bundling up is not gonna cut it in

January, Iffy. It's not even gonna cut it in October. You'll definitely freeze to death." She was serious but then stopped with her hands, clawlike, grasping at the air, as though she had been frozen in place. "Like Hansel and Gretel or whatever."

"I don't think they froze to death," Anthony said.

"Well, that's because they moved in with the witch," Corinne answered.

"That didn't really work out for them either, though," I said.

"You people," Corinne shuddered. "You are so literal."

"It's just hard to imagine now," I said. My forehead was beaded with sweat. "In this weather."

"Just 'cause it's hard to imagine doesn't mean it isn't true," she said, and I saw a flash of anger for a moment, an impatience. "It's serious, Iffy. We have got to figure something out."

"Maybe you should head south or something," Anthony said.

"Yeah," I said. "I thought of that." We sat quietly for a minute and then I added, "You know, I once heard about this guy who walked all the way to Florida by just going down the coast."

"That's not possible," Corinne said.

"It is, though," I protested. "Some places are people's private beaches and stuff so you have to be careful, but you could follow the coast all the way down."

"That sounds awesome," said Anthony. "If you do that, maybe I'll come with you."

I felt the blood rush into my cheeks, and I couldn't help it, my lips turned themselves up in what I can only imagine was the goofiest smile.

Corinne cut her eyes to me, but thankfully said nothing.

Then, something occurred to me. "What's the date, anyway?" I asked.

"Today?" Corinne said. "No idea."

"It's the twenty-first," Anthony said. We looked at him. "Of July," he added.

"We knew that," Corinne said. "Just kidding."

"It's my birthday," I said.

"What?" Corinne shouted.

"Yeah," I said. "I totally forgot."

"This is your sweet sixteen, isn't it, Iffy?"

I nodded, smiling. "Wow."

"You are such a ..." Corinne began. "Who forgets their own birthday?"

"It's not that I forgot," I explained. "I just lost track of the days."

"Happy birthday," Anthony offered. He reached out and patted me.

"Happy birthday, you *b-i-t-c-h*," said Corinne, punctuating each letter with a little punch on the shoulder. "I am totally unprepared for this. Thanks a lot."

"Sorry," I said. "I mean, whatever. I didn't mean to make a big deal."

"Stop it! Sixteen is a big deal! A huge deal!" Corinne cried, looking to Anthony for confirmation.

"It is a pretty big deal," he agreed.

I shrugged. Smiled. My face was hurting from all this smiling.

Corinne clapped her hands. Angel leapt up. "We should do a cookout tonight. Commandeer one of those grills over on the other side of Woodhaven, get us some hot dogs or something."

"That sounds great," Anthony said.

And it did sound great, but I had my reservations.

"Are you sure that's a good idea, Corinne?"

She looked at Anthony. "Iffy and I are incognito," she said. "Hiding out and all that. I mean, now that you know her real-fake-name—you don't think her name is 'Iffy' do you?—we might have to kill you." She widened her eyes at Anthony. "So, Iffy, we'll have to wear disguises. Do you have an extra mustache, Anthony?"

"I guess I could try and grow a first one real quick," he answered. "Not sure about a spare, though."

"Corinne," I groaned, warningly.

"It'll be fine, Iff," she cajoled. "We'll start late. Wear baseball caps. Pleeeease!"

Of course I couldn't resist. Corinne was irresistible.

So, it was arranged. We gave Anthony the most recent twenty bucks we'd gotten from Ann and it was his job to go to the store and get some charcoal, hot dogs, buns, and—extravagance!—sodas. He would steal ketchup and mustard from McDonald's. He said he had a couple of bucks too and that if he could afford it and they didn't proof, he'd also get some tall boys. In the meantime, Corinne and I would pick up other supplies from our stash and meet him by the picnic area on the other side of the park.

As soon as Anthony was out of sight, Corinne said, "Do you think he'll just take off with our money?"

"Nah," I said. "He brought our book back."

"Besides," she said, "he's in love."

"Yeah, right," I made a face at her, sticking out my tongue and rolling my eyes. For real, though, I had butterflies in my stomach just thinking about Anthony's face. I didn't know if he was in love, but I had a feeling I might be.

CHAPTER 27

"You just have no idea what you are missing," I said, nose in the air.

Anthony laughed, despite the fact that I had made that remark about a dozen times already.

"Um, ketchup and mustard together on a hot dog is just vile," said Corinne. "I think it might be a fact."

"Must be Jersey thing," I said, shaking my head. "And upstate. Only people in Queens understand how to do a hot dog."

Corinne started in on her third dog. I had had two myself, even though Anthony hadn't been able to get mustard, which I was maintaining was a key condiment. The hot dogs tasted so good, actually, that they didn't really need toppings at all—or even a bun for that matter.

"Say it again," Anthony teased.

"Oh my god, leave me alone!" I cried.

"Just say it," Corinne said. "You keep your underpants in your dresser ..."

"Shut up," I said.

"*Draaaaw,*" Corinne mimicked.

"What? It's a draw."

Corinne turned to Anthony, "Unbelievable."

"I think it's cute," he said.

"Well, Iffy," Corinne said. "Look no further. A man who find the Queens accent 'cute.'"

"One in a million," I conceded. "Unless, of course, the man is himself from Queens."

"Ah, Queens guys are the pits," Corinne said. "I should know."

I made a face and tried to, like, guffaw, but it didn't come out right.

I noticed that Anthony sat up a little straighter.

"Poor Angel," I said, changing the subject. "She looks totally pooped."

Anthony had bought a Frisbee, too, and he had thrown it for Angel and chased her for what seemed like hours. She was so happy playing, and he looked happy too, leaping around and falling down and rolling on the ground. It was almost normal for a few hours there. Just like we were three friends who decided to meet in the park to have a cookout, to play with the dog, to drink a few beers. Like after we had our cookout, we were each gonna go home to our houses, with our families, maybe watch some TV before going to sleep in beds, with sheets and pillows, with walls around us.

I didn't know if I would even like sleeping in a bed anymore.

Maybe it was the beer, more than anything, that made me feel so sleepy and happy and okay. I'd never really drunk a lot and I was also, I knew, kind of skin and bones. I could just hear Lizette in my head, "*I am so jealous,*" she would say, and I'd try to explain, to be serious, "*No, no, this is not a good diet, Lizette. This is not healthy,*" but she'd insist, "*Yeah, but, you know, if I lived in the park you think I would get that skinny?"* Despite myself, I smiled just thinking about it.

So, I guess I was a little drunk.

It was night and, besides us, nobody was cooking anymore. There were three other groups at the barbecue spot, sitting at picnic tables, drinking and talking. Some people had a small, yappy dog that they had on a super long cord that the dog kept getting tangled around the picnic table. It would whine and bark until someone noticed and then the whole thing would start all over again.

Another group's radio played hip-hop loud enough for us all to enjoy. They were kind of young, too, and had little kids with them. One of the kids had been asleep in a stroller literally for hours.

The group closest to us was all women, older types. They seemed to be drinking heavily and getting drunker and drunker as the evening turned to night. It was one of those great, weird, New York things, where all these strangers share the same spot and even sort of acknowledge one another but then go ahead and act like the others don't exist at all.

"It's totally unprofessional," one of the drunk women was declaring loudly, "And I will tell her that to her face. I swear to god."

One of her friends agreed, *"Totally* unprofessional."

We all overheard and looked at each other and laughed. "Totally unprofessional!" Corinne mimicked in a whisper. I giggled. She popped the end of a dog in her mouth before she lit another cigarette.

Anthony cleared his throat. "We do have desert," he said, and he got up and picked up a plastic grocery-store bag. "Corinne, if you would?"

"Don't look, Iffy," Corinne demanded and I rolled my eyes and smiled and got down on the ground with Angel, scratching her belly. I could hear them taking the Entenmann's cake out of the box, messing with the candles, lighting them with Corinne's lighter.

"We're ready!" Corinne cried.

I stood and turned and they began to sing a loud, joyous version of "Happy Birthday," Corinne harmonizing: "Happy birthday, dear Iffff-ieee, Happy birthday to you!" Angel roused herself and stood up, barking along and whining, putting her front paws on the picnic table bench and eyeing the cake.

Anthony took out one of those plastic disposable cameras. I laughed when I saw it, and he took a picture of me, laughing too, the little flash exploding at me, and then he slid the wheel to advance the camera and to get ready to take another picture of me blowing out the candles.

"You guys are the best," I said, looking from one to the other of their sweet, smiling faces. I don't know who was more pleased, them or me.

I blew out the candles. I wished. I wished so hard. I had learned my lesson from fairy tales, though, to never make your wish too specific. Like, if you wish for a lot of money, you might get a big check, but because, like, you lost your arm in an accident or something. So, I left it vague. *I wish to be okay. I wish for us all to be okay.*

"I didn't know what kind you liked," Anthony apologized. "I figured everyone likes chocolate?"

"Chocolate is perfect," I said, smiling, taking the candles out one by one, careful not to waste any cake. "Thanks so much, you guys."

They beamed back at me.

"Here," said Corinne. "Take a picture of me and Iffy." She slid her arm around me. We smiled big smiles for the camera.

"And one of you and Iffy," she announced immediately and I stood next to Anthony and he put his arm around me and without thinking I leaned into him and Corinne snapped the photo.

"Not like we will ever see any of these pictures," I remarked. "I mean, are we going to get them developed?"

Corinne stuck out her tongue at me and waved me back toward Anthony. "See if you can get Angel in the picture."

"Come here, girl," I called. She jumped up. Another flash.

"It was a stroke of brilliance to buy this, dude," Corinne said to Anthony. "Hold up—one last one." She left us there and approached the ladies at the neighboring table to ask if they'd take a photo for us. One agreed and returned with Corinne.

The lady squinted into the viewfinder. "All right now … ready?"

Corinne crammed me in between her and Anthony; Angel sat at our feet. It was perfect.

"And another—a goofy one!" Corinne announced and I stuck out my tongue and crossed my eyes, Anthony did big arms, and Corinne made a monster face. I blinked away the light spots on my eyes.

"Thanks so much," Corinne said. "Want some cake?"

The lady declined and headed back to her friends.

So, we ate our cake and laughed, Anthony telling us stories about what Corinne called "the colorful characters of beautiful upstate New York": the neighbor who hoarded dogs and played his drums all night long, the manager of a McDonald's who sold drugs at the drive-through window.

"It takes a certain kind of person to live upstate," Anthony informed us.

"I'll say," Corinne agreed.

"You seem normal," I said.

"'Seem' is the important word there," Anthony said.

"I'm gonna go pee," Corinne said, dabbing her mouth with a napkin. "And maybe take Ang for a little stroll on this lovely evening." She held up her beer in a "cheers." The little slosh betrayed how little was left. "So, you two lovebirds, well, you know ..." She did a funny little bow. Maybe Corinne was drunk too.

"Corinne," I groaned. Anthony chuckled awkwardly.

She had to rouse Angel, who was conked out at my feet. "Come on, sweet doggie," she said, tugging on her collar. "I need you to act as my guard dog." Eventually Angel stood up and stretched and looked at me.

"You go ahead, Angel," I said. "You have a good walk."

"Ta-ta," Corinne winked.

And of course it immediately became so weird being alone with Anthony. Like, five seconds before that, I couldn't shut up, I was so comfortable and happy and then suddenly I was, like, racking my brain for something to say. I sipped my beer, looked at the ground. We were sitting next to each other with our backs to the picnic table, looking at the grill and, beyond that, the people with the little dog. Anthony leaned forward, put his chin in his hand.

"Corinne's pretty funny."

"Yeah," I jumped on that, relieved to have something to talk about, "she's great."

"She's not ..." he hesitated. "I don't care or anything. But she's ..."

"What?" I said, innocently.

"Is she, like, a guy?" Anthony asked, looking at me.

I shrugged. "No," I answered a little sharply, perhaps to disguise my own confusion. She and I hadn't really talked much about it, and I didn't feel I was the right person to be answering these questions about her. "I mean, does it matter? She just is who she is."

I shot him a look. I told myself it was fine he was wondering. But not being okay with Corinne being exactly who Corinne was would be a big problem. For real. I was nervous for a minute. I liked him a lot. I wanted him to say the right thing.

He did.

"No, I think Corinne is great," he said quickly, apologetically.

"She's, like, the best friend I've ever had." I looked at him. "I love my friend Lizette and all—I've known her since I was a kid—but Corinne knows me better than anyone else on the planet." I realized these words were true as I was saying them. I had never been able to talk to anybody the way I talked to Corinne.

"I mean it. I think she's great. I really don't care about any of that stuff. I was just, I don't know, just asking."

I nodded, relieved.

"You're both great," he said. "I never met anyone like either of you."

I smiled, but I didn't say anything.

"It's weird," he said, and I could feel him looking at me. "You guys didn't know each other before, either?"

"No, we met in the park, too."

"You must just draw people to you," he said.

"What?"

"Well, it must be you. You're like the magnet. The spit that holds this whole operation together."

"Nice ..."

"Just kidding," he said. "About the spit. But really. The dog, Corinne, me. That lady who leaves you stuff. Guess you don't even notice it. People are drawn to you."

"No," I said, confused. "I never felt like that."

It didn't seem right to me, what he was saying, but at the same time, it *did* seem right. I had always been so alone in my life. I always felt so awkward, so dull, so lame. So invisible. But at the same time ... at the same time ... something else, too.

And while I sat there, enjoying what he had said, feeling embarrassed but also wonderful too, more wonderful than I had ever felt in my life before, he leaned over and kissed me.

I had never been really kissed before. Not like the way Anthony kissed me. I guess, in general, boys had kind of made me nervous—even more nervous than other people. I knew a couple of guys through skating, but they were different. We just skated together, didn't talk.

To be honest, I was terrified of boys. Maybe I was also terrified that even if I really wanted to be kissed, that some part of me would shut down, that I wouldn't be able to do it or enjoy it or anything like that.

But I guess I didn't need to have worried so much. Kissing Anthony was a revelation. It was just right. Like listening to the Ramones that first time. It felt so good, I forgot to pay attention to it.

I didn't want to stop, not ever, but eventually I opened my eyes and leaned back and looked at that face, already so dear to me. "That was nice," I said.

He let me go and turned to face forward, but he put his arm around me.

"I've been wanting to do that since I first saw you."

"Me too," I blushed.

"That's ... that's pretty cool." He laughed a little. "So crazy."

"It is crazy. Weird, right?"

"Yeah. What are the chances that we would find each other, you know? And the moment I saw you ..." he trailed off.

"That's how I felt," I said, marveling. "Like, right away ..." I knew I was acting totally cheesy, but it was impossible to stop.

"I know." He sounded just as cheesy as me. "I know." And I couldn't stop smiling. I was glad we weren't facing each other directly, but still. I could tell he was smiling too.

So, we sat there like a couple of dorks, smiling, and then I perched up on the bench so I could kiss him some more and then he held my face in his hands and told me that he thought I was beautiful.

I looked down. "Ah, cut it out."

"What?"

"I just feel embarrassed."

He grabbed me around the shoulders and squeezed me hard.

I realized that the other tables were empty; all of the other people had left and I hadn't noticed. In the dark, with only orange lights from the streetlamps, the park looked gorgeous, like a movie set.

"Iffy," he said. "Is it okay if I call you that?"

I nodded. "Yeah," I said.

"Iffy, I want to hang out with you all the time."

I breathed out, happy. "Okay," I said, feeling a little shy again.

"I mean it! Is that okay, like, okay, we can hang out all the time?"

I nodded. "Yeah. Okay."

We smiled at each other. "So, let's do something tomorrow."

"Oh yeah? What do you want to do?"

"I dunno. Let's go somewhere. Let's go to the beach or something."

"That would be awesome," I said, absolutely meaning it. Being on the beach with Anthony. I couldn't imagine anything I would have liked more.

"Yeah, I have to do this thing for my brother, but if you don't mind, we could go, like, in the afternoon."

"I would love that," I said.

"You know what? I've always wanted to go to Coney Island and, Iffy, I've never been there. So, let's do this. Let me steal—I mean borrow," he laughed, "my brother's girlfriend's car, and me and you can head over to Coney Island."

"I've never been there either."

"What? You've lived here your whole life and you never even went to Coney Island?"

"Not that I can remember," I said. "We always went to Rockaway. Or, if we were feeling fancy, Jones."

"Well, cool. It'll be a first for both of us."

He smiled at me and I looked up at him and smiled too.

"You know," I said, "if I had known they had guys like you upstate, I would have run away there a long time ago."

He pulled me closer. "If I had known that there were girls like you ... well, I woulda spent a lot more time in city parks is all."

I tilted my head up and kissed his lower lip and then his upper lip before going in for a big kiss.

"Wow, Iffy," he breathed. "Wow."

PART V:
ALL SAINTS

CHAPTER 28

We didn't have watches, so we left the radio on and at ten to two I picked up my stuff to head out to the gate.

"Have fun on your date," Corinne teased.

"Oh, shut it," I answered.

"He's real cute, Iffy," Corinne said, genuine and suddenly serious. "You nervous?"

I nodded.

She put an arm around me. "He's really nice. Anthony's a really nice guy."

"I know ..."

"What is it? Do we need to, like, talk about the birds and the bees?"

I made another face.

"Okay, for real," Corinne said, dropping her arm and facing me. "What's wrong?"

"I mean ..." I sighed, looked away. "I just, you know. I haven't, like, ever really dated. Like, had a boyfriend or anything like that."

"You'll be fine," Corinne said. "Just be cool. He likes you, you like him. Just have a good time."

"I know ..." I said again.

"You were fine last night," she pointed out.

"I know. When I'm with him I feel fine, but ..."

"So, go!" she commanded. "Go be with him." She dropped her head into a tilt. "You'll feel better once you see him again."

Rationally, I knew she was right. Emotionally, not so much. I had butterflies in my stomach, thinking about the kiss, about the things he had said. Hoping that he hadn't, overnight, changed his mind about me.

"I'm happy for you, you know."

"Thanks, Corinne," I said. "I know you are." I bent down and scratched Angel behind her ears and under her jaw. "And thanks for watching Angel." I handed her the leash; I didn't want Angel following me after I left. "You two have fun now too. Be good."

"Tossed aside, just like that," Corinne snapped her fingers, "for a guy she just met."

"Aw," I said.

"Oh lordy, Iffy, I'm kidding." Corinne rolled her eyes. "Have fun!" she demanded, sticking out one hip and opening her eyes wide, imploring me to go.

"Okay, I'll meet you back here tonight." I gave Angel a final pat.

"It's fine, Iff, go."

"Okay." I stood there.

I sighed.

She swept her hands, as though to brush me away. "And you look totally hot. I mean, for a hobo. Now go!"

"Thanks a lot."

"You do, though. Very cute." I was wearing a little tank and some short shorts—Corinne's—which weren't quite as short on me as they were on her. I didn't have a bathing suit, but after a long discussion, Corinne and I decided I could go swimming in what I was wearing and I could change into a clean(er) tee and shorts after. I carried those clothes in a backpack; I also brought some water and snacks, a towel, some cash.

"Go!"

I kissed her on the cheek, one last kiss for Angel, and I was gone.

I had gotten a late start, though, and I was sweating as I jogged through the park, worried that I'd get to our meeting place at the Richmond Hill entrance and he would've gotten there and not seen me and left, but I only waited a minute or two, scanning the street, looking hard at every car that passed, when he pulled up in a black Corolla and honked.

"Hey!" I called, hustling over to the car, as though he would pull away if I didn't get there fast enough.

"What's up?" he said as I got into the car, slamming the door shut behind me, a little harder than I meant to.

He leaned over and kissed me on the cheek. He was the opposite of me: totally unhurried. It was cool in the car, the AC on high, blowing loudly. His hand rested on the gear shaft. I grabbed it. "Hi," I said, smiling.

Someone honked. "All right, all right," Anthony said into the rearview mirror, squeezing my hand in his and then letting go to shift into drive. As soon as he had pulled into traffic, though, he reached for my hand again.

Corinne was right. I was fine.

With Anthony, I was fine.

I noticed how big his hand was, especially compared to mine. Big and calloused, but clean. My hands were small and calloused and not as clean as I would've liked. But I was going to be getting in the ocean; just thinking about the beach and the seawater made me feel fresher, more awake.

"So, I think I know where I'm going," Anthony announced, but not with a lot of confidence. "I think I go straight down here for a while?" He nodded his head at the street that stretched out before us.

"Sure," I said. But I had no idea.

There were more than a couple of false starts. We would start going one way and then get into our conversation and then Anthony would say, "I have no idea where we are right now." Then he'd pull over and I'd yell out the window to some pedestrian, "Could you tell me how to get to Coney Island?" or, after the first guy's incredibly detailed instructions, "Can you tell us how to get to the BQE?"

One guy looked at me like I was crazy. His face somehow reminded me of Lizette. "From here?" he said, as though I had asked for directions to Madrid. He sighed and walked over to the car. "Well, you're gonna have to get to the LIE first," he said.

"We can do that," Anthony called from the driver's seat.

The man settled his forearms on the window and leaned in, like he was resigned to a long conversation.

We had to ask one more person after that, but eventually, we did get to the highway. And then, on the highway, of course we hit traffic. But that was okay, too, because it let us have time, together, holding hands, listening to the radio, talking, and sometimes kissing. We got honked at more times than I could count. But it was nice, in the AC. It was nice to be in a car. It was nice to be with Anthony.

"Listen, I want you to hear this song," Anthony said, fiddling with the tape deck. "This guy's called Daniel Johnston. He's like,

I don't know, like, sort of not-all-there but he's totally amazing. I guess ... just listen." And he turned up this song, piano and vocals, just the sweetest and saddest thing I ever heard. *"Some things last a long time,"* the man sang. I turned and looked out the window and listened.

"Do you like it?" Anthony asked over the music.

"Yeah," I said. Looking at Anthony. I wanted to add, "It's beautiful," but I couldn't.

Anthony smiled and we listened some more.

I liked the song, but what I liked even more was that Anthony wanted me to like it. I leaned my forehead against the cool window.

When the song was over he said, "I have something else for you to listen to."

I smiled.

He put a different tape in and turned up the volume and I heard a spare electric guitar and drums and a voice that I recognized as Anthony's.

I couldn't make out some of the lyrics, but what I could catch was strange and lovely. He crooned,

> *"I don't know what I would do*
> *without my honey baby-bee, but I suspect*
> *it could not be much better than*
> *whatever*
> *I am doing now"*

Or something. It was like poetry.

"I like this a lot," I said.

Anthony was smiling broadly. "You do?"

I nodded. "Is it the Beat Drums?"

"It is," he confirmed.

"What is it about?"

He shrugged. He was embarrassed.

"I really like it," I said.

"I'm glad."

I saw him a little bit differently, suddenly, knowing he was so talented, that he could sing and write and play guitar. I wondered, not for the first time, why he was interested in me.

"What?" he said, looking at the road and looking at me. "What?"

"Nothing." I shook my head.

He took my hand and squeezed it. "Iffy. Tell me everything about you. I want to know everything. Like, I don't know, what were you like when you were younger? Were you a trouble-maker? A good kid?"

I laughed. My desire to tell him, to tell him everything about me, overcame my self-consciousness. His interest in me was like the warm sun shining. "I don't know," I said. "I guess I was mostly just really quiet. And then I found skating. Skate-boarding. You know? So, that was cool."

"How did you start skateboarding?"

"My friend Lizette's little brother showed up at the park one day with this, like, weak-ass Toys 'R' Us skateboard and I looked at him trying to do it and I was like, 'I can do that.' And I could."

"So, you just knew how to do it?"

"Sort of. I mean, I fell down a lot too. But it was worth it. It was kind of like, okay, this is for me. You know? You ever feel that way?"

"Yeah," Anthony grinned. "That's how I feel about music."

"Cool. So, that was you playing guitar?"

"Yeah, that's my main thing, but I can play most anything, you know, if you give me a little while."

"That's so cool," I really meant it.

"I like it," Anthony said. "But tell me more about skateboarding. Like, are you like one of those kids you see hanging out in front of the mall, getting chased by the cops?"

"I don't know what you're talking about," I laughed. "But yeah, you know, I guess it's more than just skateboarding. I don't know. You meet a lot of people and stuff too. I know it's cheesy, but it is like a way of life and all."

"Yeah."

"My friend Lizette started skating too, although she was never very good and then we met all these guys, not like that, but you know, they'd always be like, *you girls skate?* And those skater guys, they were a lot cooler than the other guys from our high school. I don't know, less … basically not assholes, you know?"

"I guess. So what, though, you like skater guys?"

"No, that's not what I'm saying," I said quickly, embarrassed. "I just meant, I don't know. Whatever." Again, I wanted to say more. I wanted to say, "*I like you. You're the only guy I like,*" but instead I forced a laugh.

He laughed too and looked out over the wheel. "I'm no athlete, but I could get a board," he offered, joking. "Shoot, I'd do just about anything you asked." It was as though he could read my mind, as though he could simply say all the things I only thought about saying.

We smiled at each other.

"But you know, when I first saw you, I was like, 'What's up with her?' Like, in a good way? Like, you just looked so … okay, whatever. You can laugh, but you looked cool. You know? I was like, 'I'll never have a chance with a girl like that.'"

I was already slapping at his arm, saying, "Oh my god, shut up."

"Really, though," he said.

"Oh my god." I looked out the window to hide my smile, pretending to be mad.

I had tingles running up and down my spine. I couldn't stop grinning.

Of course, I wanted to hear more about what he thought of me when we first met, but I couldn't really pursue that without seeming like I was fishing for compliments. So, I figured, something for something: "Well, you know, I thought you were pretty cute when I first saw you."

"Oh yeah?" He had a case of the grins too.

"But, you know, I never thought that you'd like *me*. I have been living in a park and all."

"You have no idea how good you look," is all Anthony said.

"Shut up," I said again. *Yeah? Really?* I thought.

"I'm afraid you're gonna figure it out and dump me. Like, what are you doing going out with this chump?" he said, pointing his thumb at his chest. "I don't know, Iffy, you're so smart and funny and all that."

"No, I'm not," I said, thinking, "*dump me*," thinking, "*We're going out.*"

"Let's not even pretend, Iffy," Anthony said. "Like, I don't know your SAT scores, but all that camp stuff, you had it figured out. Not everyone could do that."

I shrugged. "I don't know."

"I do. And I may not be the smartest tool in the whatever,"

he said, laughing, "but I'm smart enough to know to get together with a smart girl. That's where my talent lies."

"Well, I can be the brains and you can be the beauty," I said.

"Oh, you got them both. I can be, well, I'll just be the boyfriend."

"You're my boyfriend?" I said, my heart soaring. His easiness, his warmth, made me feel like I could be warm and easy too.

"Is that okay?" He looked at me and squeezed my hand.

"Yeah," I said, smiling and nodding and laughing. "That's okay."

"For, like, real?"

"Yeah. For real."

He laughed too and then he said, "Awesome. 'Cause I'm done, Iffy. This is it for me. I'm yours for as long as you'll have me."

I looked down, still smiling. "Well, that's gonna be a long time." After a moment I added, "But don't worry, we won't have to live in the park."

He chuckled. "Whatever you want, Iffy. It's a nice blend of city and country."

"I think I'd like to live in the country," I said. I'd said it twice now, so I guess I meant it.

"I like it too," he said. "But maybe not Monticello. Maybe we could go south or west or something."

"That'd be cool," I said.

"You know, we should really think about, I don't know, like, whatever's next," he said gently. "Like, you think you're gonna go back? Finish school someday or what?"

"I want to. Definitely. I definitely want to."

"Me too," Anthony said. "I didn't finish high school either."

I kind of snorted. "We can study for the GED together, right?"

"Maybe, I guess. But you could actually go back to high school, right?"

It hadn't occurred to me, so I didn't answer right away. "No," I said finally. "I mean, it might be *allowed*, but I don't think I would. Go back. But wait, how old are you anyway?"

"Eighteen," Anthony said.

I didn't say anything for a minute, and I guess that made him nervous. "Is that too old for you?"

"No," I said, distractedly. "Sorry. I was just thinking about something else."

"Home?"

"I guess," I answered.

"So, you wouldn't go back there?"

"No," I said bluntly.

Anthony waited.

"No," I said again. "I might not stay in the park forever, but I won't go back there."

He nodded, looking out at the traffic.

Neither of us said anything for a while and then, very softly, he asked, "Why not?"

I didn't answer at first. I was thinking about what to tell him. How to tell him.

"If I hadn't left I probably would've killed myself," I said at last.

"Iffy," said Anthony. He looked at me. He looked back to the road, but put his hand on the side of my face and left it there.

"I mean, obviously I didn't do that. But I felt, really, like I didn't have any other, I don't know, *options*. You know? I couldn't stay there. But there wasn't anywhere else to go. So, I just thought ..."

I've had this problem sometimes, when I am saying something true, I get kind of choked up. Like something's literally stuck in my throat. And then I can't talk at all. I can barely even swallow. That happened with Anthony in the car. I stared out the window.

I kept looking out the window and eventually I said, "I guess, you know, I had a stepbrother. And he was really ... abusive to me? I mean, they all were. My father, my stepmother ... but he ... he was the worst."

We sat there for a minute and I finally looked at Anthony and he was frowning hard into the traffic. "I'd like to meet that stepbrother of yours," he began to growl. "I'd like to—"

"It doesn't," I interrupted. "It doesn't even matter anymore. I mean," I took a deep breath. I had to look out the window again.

I was thinking about how, even though it seemed to somehow satisfy me, I didn't need what Anthony was offering anymore, not really. For many years I had wanted someone to say exactly what he was saying. And now, it was nice to hear, but I didn't need it. I didn't even want it. I didn't want anything having to do with my stepbrother to contaminate Anthony.

But something else had been bothering me too. I couldn't get over the idea that my stepbrother had found Lizette, had pushed her around. That maybe he was now trying to get her to trust him. Like, he was *recruiting* her or something. I didn't want to tell Anthony about that because I hadn't been able to process it yet myself. I couldn't let that stand, could I? I couldn't just let my stepbrother be out there, in the world. Maybe hurting Lizette.

I shook my head, tried to return to the moment I was in. Anthony drove silently. "I guess there's something else, too. I mean, there's actually a lot of other stuff. A lot of ... complicated stuff. But there's one other thing I need to tell you now."

I glanced over and he nodded at me.

"It's ... well. I think my mom might have been living in the park," I admitted. "So, I guess I'm in the park, really, because I'm looking for her."

"You're looking for her," he repeated.

"Yeah." I waved a hand. "I don't want to get into all of it now. It's crazy. It looks like she may be gone now or whatever. I don't even know where to look. But that's why I went to the park in the first place."

I don't know why I didn't want to talk about it with Anthony. Maybe it was because, even though the whole thing wasn't quite as insane as it had initially appeared, it now seemed more hopeless than ever.

I got lost thinking again and then I looked over at Anthony, who seemed to be thinking hard, too, focusing on the traffic. I put my hand on the back of his neck, leaned toward him, and kissed him on the cheek. He kept his eyes on the road but turned his face a little and quickly kissed me back.

"The only thing is ..." I began. "I mean, I just want you to know that, well, if you hadn't already guessed, I'm a little messed up. I'm not ... I don't know. I've had a hard time, I guess. And I have a feeling it's gonna be a while before I'm really all right, you know? I'm not saying you have to wait for me to be okay or anything. I understand if you totally want to run."

He made a face to suggest I was being ridiculous. "Um, I think I'll stick around, thanks," he said.

"No really." I wanted this out now, before I got too deep. "Like I said. It's complicated. And I don't want you to run away. But I feel like you should know that about me." I sighed. "But at least now, I feel like, I'm better enough to know that I have to get better still. Does that make sense?"

"Yeah," he said, nodding. "It's like, your parents, or your

family or whatever, you think that's what's normal. When you don't know any better, you think, this is how everybody lives. And then you find out that's not true. And it's kind of a shock."

I nodded as he spoke.

"This is embarrassing, but I had this one social worker and she was like, 'Anthony, you can choose. You know, you can *choose* how you want to be in this world.' She was like, 'You can go on fighting and being angry all the time, finding an insult in everything anyone says or does, or you can choose to be different, not be that guy all the time.' She said, 'You know, it might be hard at first, but in the end it's a lot less work. A lot less energy.' Which was kind of a funny way to put it, but it stuck with me, you know? At the time when she said it, I was pretty much like, 'Eff you, lady,' but you know it stuck with me and it was true."

I tried to imagine Anthony, with his gentle eyes, so angry.

"I'm glad you're not angry all the time anymore," I said.

"Me too," he answered softly.

"Why? Why were you so angry?"

He stared into the traffic, but I could tell he was looking way past the car in front of us. "I don't know. I mean, it was dumb. I'm not like that anymore, not at all. I haven't even, like, exchanged harsh words with anyone in literally years. You know? And before that, in my family, I always had the reputation ... I was always known as, like, the 'sensitive' one. You know? The artistic one? But then, when I was in junior high, we went into care— foster care—for a while. And, well, you don't really wanna be a sensitive boy in foster care." He smiled in that way that told me there was a lot he wasn't saying.

"Yeah," I said.

"So, I guess I was just really pissed, really angry, for a while there."

"I get it," I said. I waited a beat, watching the driver of the car next to us, a lady, singing along to a radio I couldn't hear. "Why were you in foster care?"

He made a grimace. "Aw, my folks," he started and stopped. He thought for a minute and then continued. "My mom ... my mom never met an illegal substance she didn't like. No, I'm kidding. My mom's, like, the sweetest lady you'll ever meet. But they both, my mom and my dad, they both have drug problems, you know? My dad's a really good dude too. I feel bad complaining about them. And they've been doing real good lately. They just ... you know. Drugs."

"That stinks."

"Yeah." He sighed. "My dad got sick and then my mom got arrested ... So, we were in care. Me and my brothers—they split us up. I've got three brothers. Gio, in the city, and Johnny, who's got his own problems now, and then Vince, the little guy. It was just really good when we were all back together again, you know? My brothers drive me crazy, but you know, without them what do I got?"

I nodded like I understood, but I couldn't imagine, not really.

"So," I said, "Gio and Johnny and Vince and ... Tony?"

"Nah, they call me 'Ant'—my mother's Italian, in case you were wondering."

"I see," I said. "I like that. Ant. Can I call you that?"

"You can call me whatever you want, Iffy."

Ant and Iffy. Iffy and Ant. Perfect.

CHAPTER 29

When we finally got to Coney Island, Anthony said, "Two hours, wow. We coulda driven all the way to Monticello."

"It didn't feel like two hours," I said.

"Mermaid Avenue," he said, gazing out the windshield, unguarded wonder in his voice. "That's cool."

"Spot!" I cried. The car screeched to a halt and Anthony pulled over.

"*It's ninety-seven degrees out there—hope you're keeping cool!*" the deejay on the radio chirped before Anthony turned the car off. He leaned over and kissed me and we grabbed our stuff and headed for the beach.

We stood at the shoreline and I looked left and right. The beach was so packed it might as well have been a dance club. I hadn't been around so many people for as long as I could remember.

"Let's go in," I said to Anthony. We found a little spot to lay down the towel I'd brought and piled our stuff on it.

"It's okay to leave it?" Anthony asked, nodding at our things.

"The beach is like, the one place in New York where you can

trust people not to steal your stuff," I explained. "Don't know why. Must be some kind of honor code."

"Okay then. Let's go!" He took my hand. We made our way through the people, the moms standing in the shallow water talking and watching their kids, and the little boys jumping in and out of the water in their tighty-whitey underpants, and the girls running with spilling buckets of sea water, and the other kids almost swimming, but more like crawling, with their butts in the air in the shallow water.

Once we got close enough, we just took off. Still holding hands, we ran into the waves.

It was cold. Not so cold it took your breath away, but cold for, like thirty seconds and then it started to feel right. We finally let go of each other's hands and swam out, fighting the waves, checking in with each other before going further and coming back together again. Once we got away from the other people we treaded water together, talking and kissing. We were totally those people who make out in the water. Me and Lizette used to laugh at those couples, the people who seemed to think that just because they were in the ocean, nobody could see what they were doing. But whatever. It was like nobody else really existed for us anyway. Just me and Ant in the Atlantic. It was perfect.

I'd hold my nose with my thumb and forefinger and tip my head back, get my whole self wet, and then emerge, wipe my eyes, run my hands down my soaked hair. It felt so good. I did it over and over again.

We stayed in the water for an hour, I bet, treading water and kissing and laughing and talking about all the things we were gonna do. We were gonna raise chickens, we said, and eat the fresh eggs for breakfast each day. We were gonna become lawyers and open an office together in a small town so we could work together and have lunch together and spend all our time together. We were gonna have, like, eleven kids, some biological and some adopted, and raise them up trilingual.

"We can get married, right here, under the Cyclone," Anthony said, holding me around the waist.

I kissed him on the nose.

"Anthony, I have to tell you something," I buried my face in his neck, embarrassed. We bounced in the waves.

He patted my hair. "Okay," he said.

"Iphigenia," I whispered in his ear.

"Sorry, what?"

"Iphigenia. That's my real name."

"If-fa-jen ...?"

"If-ah-ja-*nye*-ah."

"That's so beautiful," he murmured. "That's so beautiful, Iphigenia."

I smiled into his neck.

When we finally got out we were so tired and hungry and thirsty.

"Let's hit the boardwalk," Anthony suggested.

We rinsed off in the cold-water outdoor showers. I had brought a little soap, so I took the opportunity to get pretty clean. Then I went in the bathroom and changed; Anthony did the same. I'd also brought some of Corinne's lipstick and a hairbrush. Looking at myself in the cloudy, warped mirror, I felt positively dressed up.

Emerging from the dank bathroom into the bright, humid evening, I expected to see Anthony waiting where we parted, at the front of the building. He wasn't there and I lost my breath for a moment, feeling perhaps that he had never been there at all, that I had made him up and it was actually only me, alone, in Coney Island. But then I looked to my right and there he was, his faced turned to one side as he carried a huge stroller up the wooden stairs that lead from the beach to the boardwalk. In the stroller was a sleeping child and attached to the stroller was a big, unwieldy beach bag that bounced against his side.

Once at the top, Anthony put the whole apparatus down gently. A woman who had hovered around him was nodding and smiling and I saw Anthony smile back and shrug before heading back down the stairs.

He turned and saw me and loped over, still smiling.

"You helped that lady?" I asked, even though I didn't have to.

He shrugged again, a little embarrassed. "I mean, she was trying to do it herself. It was gonna be a disaster."

"Who *are* you?" I grinned, shaking my head.

He shook his head, too, like I was crazy and then he raised his eyebrows. "You look amazing."

I grabbed his arm and squeezed it. I kissed him. I wished I could tell him all the things I felt.

He took my hand and we started down the boardwalk, gliding together past the carnival games, past the clam bars and T-shirt shops.

We stopped in one of the gift shops and I lingered, picking up and putting down different bright, plastic, colorful things— Frisbees and beach-themed drinking cups, sunglasses shaped like seashells. So many things to waste money on. And yet I wanted it, all of it, suddenly and painfully. I wanted to wear pink flip-flops and a fish-print wraparound skirt. I wanted a snow globe of the Cyclone, seashell wind chimes, a conch with the words "Coney Island" emblazoned in gold.

In the end, I settled on two postcards, one a picture of a seagull on the beach and one a picture of the shops on the boardwalk. Pictures to remember our vacation.

"We should go to Nathan's," I said finally, looking once more around the shop before stepping out. "The famous hot dogs?"

Anthony widened his eyes in anticipation. "Sounds good to me. I think I saw it on the main road before."

"Let's go," I said.

I clung to Anthony's hand as we walked in the heat and the crowds. It seemed to me that every day at Coney Island was like a carnival. Every day was a celebration. A drunk woman careened into me, beer from her red cup splashing over the side, just missing me and slapping on the ground. "So sorry!" she hooted over her shoulder. I smiled indulgently. I didn't mind at all. It felt good to be part of the party.

On a side street, we had to pass this big, industrial-looking building, its face covered with huge, lurid, old-timey paintings of "freaks." There was the bearded lady and a guy swallowing swords and another lady all wrapped up in a snake. There was a real-life guy in a top hat and a woman juggling fire on a platform at the front, talking to folks passing by.

"Come on in, ladies and gents," said the man. "See the unseeable, experience the exotic. Have your minds blown." He raised his eyebrows, pulled a face of astonishment. "For only five dollars, you can have your horizons expanded ... Hey there, you sir, you look like an adventurer," he pointed to an older, tank top wearing guy in the crowd. "Come on in, now. Don't tell me you're too *scared*." The old guy waved his arm, like, "get outta here" and turned away, annoyed. I was gonna keep walking, but Anthony stopped to listen. "And you two," said the man in the top hat, pointing at us, "the lovebirds. Have you ever seen a two-headed baby?"

"Nope," Anthony answered.

"Of course you haven't!" cried the man. "So, now's your chance. Let's bring that little lady—your daughter, sir?" Here, everyone, including Anthony, laughed. "Let's bring her in. Why, she's so very small, we could put her in a jar and exhibit her. She's a Thumbelina, isn't she?"

I laughed, but grimaced up at Anthony, embarrassed.

"Come on in," said the guy.

"Can't," said Anthony. "We got places to be."

"I can see that," said the guy. "I can see that about you. There's something special about you two, I can tell that right away. Something very special about her—she's a special person indeed!" And here he clapped his hands and then stopped and looked at me hard and then looked back at Anthony and sure, I knew it was a bit, designed to make us feel like he knew something about us, designed to get us to part with five bucks each and go to his dumb show, but it gave me chills anyway. What was it that he thought he could see?

Anthony put his arm around my neck and kissed me on the top of my head. "I told you," he murmured as we walked away. "I told you you were somebody." I stayed facing the barker as my body walked away, only turning at the very last minute.

CHAPTER 30

I slept on the ride home. I didn't mean to, and I felt kind of bad letting Anthony navigate all by himself, but I couldn't help it. I had won a big stuffed Snoopy on one of those water gun games and Anthony had won a stuffed basketball on a shooting hoops game and I was leaning on them against the car window and I just closed my eyes for a minute and then the next time I opened them we were stopped at a light on the edge of the park.

"Hey, Sleeping Beauty," Anthony said.

"I'm sorry," I said, my mouth dry. "I didn't even ..."

"Don't worry about it," he said. "It was very sweet. You were right in the middle of a sentence and then, boom!"

"Really?" I said. "I don't even remember."

He chuckled. "Something about the waves."

My mind was muddy, but I remembered what I had been saying. "Yeah. I guess I was saying that I hadn't felt this way since I was a kid. Do you remember that feeling? When you'd go to the beach and you'd spend so much time in the water that when you went to bed at night you'd feel like you were still floating, rolling on the waves? That was how I was feeling right before I fell asleep."

"We didn't go to the beach a whole lot when I was a kid," Anthony said, pulling the car over. We were home. "Ugh. I hate for this day to end." He turned the car off.

"I hate it too."

"I have to get the car back."

"Thank you so much," I said. "I had such a good time with you."

"Me too." He leaned over to kiss me. It must've been the hundredth kiss that day, but it was as wonderful as the very first one. "I love you, Iphigenia. I know we just met, but it's true. I totally love you."

"I love you too." It was easy to say. It was true and it should have been scary, but it wasn't.

I smiled and I kissed him again and squeezed his hand.

I went to open the door.

"Wait," he said. "I'll walk you to your camp."

"It's okay, I'm absolutely fine. You go get the car back. I know what I'm doing."

"No way. It's late. I want to make sure you're safe."

"Anthony," I groaned. "I *live* here, remember? Believe me. I did this for a while before you and Corinne came along. I'll see you tomorrow." I kissed him again and then I said it again. "I love you."

"Sorry, babe," he said. "You're either walking with me or I'm following along behind you. And I, for one, would prefer not to feel like a stalker."

"Anthony," I said warningly.

"If-ah-ja-NYE-ah," he warned back.

We stared each other down, but I had to smile a little. I sighed, resigned. "But whatever. Fine. Thank you."

So, we both got out of the car. I waited on the curb for him, clutching our stuffed prizes, and when he came around the car he took my hand and we skipped the path, walking straight into the woods.

"It's funny, like, a few months ago if you had told me to walk through this park in the middle of the night I would've been scared for my life. But now, it's like, my park, you know? Like, other people should be scared of *me*."

Anthony laughed. "Um, Iffy, I think you have, how do you say it, like, an inflated sense of your own self or something?"

"I'm serious! I mean, I don't have my mace with me, but I do have a couple of tricks up my sleeve."

"What are you talking about?"

"Just saying, is all. Remind me to tell you about the hot beans sometime."

When we got to the camp, Angel rushed over to greet us, jumping up on me and knocking me down, licking my face and nudging me around with her snout. She was totally intrigued by the smell of the ocean, I think, and she couldn't get enough of it. I threw the basketball for her and she immediately attacked, growling and tearing at it.

Then I noticed that Corinne hadn't gotten up or said anything.

"Hey," I said, walking over to where she sat on a stump next to the tent.

There was a lantern on the ground in front of her, illuminating the area and she had the radio playing softly. She looked up.

"Hi," she said.

"What is it?" I asked, coming to sit on my knees in front of her. I put my hand on her leg.

"Nothing," she said, but covered my hand with her own. Her bony fingers were cold.

"What's going on?" Anthony asked.

"Whatever, you might as well hear this too." Even in the lantern light, I could tell Corinne had been crying.

"What's up?" I said.

"You're gonna hate me."

"I couldn't," I said.

"Well ..."

"What's up?" I asked again. I pushed some hair out of her face, tucked it behind an ear. It popped right back out. Anthony sat down on the ground with us, but a little way off. "Henry?" I guessed. My heart began to beat faster.

"Yeah. But not what you think."

"What?"

"I called him."

"What?"

"I went to the pay phone and called him."

"Why?"

"Because I needed to."

I was suddenly aware of Anthony, wondering what he would make of this. He looked calm, leaning back on his hands, his legs bent in front of him and his face lit from below by the lantern. Would he wonder what he was getting himself into? Would he want to rescue Corinne, or me, or would he simply want to get as far away from this kind of nonsense as possible?

"I'm going back to him, Iffy."

CHAPTER 31

She didn't say it outright, but she blamed me. If only I hadn't gotten together with Anthony. If only we hadn't run around, making her feel lonely and sad ...

She never said that, but I could feel it. Perhaps I'm being uncharitable, but she *wanted* me to feel that. I loved Corinne; I still do. But that was pretty crappy. The way she made me feel like it was my fault.

She told us that she had walked and walked and walked looking for a pay phone, dragging Angel all around the circumference of the park on that hot July afternoon, because she wanted to call Henry and curse him out. It had been her apartment too! She had a right to be there, to shower there, to get her stuff. She worked her anger up; she was ready to really let him have it. How dare he threaten her! How dare he touch her! Didn't he know she was the best thing that had ever happened to him? That she had put up with so much of his nonsense that it was ridiculous? She was calling to tell him she was done, that it was the last straw, he had crossed a line. She wanted Prince back and she was coming to get him tomorrow and she'd bring a cop with her if she needed to.

By the time she had found a phone she was hopping mad. But also maybe a little tired too, after all of that walking. When he answered, she just lit into him, although, admittedly, maybe with not the same enthusiasm she would have had if she hadn't done all that walking.

"Henry?"

"Who is this?"

"You know damn well who this is," she told us she had said. But then.

But then.

But then.

But then he wasn't at all what she expected. He was so sad. It was "oh, baby" this and "oh, baby" that.

"It was like, if I coulda written a script of all the things he would've needed to say ... like, somehow he got hold of that script. Because he said everything just right."

"Corinne ..."

She delivered the rest in a rambling monologue, pausing only to smoke and sometimes not even doing that, the ash on each cigarette growing longer and more precarious until a quick gesture would send it flying. "I know you don't believe me. I know what you think. But I have to do this. I have to give him one more chance. I spent two years of my life with him. I've already gone and spent two years of my life trying to make this work with him. I cannot give up now. I know we can do this. He is going to get help. He is going to quit drinking and all that other stuff too. He never said that before. He never said that he would actually quit for good. Sure, for like a couple a weeks he would take it easy or 'I'm gonna cut back,' or whatever. But this time it was for real. I think he really realized it. Like, you know, except for that one time, I never left him for this long before. And I think he finally is maybe starting to appreciate me. He was all like, 'I know you want to go back to school and I think you should do that, and we're gonna turn it around, and I'm gonna support you in your dreams, 'cause it's your turn now.' And it was like, that was exactly what I needed to hear. Because it should be my turn, you know? And I am not gonna find someone else who understands me like he does. It's a rare thing what we have. I've never felt this way about anyone else. I can't even really imagine myself without him in the long term. Like five years from now, where am I gonna be? With him. You know? And he just acts like that because, I don't know ... I love him so much, Iffy. You would understand if you just knew how much I loved him."

What could I say? I have asked myself that many times since that night. What could I say?

What I wound up saying was, "Whatever, Corinne." I sighed, looked at the ground because I couldn't look her in the eye. "Fine. You should go back to him if that's what you want to do."

Did I say that because Anthony was there? Because I didn't want to beg her in front of Anthony? Or did I say that because I knew it didn't matter at all, not at all, what I said?

"Don't be mad, Iffy."

"I'm not mad."

"You obviously are."

"I'm just worried."

"Whatever, Iffy. I need you to support me."

I looked up for a minute, almost incredulous. "Support you? What are you talking about?"

"We can't all live in the woods, Iffy." Her voice was quavering, but increasing in volume, until she was shouting. "What do you think this is? *Peter Pan* shit? People have real lives that they have to live. We can't all be like, wood sprites," she added nastily.

"I don't even know what you're talking about."

"You just want me to stay here so that you have company. But whatever, you have company now," she pointed her cigarette at Anthony.

"*Corinne.*"

"You were just using me to find that Dougie dude for you. Whatever, you're on your own." She turned her attention to Anthony again. "*He* can help you. What'd you bring him back here for anyway? I suppose you two want your privacy." She flung the words at me.

"Don't do this, Corinne."

She rose, picked up her bag. She had already packed. She had been waiting to go.

"Peace out," she said sarcastically.

"Please, Corinne," I said, I was begging because I didn't know what else to do.

"What?"

"You have to leave *right now*? Can't we just ... I don't want you to leave like this."

"I don't either, Iffy. But I've got to go. I've got to go *now*. Look, you've got him now anyway. He'll keep you warm tonight."

"Stop it, Corinne."

"What do you think, country boy? You haven't said a word."

Anthony shook his head. "I don't have anything to say."

"Come on, Corinne. Stop trying to pick fights. *Please.*"

"See, Iffy. I told you. I can be mean. You should watch yourself. I haven't even gotten started yet."

"You go, Corinne. But I'm not gonna move camp. Not for a few days. And when I do, I'm going to go back to the last spot we were at. So, if you want to find me—"

"Whatever, Iffy."

"I'm just saying, I'm not mad. I know you're doing this, acting like this, so it's easier for you to leave. But I'll be here. I'll be here until the winter comes, Corinne. So, you can always come back."

"Fuck you, Iffy," she said, and she turned around and got gone.

CHAPTER 32

Anthony wouldn't go. I told him I was okay, that I wanted to be alone, that it was fine, but he wouldn't leave.

"You have to get the car back."

"I will," he said. "I will. But I need to be with you right now. I can't leave you like this."

"I have Angel," I said, pointlessly.

"Iffy," he said, "the car—it's not that important. I'll get it back when I get it back. I'm not gonna leave you all alone."

And there was a part of me that was grateful. I knew I'd be okay by myself. But I didn't want to be alone, not after that scene.

"I guess she was right," I told Anthony as we climbed into the tent together. "Maybe I don't get it. She didn't have to go back to him, not really, not even if she felt like she had to. If she had just stayed with us overnight, if we could have just convinced her to stay until the morning, she would've seen it all again with clearer eyes and she wouldn't have gone back."

"Maybe," Anthony said. "Maybe."

"I hate this so much." I didn't want to cry. I let myself be pulled into his arms.

"What was that other thing all about?" he asked. "Dougie?"

I explained. "A girl Corinne knows recognized one of my photos of my mom. She said this guy Dougie used to hang out with her. She said to ask him about her, but we haven't been able to find the guy."

"He's like, a drug addict, junkie, or something?" Anthony had gone still.

"Yeah," I said, my head jerking up involuntarily. "How'd you know?"

"I think I might know the guy."

I sat up straight. "*What?*"

"I was at this bar a few blocks away with my brother and he was talking to this guy. My brother ... well, let's just say he is familiar with the kind of people who use and sell drugs. So, he introduced me to this skinny, scary-looking dude called Dougie. I mean, it was like, for five minutes, but I think that guy Dougie is always at that bar. Like, it's his hangout."

"Will you take me there tomorrow?"

"Of course."

I squeezed my eyes shut and tried to think. I was elated by this news, that we might be able to get more information.

My heart sank as it registered that I wouldn't be able to tell Corinne. That she wasn't with me on this. And then I thought again about what she had done and I was scared for her. And I was scared for me too; this man Dougie terrified me for some reason. Maybe it was because I was getting closer to something, maybe he might have actually known my mother.

I went over this in my head, and then I thought of Corinne, again, and how awful her leaving had been.

But it also felt so good to be in the tent, in Anthony's arms.

He held me until I fell asleep.

I woke up a little at dawn, as he was leaving. I was embarrassed, because I woke up with my thumb in my mouth.

"Hey ..." Still groggy, I sat up, pushing my wet thumb down into the sleeping bag.

"I'm gonna go, Iffy," Anthony whispered, leaning in to kiss me. "But go back to sleep. I'll come back this afternoon, okay? We can talk then?"

"Okay," I murmured, burying my face in his neck, kissing him again. His skin was still salty, still smelled like the beach. Despite it all, my sleep-heavy body felt so good in his arms, in my tent, on the ground. He gave me one final kiss before leaving. I fell back asleep pretty much instantly, with my arms around Angel.

When I woke again, I lay in the tent, indifferent to the rising sun. I almost didn't care if someone, a cop, a hiker, stumbled upon us in our vulnerability. Everything about the last night and about Corinne came back. I was slow and sad, but then I was suddenly, urgently ill, and I scrambled from the tent, my hands barely unzipping quickly enough. I stuck my head through the open slot in the door and puked.

When I finished throwing up, I unzipped the whole way. Angel came out too and I saw her going to sniff the puke and I yelled "*Stop!*" so loud that she jumped and looked at me. I put the cord around her neck and tied her up so she couldn't get to it. "Ugh," I grumbled. "Not okay."

Luckily, I didn't get any on the tent itself. I also felt an overwhelming relief that Anthony had already left. I gave Angel something not horrifying to eat for breakfast while I packed up the tent and shoveled some dirt and leaves over the vomit.

I brushed my teeth, rinsing with a bottle of water I'd kept

refilling at the water fountain. *Probably just had too many world-famous hot dogs at Coney Island*, I told myself.

When our morning stuff was done, I told Angel we had another appointment.

"We're going to meet your big old friend," I told her, disapprovingly. She wagged her tail.

Ann had continued to leave us gifts and supplies at the rock and we'd continued to retrieve it every couple of days. But in her last note, Ann had written, "Would it be okay if I bring some coffee and we could drink it together? Day after next, around 10?"

I had left a note in response. It said, "OK."

We headed over to the rock. Despite how terrible I felt, the weather was perfect: warm, with the most wonderful breeze, the wind making its way through the trees just enough to keep me cool and tickle my legs. We emerged from the deep woods and made our way over to the main trail and then past all the joggers and to the spot.

I brought *Watership Down* along, but I didn't do any reading. I sat there, a pit in my stomach, playing the scene with Corinne over and over in my head. My stomach continued to churn as I wondered what she was doing, if she was okay. I wished she hadn't taken off. I wished that we had left things on better terms. I hoped she knew I meant it when I said come back, find me.

I was pretty lost in thought when I saw movement. I looked up and there was Ann. She hadn't seen me yet, but then Angel jumped up and barked and she looked over at us and waved.

"Hey," she called, sounding happy and maybe even surprised that I had kept the meeting.

Angel bounded and started jumping up on her and everything. *Shoot, maybe Angel had been her dog*, I thought. Who knows.

"Hi," I said, and took my time walking over. She was carrying one of those to-go trays with two coffees on it and really only wanted to see Angel and not me. I took a minute to look at her again; she was different than I remembered. Maybe it was just that she wasn't wearing jogging clothes; this time she was in jeans and a short-sleeved button-down. She was wearing jewelry, a small gold cross around her neck, and one of those Irish rings with the two hands holding a heart on her right hand, but she was otherwise very plain-looking, no makeup on her angular face.

She was still down on one knee and looked up at me. "Hey! It's nice to see you, Brenda." She stood, but kept one hand on Angel's head, and said, "Here, I brought a few things," letting a bag fall from her shoulder into her hand and holding it out to me.

I took the tote: it had cans of dog food, cans of lentils and beans, a sack of those little oranges and couple of bottles of Gatorade. There was also a wax paper bag from Dunkin' Donuts.

"Okay, thanks."

"Is there somewhere we can sit for a little bit?" Ann asked.

"Yeah," I said and nodded back at where I had come from. "There's a spot over here."

Ann and Angel followed me to a little clearing that had a good flat log in it and we sat down and she kind of chattered away at Angel, all "How are you doing, sweetie?" and "What a good doggie!"

When we were settled, I said, "Thanks a lot for all the stuff and all."

"I'm happy to do it," Ann said. "Really. Here—" She handed me a coffee. "I take mine black, but there's milk and sugar in the bag. And there're some doughnuts in there too."

I don't usually drink coffee, but I was suddenly ravenously hungry and it smelled good and I loaded it up with milk and sugar. It still seemed bitter to me, but it was a treat and I drank it. I also got myself a chocolate doughnut out of the bag. I kind of wanted to save it, to eat it in private so I could eat it real slow and not be distracted and truly enjoy it, but I also wanted to eat it up, scarf it down right there. So, that's pretty much what I did. I couldn't remember eating anything so delicious. It didn't escape me that there were still two other doughnuts in the bag. At first I thought it might be nice to bring one back to Corinne; then I remembered that Corinne had left and my stomach flipped over. I thought for a moment I might be sick again.

I passed the doughnuts to Ann and she fished one out of the bag. "So, how have things been?" she asked.

"Fine," I said. I sipped on my coffee, but then put it down and to the side. I knew I'd throw up if I drank any more.

"You know, I think about you and Angel a lot, especially at night. When it's chilly or rainy, I think of you two, sleeping out here."

"We're okay. We usually keep warm, and mostly dry."

"That's good." And we kind of just sat there in silence for a minute. "Well, we really worry," she said lamely.

"We? You and ... your husband?"

"No," she said. She smiled, kind of tight though, so I could tell she was embarrassed. "I have a roommate. She was the one who let Lola ... who left her outside. Our Lola, that was our dog who looks like your Angel. Jeannie, my roommate, she put her out in the yard and forgot about her." Ann frowned. "Lola didn't have her collar on. Jeannie never had dogs growing up. I don't know." She continued to pet Angel, frowning into the distance. She caught me looking at her and said, "I was so mad. I'm sure you can understand. Jeannie felt terrible." Ann looked off into the distance.

I nodded but didn't say anything. Ann continued. "But you know, animals have much more acute senses than humans. They say they know when a big storm, like a tsunami is coming, they just know and they head for higher ground. So, maybe our dog, maybe it was time for her to go. Maybe she knew she was needed elsewhere." She looked meaningfully at Angel.

I thought she was being a little heavy-handed, but I appreciated what she was trying to do. I gave a short, vague smile and then looked back down, stared at my knuckles.

We sat in silence again and she sipped her coffee.

What she was saying, it made me feel sort of indebted. Like she had just actually given me her dog. Plus, she had given me so much other stuff: the food and the money. I don't know, I figured I owed her at least a conversation or something. I took a breath. "So, what do you do? I mean, when you're not harassing homeless kids."

She laughed. "Is that what I'm doing?"

"No, I was just kidding."

She looked at me with half a smile. "I teach gym at a high school," she said. "All girls. Catholic."

"You Catholic?" My mother had been Catholic. So had my dad, although he hadn't taken us to church since I was really little.

She didn't answer right away, but again sort of looked up at the tree line. "I am," she said, and I braced myself for a lecture, but she surprised me by adding, "I have my problems with the church, but I am."

I didn't say anything for a while and then I muttered, "Cool."

She nodded. I waited. *I have given her enough,* I thought. *That was enough.* I thought, *Can I go now?* I shifted how I was sitting. The first preparations for leaving.

"Well, what do you want to do?" she said quickly, obviously stalling. "I mean, as a profession?" She looked abashed, like she immediately regretted the question.

"Um, I dunno?" I thought about Anthony, about swimming in the ocean and talking about our future. Again, my stomach did flip-flops, but these were good, Anthony ones. I wanted to talk about him, but not with her. So, I said, "I kind of want to be a lawyer. That would be cool."

"Sure," she said, looking relieved.

"I also like animals," I said. "But no, I think I would want to be a lawyer. They make a lot of money, right?"

"Depends on what kind of lawyer you are."

"Well, I'd want to be the kind that makes a lot of money," I said and Ann laughed. "I guess you have to do a lot of school for that."

"You do," she agreed.

"Maybe not that then." I was aware that I was acting younger, dumber than I was. That I was playing up the whole, sweet, naive kid thing, maybe. Was I trying to get her to feel sorry for me? I wasn't sure.

Ann didn't say anything for a minute. "Well, you could get back in school at some point," she said. "Don't you think?"

"I don't know." I wondered if she was going to try to make me go to her all-girls Catholic school. Ha. "Maybe a GED, you know? My boyfriend and I were just talking about this."

She frowned, maybe a little startled by the word *boyfriend.*

"But maybe I wouldn't be one of those lawyers who makes a lot of money. Maybe I'd be a lawyer who helps kids."

"I think that would be wonderful," Ann said, recovering.

"Are there any lawyers who help animals?" I knew it was a stupid question as I was saying it, but I said it anyway. I knew that it would make her sad for me to say that, and I wanted her to feel sad for me. It was messed up, I knew, but I didn't care. It felt good to have someone feel sad for me.

Ann kind of sniffed a laugh. "Well, I guess," she said. "There are environmental lawyers and lawyers for the humane society and stuff. They have animal cops, why not animal lawyers?"

So, then we sat there awkwardly again, having finished that topic too. I figured I'd done enough—she could go home and tell her roommate Jeannie about the homeless kid she was helping, how she gave her money and food, and how the kid opened up to her about her career aspirations. How it was all so tragic, 'cause it was so obvious the kid was never even gonna get that GED, not living in the park she wasn't.

I picked up my coffee. I was about to get up, brush myself off and go, when Ann said, "Okay, Brenda ..." She took a breath. "Let me give you this and you can throw it out as soon as I'm gone, if you want. Let me just give it to you," and she took a bunch of papers out of the tote. There were cards and brochures and notebook paper with handwriting on it. She held out the brochures and printed-up papers. "This is information about Covenant House. It's a safe place for kids who are runaways. They'll take care of you, no questions asked. The address and phone number are there. It's in Manhattan, but if you can get to a phone and call them, they will pick you up." She put the pages between us. "The only thing is, of course, they won't take Angel. But," she took a deep breath and continued her speech, something she had obviously rehearsed, "of course Jeannie and I would, if you ever needed us to. Here is our address and phone number." This was the notebook paper. "I'm not trying to take your dog away. I'm just trying to tell you that if you want to go somewhere, if you need to get out of the cold, you can leave Angel with us. We will take care of her for you and I promise we will give her back to you when you are ready to take her back. I want to encourage you to really think about it," she said, trying to meet my eye. "You need to really think about getting yourself in somewhere ..." Here she trailed off, furrowing her brow, as though she had lost her place in the script and wanted to start over again.

I couldn't bring myself to look at her. Instead, I stared at the papers on the log, my hands curled around the coffee cup. "And Brenda," she said, tapping the paper with her address on it, jarring me for a moment, "our house is only about a half a mile from the park. Walk out the Doughboy entrance and take Myrtle. You know, if you need anything? You know, if you're in a pinch? Or even if you're not. You are welcome to stay with us. We have a guest room. We can help you get a plan together. Get you what you need."

I bit my lip and kept looking at the papers. I ran my fingers through my hair. Even though I had rinsed off at the beach, I was still sandy, my hair now stiff. The sand made me think of Anthony, made me think of Corinne.

"What's wrong?"

"Nothing," I said. "This is just really nice of you and all. Don't worry, I'm not gonna show up at your house."

"I'm not worried. You can show up at my house."

"No, it's okay," I told her. "I'm okay. I really am."

She looked into the trees. "You kids ..." I wondered who she was talking about. "You know, you're not okay," she said, almost angrily. "It shouldn't have to be like this. You shouldn't be living all by yourself in a park."

"I'm not all by myself."

"This boyfriend ..." she said. She looked at me, and I could imagine how she was as a teacher. "Is he why you're in the park? Is he ... manipulating you?"

I actually laughed. "No!"

She didn't laugh, though. And I felt myself shrinking a little bit under her gaze.

A bird called out and then another bird called back. I looked up into the trees but I couldn't see them.

And then I swallowed, hard, and the next thing I knew words were coming out of my mouth and I didn't even know they were there, didn't even plan on saying them. And even more surprising, it didn't hurt.

"I think I might be pregnant. Not my boyfriend. Not Anthony. My stepbrother."

Her gasp was almost inaudible. I stared straight ahead and thought about what I had said.

"Well," she said. "You'll get an abortion. I'll take you."

It was my turn to stifle a gasp. I did look at her then. "Isn't that, you know, a sin?"

She looked at me too, hard, in the eye. "You don't have to have your rapist's child. And you can't have a baby living in the park."

I almost started crying right there, but I didn't. I stuck the tip of my thumb in my mouth and kind of nibbled.

"I don't know for sure," I mumbled. "I might not even be."

"Well, let's go to a doctor and find out."

I waited a minute. "Yeah," I said. I took my thumb out of my mouth. "I guess I should do that."

"Do you want to go right now?"

"I can't now," I said, nervous and awake suddenly. "I've got to go." I stood up a little too fast. "I've got to get back." Angel stood too, but Ann held out a hand, trying to get us to stay, to sit.

"This isn't something you can postpone, Brenda," she said.

I was thrown for a moment by the fake name but refocused. "Can't I, like, get a test at the drugstore?"

"Probably. This isn't really my area of expertise. But let's think of it this way. If you aren't pregnant, fine, you got a checkup. If you are, well, you're going to need to see a doctor, so you can get proper care or so you can ... well, figure things out."

When I didn't respond, she went on. "Do you have any idea how far along this might be?"

I shook my head, no. "I mean, not long. Two months? Maybe a little more."

"This is important," she said. She lowered her voice. "It could be unhealthy, dangerous for you to wait longer. Please let me bring you to a doctor."

I wanted to run, just dart away. But I stood, in limbo, before picking up the tote and grabbing Angel's leash. "I will," I said, holding Ann's gaze. "I promise you, I will. Just not today."

"When? I can meet you here again. When?"

"How about, a couple of days? I need some ... time."

"Tomorrow?"

I was regretting having told her, already knowing that if I left with her, even if it was just to go to the doctor, I wouldn't be coming back to the park. That it might have all been for nothing. "I'll let you know. I'll leave you a note. Here," I nodded toward the rock where she left things. "I just ... I can't go right now."

"You don't have to get an abortion or do anything you don't want to do." She was pleading. "But you need to talk to a doctor."

"I know," I relented. "I promise I'll go with you soon. I need a few more days."

I met her eye and offered what I hoped was a reassuring smile. "A couple more days. It won't really make that much of a difference."

She frowned, as though to say, *it could*, but instead she said, "Oh, Brenda, the world shouldn't be like this."

I needed to get out of there, now, and started to move off with Angel and the tote and my coffee. *No kidding*, I thought. *Tell me about it.* But I swallowed my bubbling outrage. I knew she meant well. And I knew it wasn't her fault that my father was a loser and my stepmother was a bitch and my stepbrother was, like, a sociopath.

"Brenda," she called after me. "Don't forget to leave me a note. If you don't, I'll have a squad of nuns from the Catholic school out looking for you. And you don't want to mess with those sisters."

I kind of laughed in spite of it all.

"Okay? Brenda?"

"Okay," I yelled back, turning. "And Ann?"

She was standing, watching us. "Yeah?"

"My real name is Iphigenia. But everyone calls me Iffy."

"Wow," she called back. "That's some name. Quite a history there."

"You're telling me."

CHAPTER 33

I left the park.

Now that I had said it, out loud, to someone, I couldn't *not* think about it.

I wasn't lying. I didn't know how far along it could be. But maybe two months? That was almost how long I'd been in the park. But it could have been more. Maybe more like three months? I really didn't know.

There was a lump in my throat, like I'd bitten off too much of the doughnut and it hadn't gone down right, although I knew that wasn't possible. But it was there, a mass, and I felt like it was choking me. I chugged some water as we walked, but it was still there.

I went to the pay phone and called my stepbrother. He had his own phone in his room. I knew the number.

It rang and my breath got faster and shallower. It was weird how calling a phone number could make me feel like I was gonna have a stroke. How did I think I could face him if I could barely even call him on the phone? I considered hanging up. I almost did.

But then I heard his voice on the answering machine. And I thought of him bothering Lizette.

So, I swallowed hard and said, my voice almost a whisper, "I heard you were looking for me. Yeah, it was me that got you in trouble with Oscar. And the cops. And I'm not even finished yet. You know, what you did to me was wrong. And if you want to find me, you come to Forest Park. I'll be waiting for you."

I hung up.

I closed my eyes and leaned my head against the slippery inside of the phone booth. It was gross, but my knees were weak and I needed to collect myself.

I wanted to stay there, like that, not thinking for a moment, but Angel was tugging at the cord, trying to sniff something just out of reach of her nose. So, I moved. In a daze, I went on.

What had I done?

And what was I going to do next?

We headed to the southern part of the park, to a spot where I had some stuff buried. It was my most secret site. I had carved a moon into a tree stump and from there I would take ten big steps to the right. Under a pile of leaves there was a flat stone; under the flat stone was a hole I had lined with plastic bags to keep my things dry and safe.

I memorized Ann's address, just in case, and then put it and the other papers in a plastic bag and then buried it with some of my other gear.

Then I took out the gun that I had found all those weeks before.

Corinne was right to ream me out, because the truth was I didn't know a thing about guns. I couldn't even tell if the safety was on, so, like a total dork, I put the gun in a bag and held it way out in front of me, so that if the gun accidentally went off it wouldn't shoot me.

I carried it like that all the way to the bridge. I passed some hikers and we all nodded our heads at each other. I felt a little paranoid, but I reasoned that they probably thought I was carrying some dog poop or something.

When I got to the bridge, Anthony wasn't there yet, so I made a pile of leaves in a spot where the sun broke through the trees, covered it with a towel, and called Angel over to snuggle down. Even though I didn't think I'd be able to sleep, I did; the next thing I knew, both Angel and I were stirring, sensing someone approaching, and it was him.

He didn't look happy.

"Iffy," he said, coming to me, getting down on the ground and taking me in his arms. "You okay?"

"Of course," I said. "What's up? Is something wrong?" I craned my neck to look at his face. He was stricken.

"Yeah," he said. "It sucks."

"What? What's going on?" I had to push his arms away so that I could sit, but once I was up, he encircled me again.

Anthony kissed my head, took a deep breath, and blew out. "More trouble, of course. When I brought the car back, which, was like a whole other scene, my brother told me that my parents got arrested again." He leaned his head and rested it against mine.

"Arrested?" I had to pull away, to look at him. "For what?"

"Drugs. Of course. They had people over at their place and there was a fight and the cops came and then they all got busted. I'm sure they're claiming the stuff wasn't theirs, but it probably was. They're both already on probation. So, now I have to go back upstate. My little brother, Vince. He's already in care. But if I head up now, maybe I can get him back."

"What about your other brother?"

"He's got a record too. I'm the only one who can do it. So, I have to go. Gio's driving me up today, Iffy."

I must have looked as heartbroken as I felt, because my eyes filled with tears.

"Will you come with me? I'll be honest, the house is a dump, but there's room. I mean, there's a lot about the whole situation that stinks, but it's probably better than staying here by yourself."

"I can't," I said.

"I can't leave you here alone," he argued.

"But I need to stay. I have to find that guy Dougie and ask him about, you know, what he knows or whatever. And then I have to wait too. In case Corinne comes back. In case she needs me." *And my stepbrother*, I added silently to myself. *I'm expecting him soon too.*

"Iffy." Anthony's brow was furrowed.

"You have to go, but I have to stay. It will be okay." I looked at him squarely in the face. "I'll get up to Monticello as soon as I can. I'll take a bus or something. I just need to stay here for a few more days. Maybe a week."

His eyes filled with tears. "But we just found each other."

"I'm not worried." I suddenly found I was crying too. "I know how I feel about you. We'll be together again soon."

"Iphigenia," he said, pulling me close, "you know how I said that when I came to the city, I was looking for something? I didn't even know what I was looking for, only that I have been so, I don't know, discontent? Dissatisfied? I thought maybe I could find what I needed in music or maybe in the city itself."

He looked at me. "But it was you. It was you. It was feeling at home. Feeling at home with you. That's what I was looking for."

I knew what he meant and, despite everything else, a thrill ran through my body.

"I feel the same," I said. "I really do."

"I just hate to leave. I hate to leave you so soon after finding you."

I buried my face in his neck. He smelled good, a little like sweat but also like the outdoors, like the park and the fresh air. I wanted to store up his scent and the feeling I had when I was with him, to sustain me in the weeks ahead.

And I wanted to tell him then, too, what I had told Ann, but I couldn't do it. I couldn't pile that on top of everything else. And I knew if I told him, that it would change things. I didn't know how they would change, I just knew that they would. And I didn't think I could bear that.

We lay back into the leaves, our arms around each other, looking into each other's eyes. "I think it's good that you're going to take care of your little brother. He's lucky to have you," I said.

Anthony caressed my hair, touched my cheek as we talked. "He deserves better than all of this. He's such a sweet kid, Iff. You'll see when you meet him."

"What's gonna happen with your parents?"

He closed his eyes, but the deep lines on his forehead remained, as though he was working hard to figure out a problem. "Who knows." He let out a breath through his nose. "I don't know how bad things are. This might be it for my dad. He might be going away for a while. My mom. Jeez. I'm worried about her. It pisses me off that she's using again, but ... I'll know more soon, I guess. But listen. Give Corinne a week, okay? I'll come back a week from today and pick you up? We'll meet right here?"

"I guess, but I can't promise," I said. "I don't think I can leave unless things are settled. Unless I know she's safe, that she's okay or whatever."

"We don't have a number for her or anything?"

I shook my head, no. I didn't tell him I knew where the apartment was, that one of my ideas was to go, watch the door and the window. Wait until Henry left and try to see her.

"But maybe we can look her up, find a number for her. You know, then we can figure out some way for her to get in touch. You know, so you can come with me but she can find you if she needs you."

"Maybe." I didn't want to make promises I couldn't keep.

"I don't have long, Iffy. My brother's waiting. I told him I had to see you and tell you what was happening. I told him you didn't have a phone and he was like, 'What century does she live in, Ant?' But I didn't tell him that you actually lived in the park. Not yet."

I laughed and rolled my eyes. "People are so judgmental these days."

"Whatever. Our mother is a crackhead, so he really can't be making fun of other people."

I tsked my tongue. "I hope your mom is okay. And your dad."

"Me too." He handed me a piece of paper. "Here's the address up there. Suffice it to say, their phone has not been connected for some time now. I've written my brother's number underneath. So, you know, just in case."

"Getting a lot of addresses today."

"What d'you mean?"

"Nothing," I shook my head. "I'll tell you some other time. Right now I need you to help me with some things real quick before you go."

"Whatever you need."

"Okay. Well first, you gotta tell me where to find that guy."

"Dougie?"

"Yeah."

"Iffy, can this wait until I can get back?"

"If you're worried about me going to that bar on my own then you need to get over that right now."

We stared at each other. I didn't look away. Didn't flinch.

"Iffy," he sighed, finally, and I knew I had won. He threw his head back, looked into the trees.

"Anthony," I sighed, in imitation. I grabbed his arm, shook it playfully. "I promise you, I will be fine. It will be fine. I have actually been in a bar before." This much was true. Lizette and I went through a stage when we'd go to the dive bars in our neighborhood, after school, and order drinks. Most of the time, the bartenders didn't even look up at us, just went ahead and served. We thought it was so cool and kind of funny. We'd probably have done it more if we'd had the money.

So, I figured, how bad could it be?

Anthony squeezed his eyes shut, not looking at me as he answered. "The bar is called All Saints and it's on Woodhaven and 68th. It is not a nice place, Iffy. It's no place for a—"

"Girl?" I finished for him.

He shrugged and looked at me, frowning.

"That's a nice name though," I said. "The All Saints."

"It's not a nice place," Anthony repeated.

I shrugged. "That's us," I said, ignoring him. "If we ever start a band. Me and you and Angel and Corinne. We would be the All Saints."

Anthony smiled. "I gotta go. Gio's waiting."

"Wait, I have one more favor." I reached under the towel for the plastic bag and gingerly removed the gun. I held it awkwardly, pointing down. It felt pretty dramatic, but maybe that was all right. "I need to know how to use this."

"Whoa, Iff," he said, in evident alarm. "What are you doing with a pistol?"

"I found it. A couple of weeks ago."

"This is kind of nuts, Iffy."

"Don't worry," I reassured him. "I don't want to use it. I just want to know how. I'm not exactly familiar with guns."

"I don't know if that should make me more or less worried."

"Do you know how to use it or don't you?"

"I do." He was still weighing the situation, then sighed. "Fine. Here, okay." He took the gun from my hand, carefully, keeping it pointed down. He stood up and raised the pistol and directed it into the woods. He pointed to a switch. "This is the safety. Right now it is not on, and that is really dangerous. I mean *really* dangerous. This isn't like movie stuff, Iffy, where you can—"

"I know, I know, I get it," I interrupted, getting up and standing at his side. "Just show me how to put the safety on."

Despite himself, he smirked. "Fine. This is on, this is off. It's on. Let's leave it that way, okay?"

"Okay," I said.

He opened the barrel and peered inside.

"This has four bullets, Iffy, okay?" He closed it again and pointed it back into the distance. "You want to shoot it, you take the safety off, point, and squeeze, hard. Pretty straightforward."

"Okay."

"It'll kick back." He threw his arm in the air to demonstrate. "So, you probably want to steady yourself, hold your arm like this. Otherwise you'll wind up shooting the trees. Which might be a best-case scenario, really. But if you needed …" He stopped. Like it just occurred to him what he was doing, showing his girl-friend how to shoot a loaded gun. "Who are you … what do you want this for, Iffy? Are you gonna bring this to the bar? Or is this about Corinne's boyfriend?" He looked at the gun in his hands. He seemed uncomfortable holding it. He bent down and laid it in the leaves.

"I just want to be prepared."

"You think Dougie's gonna come after you?"

"I don't," I said. "It's just, you know, a precaution—"

He talked over me. "'Cause if you have a reason to think he's gonna come after you then there is no way I am leaving you here alone."

"I'm telling you, it's fine," I said. "He doesn't even know I exist. Please. I will be fine. Don't you think I can take care of myself?"

"I do," he conceded, facing me. "I really do. That's one of the things that's so cool about you. But I'm still worried."

"And Angel watches out for me," I assured him. "Don't you, girl?" She looked up at me.

"Iffy," he said, taking my face in his hands, kissing me, and putting his hands on my shoulders. "It's okay to need backup."

"That's what the gun is for," I tried to joke. I brought my hands up and rested them on his.

"Okay, I am definitely not leaving."

"Anthony," I said and I wasn't joking anymore. "You know what one of the things I like about you is?"

"What?"

"You understand that—" I stopped and started again. "You

get me. You really do. And so I'm asking you to get what I'm telling you now. This isn't ... negotiable."

We regarded each other. "You get outta here. I'll be all right," I said at last.

I looked again at his sweet face. Then I kissed him and he kissed me back. "God, I don't want to go. I love you so much, Iphigenia."

"I love you too, Anthony."

He shook me gently. "Please, please, please be careful."

"It's not me you should worry about, Ant," I smirked, playing cool. Being with Anthony gave me confidence. "It's anybody who messes with me."

He made a face, shook his head. He kissed me again and then he was gone.

PART VI: MOTHER

CHAPTER 34

It was late afternoon and I was tired when Angel and I headed over to All Saints.

I buried the gun again, but I wasn't sure what to do with Angel, whether I should tie her up in the park or take her with me and tie her up outside the bar. Just thinking about her alone in the woods, where anyone could come along and snatch her, got me feeling sweaty and panicky, so I brought her with me, figuring that, at the very least, our time apart would be shorter that way.

It looked like any other hole-in-the-wall in Queens. Small, high, dark windows covered over with beer ads featuring sexy girls wearing bikini styles that were last popular in the early '80s.

"Okay, girl," I said to Angel as I tied her to the lamppost in front. "You sit here and wait. I'll be right back."

She strained against her leash and tried to follow me as I went to the door. "It's okay," I said over my shoulder. "Don't be afraid to bite."

I turned and pushed the door open.

It was dark and somehow quiet and noisy at the same

time—a humming air conditioner, murmured talk, muffled classic rock.

You'd expect it to be like, *screech* and the music stops and everyone looks up and stares, but it wasn't like that.

I walked up to the bar. "You're too young to be in here, little girl," the bartender said, wiping down the spot in front of me.

I nodded. "I'm looking for someone."

He waited.

"Is Dougie here?" I ventured.

He looked surprised and then nodded his head down the bar.

I looked beyond the bartender and saw a guy staring at me: skinny, dirty hair, dirty face.

I walked toward him and he said flatly, "I don't know you." He said it like he didn't want to, either.

"I know," I said. "I just ... I heard you might know my mother. I'm looking for my mother," and I held the photo out to him, curled and creased from my pocket.

He didn't take it. He didn't hardly move at all, just cut his eyes from his beer down to the photo. I laid it near his hand on the bar.

Nothing happened. I thought of Angel, waiting. I could feel the bartender watching. My breath was becoming shallow. I reached out to take the picture and he put his cold, wet hand down on top of mine.

I looked at him and then he nodded slightly.

"You got any money?" he asked.

"Yeah," I said, *Thanks, Ann.* I pulled my hand out from under his and reached into my pocket again and for a ten-dollar bill and I laid it on the bar next to the photo. Dougie nodded at the bartender, who took Dougie's pint glass and refilled it and then plucked the ten from the bar, returning a moment later to put a few bucks and some change back in the same place.

A fly buzzed. It landed on my forehead, I think. I shooed it away.

Dougie took a long sip.

"They put *her* over there in Bellevue a while ago," he said. "That's how it went with her. They pick her up, but she always comes back." He looked at me and added, "To me."

My pulse pounded in my forehead. It all seemed surreal and I was struggling to stay focused, to listen and hear. "Do you know where she is now?" I squeaked.

The man turned his whole body to look at me.

"What makes you think she wants to see *you*?" he snarled, staring at me, making me squirm in my seat.

I was struck silent.

I looked at the bar and neither of us said anything for what seemed like an eternity. My mind was racing. Did this mean that he knew where she was? Did this mean that she *didn't* want to see me?

"You can leave a phone number," he said, finally, turning to signal the end of the conversation.

"I don't—can't you take me to her?" I asked, speaking to his profile.

Again, he said nothing. I wondered if he had heard me. He swallowed the rest of the pint of beer in one cartoonishly long gulp.

"No," he said. He pushed the money forward on the bar and the bartender, watching silently from a dim corner, emerged and refilled the glass.

"I live in the park," I said quickly, quietly, as he drank this beer. "I stay over by that playground off South Lane, the one with the frog sprinklers? Straight back from there. There's some bookshelves in the park, near a bridge. I've got a spot set up right behind there. That's where she can find me."

He drank some more and turned to face me for a moment and his look revealed surprise, interest even. "Bookshelves? You've got a park apartment?"

I nodded again. Suddenly, shockingly, he barked in laughter. The laugh died as abruptly as it started.

I felt sick, nauseated, like I was the one downing beers. Perhaps the initial shock had worn off, because I was suddenly elated and terrified by what was transpiring. Could I trust this man? Was any of this even for real?

And then the spinning got worse. I could feel myself losing control, but I couldn't stop it. I was distantly aware of my head hitting the floor.

When I woke up, the bartender was peering into my face. "You okay?" he asked.

I couldn't breathe. I tried to talk but nothing came out.

A moment later he was lifting me and I somehow found my feet. He steered me to a booth and sat me down.

I began to breathe again.

He crouched in front of me, looking into my eyes. "I don't particularly want to call the cops, but if I do, you need to say that you came in here 'cause you were feeling sick, you got it?"

I nodded. "You don't have to call the cops," I said. "I'm okay. I just ... is he still here?"

"Dougie? He booked before you even hit the ground."

I closed my eyes.

"My photo?"

"What?"

"Did he take my picture of my mother too?" I squeaked.

The bartender turned around and looked at the bar and said, "Yeah. Sorry." When I opened my eyes he was still staring at me. "Let me get you a coke, kid. Sugar is good for the system in times like these. Or something."

He walked around the bar and I watched him fill a pint glass with the soda gun. He came back and sat at the table across from me, a straw bobbed in the dark liquid, threatening to fall out of the glass he set down.

"Scotch," someone called from down the bar.

"Just hold on a minute," the bartender growled back. "Didn't you see the kid knocked her head? I'll be right with you."

"Thanks," I said, taking the straw between my lips. The soda was cold and sweet.

"So, what'd he say to you? Why'd you faint?"

"He said ... he said he knew my mother," I said. The man looked at me. "Hey," I said, strangely calm. "I left my dog tied up outside. Will you look out the window and check on her for me?"

"Sure," he said and he rose and went to the front. He peered out. "Why'nt you just bring her in here for minute?" his face still pointed at the window. "She looks scared." He looked at his clientele. "None of these bums is gonna mind," he said loudly into the back of the bar.

I nodded and slid out of the booth. My legs were wobbly still, but I could walk.

Angel did look scared, watching the door with an arched back, her tongue hanging out her mouth. She cried out and wagged her tail when I opened the door, and when I leaned down to untie her she was panting and I could smell her fear. I kissed her head and led her into the bar.

She set right to lapping at the bowl of water the bartender placed on the floor near the booth. I sat back down and drank more of my coke.

The bartender had returned to the bar to take care of the paying customers but then he came back to the booth and sat down across from me. "My mom died when I was a kid," he said. "I guess I'm saying I know how it is, sort of. In a different way. If you know what I mean."

I nodded. "Thanks for being so nice to me. We'll get going in a minute. I think I just need to sit a little longer."

"You sit as long as you need to," he said, and I started to cry, to weep, because this tough old pot-bellied bartender was being so kind and because my dog had been worried that I left her and because I might be pregnant and that was totally insane and because Corinne had gone back to Henry and because Anthony was gone too and because, in the end, my mother wasn't dead, she hadn't been dead, she wouldn't be dead. *She might even,* I thought, *come back to me.*

CHAPTER 35

The rest of that night, I waited, sleeping fitfully, waking to review the new realities.

I resolved to go to Monticello. Eventually. I knew Anthony would be back in a few days and I would tell him what happened, that I had to wait, just a little longer.

I would find my mother.

I would go to the doctor.

And after that, someday soon, me and Angel, we would go with Anthony and live in Monticello.

So, I was waiting. Waiting for Anthony and waiting for my mother and waiting, too, for Corinne.

The next morning, I spent some time leaving notes. I left notes for Corinne, going to our spots and tying little pieces of paper to branches and twigs. "So much to tell you! Find me by the bookshelves" and "We miss you! We are in our spot." Walking around the park, collecting my stuff, writing little message for Corinne, wondering if I would ever get to see her again, get to tell her about what had happened.

I thought about leaving a note for Ann, who had left me

another note, telling her I would meet her again soon, but I didn't do it. I didn't want her to worry, but I couldn't leave the park. Not yet. I couldn't leave now and never know.

It was the next night when Angel sat up and gave a bark. I reached for the gun next to my head. But then I heard a weak sound, like a whistle, and I knew who it was. It was Corinne. She had come back.

I unzipped the tent. "Iffy," she rasped, standing there.

In the half darkness of the city, I could tell she was a mess, from top to bottom.

She had cut off the braid-dreads and there were clumps of her blond hair missing. Two black eyes, a broken nose, swollen lip. Who knows what else was broken underneath all the bruised and bloody skin on her face. One of her ears was nearly half off. There were bruises on her neck, on her shoulders and her arms. I think she had a broken finger. She was bleeding. Even her feet looked bad.

As I looked over her body and wounds in the lantern light, I kept saying, "*You're okay.*" I whispered as I held her, as I got out the supplies, as I touched her face, her head, her neck, "*You're okay.*" And then that changed and what I was saying was "*You're going to be okay. You're going to be okay.*"

"I know. I just want to go to sleep," she would reply. "Just let me lie down."

I did as much as she would let me, putting peroxide on her ear, above her eyebrow, trying to turn over her arms, pull up her shirt. She began to push my hands away. "Please, Iffy, we can do this in the morning. I'm just so tired." She literally began to crawl, on her hands and knees, to the tent.

"You're going to be okay," I said again, standing there,

uselessly. I couldn't help myself. And then I changed it again, following her, crawling into the tent after her: "We're gonna be okay, Corinne. We're gonna be okay."

In the tent, she cried silently, not hiding her face. "I'm so glad you were still here," she said.

I held her in my arms and I told her about my mother. I told the story over and over again. Even after her body was calm, after she started slightly snoring, a low rhythmic wheeze from her broken nose, I kept telling her. Over and over again.

"I went to this bar, the All Saints. I saw that guy Dougie. He *knows* her. I told him where our camp was. I passed out and fell on the ground. He stole my photo. I think she's gonna come, Corinne," I whispered to her. "I think she's gonna find me."

And then I was sleeping, too, and then I was awake again and Corinne looked awful in the yellow light of the tent.

Angel and I slipped out to wait.

When Corinne finally stuck her head out of the tent, she squinted in the sunlight. I stood and solemnly handed her the sunglasses, the same ones Lizette had given me. That seemed like years ago now. It seemed like another life.

Corinne put on the glasses and crawled out.

She looked worse in the daylight, her skin waxy and her neck and arms and face covered in blue bruises that promised only to darken with time. Her right ear looked terrible, deformed, and I was right about her hair: clumps of it were missing.

But there was something else. It was like she was broken in some other way too. She wasn't herself; she wasn't funny or sarcastic or wry or even angry. She just seemed sad as she took the granola bar I offered, winced as she tried to wedge it between her swollen lips. "Water," she said weakly and handed me back the bar.

I didn't know what to say, so I didn't say anything for a long time and we sat there, outside the tent, Angel panting on the ground between us.

Corinne sighed. "I don't even know if I should go to a hospital or what. I hurt all over, Iffy."

I looked at her face and then back at Angel.

"Don't cry, Iff," she said.

"I'm not," I said, but my voice broke.

Out of the corner of my eye, I saw Corinne put her face in her hands and then she was crying too.

More time passed.

"You have to go," I said finally. "You have to go back to your mom's."

She looked at me blankly.

"Corinne. Listen to me. I called my stepbrother and told him where I was."

"Your stepbrother? Why'd you do that?"

I shook my head. I couldn't answer that question. "I don't want you to be here when he finds me."

"Iffy," she said.

"I'm gonna kill him," I said flatly. "Or maybe he'll kill me. Either way, I don't want you to be here. You need to go to your mom's."

She nodded, resigned.

"I'm gonna go," she said, gingerly wiping her face. "But you come too, Iffy. It's too dangerous to stay here."

I shook my head.

"Iffy, I can't leave you here. We'd do better if we stuck together. Screw him—you don't need to get revenge. Just leave, disappear with me. You'll never have to think about your stepbrother again."

"No," I said, my mind swirling. "That's not true. I have to be here. And my mother ... I'm so close, Corinne, to finding her. I really am."

She looked at me doubtfully.

"I think it's a good idea for you to go to your mom's," I repeated. "In case I wasn't clear."

"Oh yeah? Trying to get rid of me?"

I made a face. Her attempts at joking were heartening, but also a little heartbreaking. She made a little noise and shrugged.

"God," she said, into her hands over her face. "When is it all gonna get easier?"

CHAPTER 36

And then she was gone again. She promised to go straight to her mother's and then to a hospital.

I gave her most of the money so she could get the subway and then a train. She gave me her mother's address and phone number, said that if she didn't hear from me soon she would come looking for me. ("And for god's sake, Iffy, please don't make me come back here if I don't have to," she added). And I hugged her and held her and we said goodbye.

And so I went back to waiting.

Who would come next?

It was like playing a bizarro game of Russian roulette. I had given out my location to a number of people. To Anthony. To Dougie. To my stepbrother. It's possible, too, that Henry would be in the park, looking for Corinne. And I'd never left a note for Ann. Was she going to come storming through with her gang of nuns? So, which one would come? Would it be no one at all? All that build up and it would be nobody? *That*, I thought, *might hurt more than anything.*

I couldn't even read. It was like when I'd first arrived in the park. I was jumping at every crack of a branch, every squirrel darting by. But another day passed and I started to settle down in a resigned, numb kind of way. I imagined myself here for the rest of my life: an old smelly bag lady, reading the same page of *Watership Down* over and over again in the summer sun and then in crisp autumn, then looking like a snowman in the winter, and thawing out again in the spring, still stuck on the same page, faithful dog beside her, still just waiting.

But I knew it was all coming to an end. And even though I hadn't gone to meet Ann, I knew she was right about not wasting time. Because ever since I'd said it out loud, I started to know it was true. Something was happening to me. Something was done to me and now something else was happening to me.

And I needed to stop it if I could.

It was dusk on the next night when I realized I was hungry, that I had been forgetting to eat. I dog-eared a well-dog-eared page, tossed the book toward my tent, and stood, resolved to dig out one of the last cans of beans, force them down my throat. Angel stood and wagged her tail. I felt a little sick and sad, realizing she was probably hungry too.

"Sorry, girl." I patted her head and she tagged along behind me as I took the two steps over to the tent to get us food. When I turned back around and looked up, there was a skinny woman standing a few feet away, staring at me.

I screamed a little. That kind of weird, startled scream.

"Sorry," the woman said.

Angel stayed next to me, let out a quick bark.

"It's okay. You just scared me."

We stared at each other.

She had a thin face, sunken cheeks. The kind of face that

doesn't have a whole lot of teeth to hold it up. Her long, dark hair was pulled into a dirty and tangled ponytail. She was wearing a gray tank top and track pants and flip-flops. Her arms were skinny and rangy and scarred.

But she had the most beautiful face I had ever seen.

"Mommy?" I whispered.

One side of her mouth twisted up in a smile. "Iphigenia? That you baby?" she said. "You been living here, just looking for me?"

I didn't say anything. We stood.

She looked old, so much older than I ever would have imagined, and so terribly fragile. She looked so old, but she made me think of a newborn baby. She was changed, but I still knew her, knew her in some way beyond just what someone looks like. My heart recognized her. Like when you go somewhere you haven't been since you were a kid, a little baby, and you somehow instinctively know the place, know your way around. That was how it was. I knew every inch of her. I knew her even though I didn't.

I started to feel weird, dizzy again, like I had felt at the bar, so I sat down on the ground, straight down from where I was standing.

She walked over and knelt next to me. She put a palm on the top of my head.

"I was worried you wouldn't come," I said.

At first I looked at the ground, but then when I looked at her face I couldn't stop staring at her and she kept looking away. It felt so good to look at her face. Angel nudged my elbow so that my arm was flung over her neck. I slowly let my head down until my cheek rested against the top of Angel's and my mother's hand fell to my shoulder. We sat for a long time and I watched, as the dusk grew darker, as the shadows grew longer.

Still, she didn't say anything.

I was trying to feel it, to understand it. *I was with my mother.* My mother had come. I was trying to appreciate it, the way you do when you wake up a few minutes before the alarm clock goes off and you remember to enjoy being warm and half asleep. But you can't really, knowing your comfort will be short-lived, that you'll have to spring up in a moment. Just the feel of her hand on me, her body next to mine. I wanted to be aware of it.

Because I knew it couldn't last.

My heart hammered. Already, in those first moments, I sensed something wild about her, something unpredictable. But also something hard, something guarded. I was afraid, really, that she would be cruel to me.

When I finally did talk, it was the words that had been waiting there all along: "You came."

She didn't answer.

"I'm so glad you came. I thought, sometimes, that I would never see you again."

I wondered if she hadn't heard me at all. Then she grunted, softly, and said, "Maybe that woulda been better."

Her voice, like the rest of her, sounded familiar and strange at the same time.

I didn't say anything and again we sat for a long time. It was hard for me not to look at her. I would stare into the distance or at the ground and then cut my eyes back to her.

She shifted a bit and she said, finally, "I can't take care of you, Iphigenia."

My heart sped up and I felt panicky. "I don't need you to take care of me," I said, stealing a look at her.

"Then why you showing up here, looking for me?"

I shook my head. "I'll take care of you. Let me try to help you."

She put her arms around me. She smelled rotten, but I didn't care. I leaned into her and put my arms around her too.

"Mommy," I said.

She put her lips to my ear and breathed into it. "You're just my little baby," she said. "You're just my sweet little baby."

The tears streamed down my cheeks. "I don't know why you left me," I whispered. I made a noise—a crying noise—that I had never heard myself make before.

"I left you 'cause I was sick, baby," she said. She mumbled something that I didn't understand.

"Please, Mommy," I said. "Please let me take care of you."

"You can't, baby."

"I know a lady, a teacher, she has a place near here. I can take you to her."

"No thanks, baby. I can't do that."

"Please. She's nice. For real. And I'll come with you."

"Nah," she said, dismissing me. "I'm here with you now. Isn't that enough?"

"It isn't."

"What do you want from me?"

"I want you to let me take care of you."

I wanted to claw at her, crawl all over her, pin her down and curl up on top of her. I wanted to wrap my arms and legs around her, bite her, squeeze her head against my chest.

She pulled away a little from my grasping hands. "You know, I checked up on you. You know that?"

I sniffed, rubbed my hands, hard, across my cheeks.

"That's right, Iphigenia," she said pointedly. "I didn't just forget about you. I used to check on you all the time."

I let out a fresh sob. I felt out of control. I felt like all the crying that had never happened before was happening now.

She seemed unbothered by my hysterical wailing. She nodded and continued. "Oh, yes, I did. PS 37 and then IS 227, that school with the big mural over the front door. I used to go over there, see you walking out the gates with all the other kids. Don't know where you are now, though. What school are you at now?"

In between gasps, I got out a garbled, "Not anywhere right now."

"But it's true, though," she continued. "I was always checking to make sure you were okay."

I inhaled deeply. "But I wasn't okay."

"What?"

"I *wasn't* okay."

She didn't ask, but again descended into silence. I was still hiccuping, unable to catch my breath, but I was calming down, at least a little bit. She reached for me and squeezed me tightly and then let me go.

It was fully dark when I was able to breathe normally, finally. After a while I stood up and got out the lantern.

"Don't need that," she said and I flicked it off again. "You got any cigarettes?" she asked.

I crawled into the tent. When my head was inside, when she couldn't see me, I felt my face writhe into a grimace of pain. I wanted to scream and sob some more, but I couldn't. I was afraid my need would scare her away. And so I held it in and held my breath.

I returned to the deepening darkness and handed her the pack and a lighter.

Her face illuminated briefly as she lit the cigarette. In that light, she looked like herself again, if only for a moment. She looked beautiful.

She scratched her head, sucked her lips. "I didn't know that. I didn't know you weren't okay. I thought he would take care of you. But what do you want from me? I wouldn't have been any good for you either. Maybe you shouldn't have even been born." She shook her head. "I don't mean it like that. I just mean that I couldn't take care of you no more. I couldn't even take care of myself. I always had problems, Iphigenia." I wanted to record the sound of her voice saying my name. "My whole life I always had problems." She took a drag on the cigarette and considered. "I could never get along with anyone. My family. Even before I met your father I could never get along with them. They didn't ... they were always ..." She exhaled a plume of smoke. "But then it got worse when you was born. I got the depression. And they say I'm, what you call it," she waved her hand, and I could tell she was only pretending to have to search for the words. "You don't have to worry about all my di-a-noe-sees." She said it like she was making fun of an immigrant, someone who didn't know English. She smoked and stared off into the woods. "That's all a bunch of bullshit really. I know I have problems, but my situations weren't good either, you know what I mean?" She snorted and wiped her nose on the back of the hand she held the cigarette with.

She looked into the darkness and continued, "But what is true is that I can't stop it with the drugs. I'm clean now, baby. I am, I swear. I would'na come here if I wasn't. But that ain't gonna last. I'm just trying to be honest with you right now. You know. If I could, I would. I woulda come home and taken you away from that bastard. You and me, we always got along. That's true. I never loved nobody the way I loved you."

I felt my face growing hot, my eyes filling with tears again. I was glad for the dark.

"So, yeah, I used to plan to go back and get you and take you away with me. But I couldn't never get it together, you know? You know I got pregnant when I was eighteen, Iphigenia? You know that I was just a baby? I didn't think so at the time," she laughed mirthlessly. "I mean, I was happy, just happy to get out of their house, really, I didn't even care. You think your father is a bastard? Believe me, your father is a saint compared to what I grew up with. But, whatever. I'm not making excuses. I'm just saying it was hard is all. But when you come along, I changed. I took real good care of you, no matter how bad I was feeling or how bad it was for me. You were always fed and clean and I always told you I loved you and played with you and stuff." I could hear a real smile in her voice. "I read you books. Do you know I read to you all the time? We always went to the library and we'd come home with a whole stack of books. I mean, I never even had a library card before, but I got one so that I could take out books for you. Do you remember that? And I took you out to the park. And I let you get away with everything. Your dad said I spoiled you and I would say, yeah, well, she's my baby, of course I'm gonna spoil her. I wasn't gonna do to you what they did to me.

"And you know, before you were born, I said, I'm gonna turn it all around. I am going to go to college. I am doing this for my baby girl. And you know I did that. I went to school for a while. Before you were born and for a little while after too. Got good grades too."

She paused. "You remember me at all?"

I couldn't speak, so I nodded.

"Good. You know where your name comes from?"

I shrugged.

"Greek myth stuff. Girl gets sacrificed by her father. So the winds will blow his ships."

I stayed quiet.

My mother looked at me and even in the darkness of the evening, I felt she could see me. See right into me. A chill ran down my spine as she added, "But her mother avenges her, Iphigenia."

What she had said, what she was saying, revolved in my brain. It was like food that was too rich—I wanted to slow it down, take it in smaller portions. But I sensed our time together was limited; we had to get it all done now.

"It's a big name," she said, ruminative. "It's a big name and you deserve it. You can carry it, girl." She paused and then her head twitched and she was angry again. "I gave up everything for that son of a bitch and all he ever did was run around on me. And get me started on the drinking and all that." She pounded her fist, hard, on her leg and then left the fist there, clenched. "No, that's not true. I think I was always wild, Iphigenia. But he didn't help. He was a bad influence. You wild, Iphigenia? Are you wild too?" she demanded angrily.

I shook my head, no.

"Good. You better not be. You better watch yourself. Your father. He still with that tall bitch?"

I nodded.

"She looks like me, though," she said, but not to me. It was as though she was talking to someone else, someone I couldn't see. "But she'll never be me. So funny that she looks like me." My mother made a noise like a laugh. I had never thought, not once, that my stepmother looked like my mother.

"It was right after you were born I got really sick. Couldn't get out of bed I was so depressed. But I did it," she pointed her cigarette at my chest, "I did it for you, little girl. I kept living for you. And I made it through that time. But that was just the beginning."

I watched the red end of the cigarette and then watched her stub it in the dirt. I suddenly became terrified that she would leave.

"You hungry?" I asked.

She shrugged.

"I got beans," I said. "Let me open them."

I turned the lantern on and she didn't object and I took out a jug of water and handed it to her. She drank from it as I opened the beans. I got two spoons and I put some on a paper plate for Angel and I put another portion on a paper plate for myself and I put a spoon in the can and gave my mother the rest. Angel ate hers in one gulp and then held the plate between her paws while she licked it and gnawed on it. I shoveled the cold beans into my mouth, drinking water to wash them down, thinking of them as raw energy, strength, fuel. What I would need to get through another night, to get through another day. To stay alive. To do whatever it was that I would need to do next.

We didn't talk while we ate, but as soon as the food was gone I felt the need to do something else, to keep us busy, to keep her with me. I started straightening up and said to her, "Stay here with me tonight. Stay with me in my tent."

"What is all this anyway?" she said. "Bookshelves?"

I shrugged, embarrassed. "The bookshelves are just a joke," I said. "I just ... I made a camp for myself."

She shook her head, not understanding. "Yeah, that Danny told me where you might be. I really had to look, though."

"Danny told you? Danny?"

"Yeah. Why? Who else you got looking for me?"

I didn't want to tell her about Dougie, that I'd met him. I shrugged.

She asked, "You disappointed now that you found me?"

I squeaked, "No. Not at all. I'm glad I found you."

She stared at me and said, "You been safe around here?"

"Yeah," I said. "Angel is good protection. And I got a gun too," I said.

"A gun?"

"Yeah," I said.

"What's going on, Iphigenia?" she asked.

I shrugged. "Nothing."

Her eyes bored into me.

"Really," I said. "There's, I don't know, there're a couple of people I have to watch out for is all."

"Oh yeah? Like who?"

I shook my head.

"I'll stay here tonight," she said. "But I'm not going to your teacher in the morning."

"Okay," I said. "Okay." I was flooded with relief and I had to stop myself from sobbing. I swallowed hard and said, "I ..." I had to stop. I tried again. "You know? I just ..."

"I know," she said. And she embraced me again. "I think I know, baby."

CHAPTER 37

It was as good—even better—than I had ever allowed myself to imagine. She held me in her arms as we lay in the tent and in the dark it was easy. I told her things, about myself, about my life, about the kinds of foods I liked and the movies I liked and some of the bad things that had happened and some of the good ones. She listened so hard and told me some things about herself too. That when she was a kid, she'd wanted to be a farmer when she grew up, but then, later, she fell in love with books and decided to be a teacher. That she'd majored in English when she was in college.

It wasn't enough; it wasn't nearly enough. But it was something. I felt a shift inside myself as well as an even more keen longing, as though filling the empty space inside myself a little bit let me know just how big that space was. My heart was a bird, wings hitting the bars of the cage.

After so much talking, we fell silent. I thought she had fallen asleep. Then she asked, "You gonna go to college, Iphigenia?"

"I don't know."

"You want to?"

"I guess."

"Hmm," she said.

"I'm just thinking," she said after a while. "About that one book you loved so much when you were a kid. Do you remember that one?"

"I don't know."

"The one with the bunny and it lived in the woods?"

Something stirred in me, like a tune I knew I knew but couldn't quite remember. "I think I do," I said. "I think I do remember."

"God, you made me read it over and over again. At the end there was something about curling up and dreaming about the spring."

"Yeah," I said, ready to cry again, "Yeah, I do remember that. 'I curl up in my hollow tree and dream about the spring,' I think." I could see the picture of the rabbit in its tree and it seemed like the rabbit was us, curled up, together and safe.

"That's why you love reading so much," she told me. "You're just like me."

And then she was quiet again and this time I thought she really was asleep. And so I said, "Mommy, I need to tell you something."

She didn't say anything. I imagine her eyes closed in the dark. I felt her breath even on my neck. So, I said, "I think I might be pregnant and I don't know what to do."

She was suddenly even more still, so I knew she was awake. She made no response for a moment, but then, "Baby. What do you want to do?"

"I mean, I don't want it. I don't want to keep it. If I am pregnant. I think I am. But it's not ... it's not a good thing," I told her.

I felt her head moving in a nod. "I didn't want to be pregnant either, but you were the best thing that ever happened to me," she said. "I know I messed it up. But I didn't mean what I said before. I wouldn't take it back, take you back, if I could. I'm glad I had you even though I wasn't ready. You were the best thing that ever happened in my whole life."

I didn't respond. Finally, I said, "But."

Her breath was even and I wondered again if she'd fallen asleep when she said, "Whatever you decide is gonna be the right thing." She turned onto her back. "I know that. I can feel it in my bones. Either way you go, it's gonna be the right thing. You can have a baby later. I know you'd be a good mom. But maybe later."

"How do you know?"

"Don't you think I know you?" she said sharply, but not unkindly. "And here's what else I know, Iphigenia. You know why the trees lose their leaves in the winter? 'Cause they have to save their energy. They got to let those leaves die, they let that part of themselves die, so that they can survive. So that they will be strong again in the spring. So, you don't have that baby right now, Iphigenia, because you need to make sure you are going to make it to spring. Because you are my baby. I need my baby to make it, do you understand?" She reached out and her grip was strong on my shoulder and back. My breath was sharp in my lungs. I nodded.

"You're like me. You're like me, Iphigenia, only you're better. You're like me. We're strong and we have to be free, Iphigenia. And we have hearts of steel."

I was suddenly very light and dizzy and I felt myself rising, gliding, blowing a hole and flying right out the top of the tent.

She was right. I had wings, wings that would carry me away and would take me somewhere else, where I would know it hadn't all been for nothing.

I wasn't alone anymore. I was with my mother.

Tears streamed from my eyes, but I was smiling when I put my hand on her cheek and then moved it to her ear. I rubbed her ear lobe between my thumb and forefinger and I put my other thumb in my mouth and fell asleep.

I woke up before dawn, still facing her. She was on her back, with an arm flung across her face. She was snoring softly. I wanted to stare at her, but I was afraid she would feel my eyes and wake up. I was afraid that she would leave.

I took the gun from where I had tucked it next to me and I gestured to Angel, who was watching me intently. We slipped out of the tent. The birds were calling, the sky was just beginning to lighten.

And then Angel started barking.

It had been so quiet. I had been waiting and waiting, and it had been so quiet and then suddenly they all came at once.

My stepbrother was staring at me, shaking his head in disbelief.

"Shoot, I been looking all night and here you are," he said. He had a baseball bat slung over his shoulder. "So, Iffy. Long time, no see," he sneered.

I didn't answer. Angel stood growling next to me, hair standing up all down her spine.

"You know, I didn't even know what to think when I heard that message," he said. He laughed. "You know, I forgot you even existed. But I just had to check it out." He dropped his smile. "Because me and you, we've got some unfinished business."

"We do," I agreed.

"So, I heard you were looking for your bag lady mother?" He laughed again, nastily. "Yeah, that's what that dude Dougie told me. I knew you were fucking crazy."

His eyes roamed around the campsite, taking it in. The tent and the bookshelves and the little firepit.

His gaze settled on me and I took the gun from behind my back.

"Huh. No need for that, now. I come in peace."

"That why you brought a baseball bat?"

"This?" he said, bouncing the bat on his shoulder. "Thought I might play a little ball while I was out here in the park. Thought maybe I could get in a little practice."

"I'm not afraid of you anymore," I said. I was calm and I looked him in the face. "Don't you see?"

And it was true. When I was a child and I had a fever, sometimes I had felt like this, like my brain was so quiet I could hear the blood in my veins. "You don't scare me anymore."

And I saw on his face a flicker of fear.

Everything seemed to be moving very slowly. So slowly that I had time between each word and each breath to think and to understand. And I was so relieved. Relieved because even though it wasn't how I imagined—I had imagined being full of rage and fury—it also wasn't going the way I feared it would. I had been afraid I would have become small again and I had seen myself, my hands shaking, my head bowed, my pants wet.

I cleared my throat and made a little noise to test my voice.

"Put the bat down," I ordered.

He laughed. "Aww, don't be like that. Come on, Iffy. You ain't gonna shoot me. Is that even a real gun, sweetheart?" He was so cocksure. He put up a pacifying palm and stepped closer, looking at me and casting a wary but casual glance at Angel, who crouched by the tent, watching. "You really messed my business up for a while there," he said. "That was really a problem for me, you know."

I cleared my throat, again. "Yeah, I heard you went to jail. You find your own stepbrother in there or what?"

He stopped in his tracks, confused. "What?"

"Probably even harder for you. You know, the shame and all. Asking yourself what it was you did that made him think you were asking for it." I forced out a sound like a laugh. "Did *he* say you should be thanking him?"

I'd been thinking of that line for a while. But I was surprised, again, by my own reaction. It didn't feel good to say it.

And then I realized that even though I still wasn't scared of him, I didn't want to do what I'd thought I wanted to. I realized, too late, that I shouldn't have brought him to the park at all.

His face was ugly and angry. Suddenly, he came charging at me, lifting the bat, aiming for my head. I ducked, fell to the ground, and rolled away, and he raised the bat over his head, ready to bring it down on me, but Angel launched herself at him, her jaw ready to sink into his arm.

I watched from the ground as he slammed her in midair, chopping at her body with the bat. She cried out once and fell with a thump.

I sat up, fast and slow, somehow, at once. I pointed the gun at him. "Stop," I said. "Stop."

He swung and he hit the gun out of my hand as though he was hitting a baseball. I heard the pop of my fingers breaking as I watched the gun fly through the air and land near the tent.

He stood over me, the bat angled over his shoulder, his elbows jutting out, ready to play ball, his face closed. I wondered, sincerely, what I had done to make him hate me so much. I looked at Angel, who lay not far away, one leg jerking. I shut my eyes. I put my face in the crook of my arm.

The crack was deafening and I kept my eyes squeezed closed. When I took my arm away and opened them again there was only the trees and the sky.

My ears were ringing, but I could hear my stepbrother screaming. He was sitting on the ground, looking at his leg, his eyes and mouth wide. He was bleeding. My mother stood holding a gun, the one that had flown from my hand.

My mother walked over to him, the gun trained on his torso.

"This is the one that hurt you, Iphigenia?" she asked.

I started to stand but got tangled in my own feet and I fell again to the ground.

"Stop, Mommy. Stop."

She approached him. As she spoke, she thrust the gun at him in sharp, aggressive bursts. He winced each time.

"You hurt my baby?" she asked. He put his hands on the ground behind him and tried to drag himself backward. "You touched my baby? I should shoot your—"

"Mommy," I called again, finally getting to my feet and standing a few steps behind her.

She kept the gun pointed at him and spoke without turning to me. "What do you want me to do, Iphigenia?" My stepbrother was alternately begging and swearing, sometimes trying to rise and then putting his hands back on the ground behind him, his wounded leg straight out before him. Before I could answer, my mother shouted, "Shut up!" He brought his volume down to a whimper.

"Let's get out of here," I said.

I watched the back of her head and she nodded. "You got to take care of your dog," she said. "You go. I'll stay here with him. You want me to shoot him again?"

I didn't say anything. I looked at Angel on her side, her chest heaving. She raised her head and moved her legs like she was trying to get up.

My eyes returned to my stepbrother. He wasn't sitting up anymore, but instead sprawled out on the ground.

"What happened to him? Is he dead?" I asked.

"Passed out," my mother said, her arm still extended. She reached out her other hand and grabbed my shoulder.

She pulled me to her face. "What do you want me to do, Iphigenia? Do you want me to shoot him again?"

"No," I said in a hurried exhale. "No, please don't. I don't want that. I thought I did, but I don't. I don't want that for us," I said.

Our eyes locked. "Go," she said. "Get away from here." Her voice cut through, deep and steely.

All I could say was, "Mommy."

She glanced back at him and then continued. "They're gonna know it was me. I'm the one who shot him. Maybe I'll even turn myself in. I don't know. But they'll know it wasn't you. So, you gotta go, now."

"I can't," I shouted back, my ears still ringing, "I can't leave you. I just found you!"

"You have to, Iphigenia. You've got to go. *Go*," my mother growled, her face angry. "You don't need me," I think she said.

"I can't," was all I could say.

"You can," she said. "And I can too. I will handle this. I should have handled it a long time ago."

With one arm, she squeezed me to her and then she pushed me away.

I walked over to where my stepbrother lay on the ground. He didn't look good, but he was breathing. "He's gonna need help," I said.

"I'll handle it," my mother said again.

I had seen my stepbrother asleep before, but this time he looked different. He looked younger now, somehow, without his smirk or his scowl.

"Your dog," my mother said. "You better get going."

I turned away from Marco and walked back to my mother.

"We'll see each other again," my mother said. She put her cool palm on my cheek. "Don't cry," she said.

I grabbed her and held her.

"Don't never forget," she whispered in my ear, her breath hot and sweet. "Her mother avenges her, Iphigenia."

She kissed my head and pushed me from her.

"Now, go."

CHAPTER 38

I did. I let go of my mother.

I went to Angel. Her big, dark eyes rolled up and looked at me standing over her. She was breathing hard and whimpering.

"Oh, Angel," I said. I fell to my knees. "I am so sorry. I am so sorry this happened to you. I'm gonna have to carry you, Ang. Okay?"

They were still there, my mother and my stepbrother, a frozen scene in my periphery, but I focused on Angel, on the whooshing noise in my head and Angel and on trying to tell her it would be okay and, then, trying to pick her up.

My right hand was pulsing, and when I looked at it I saw it was misshapen. But there wasn't any pain, not yet, so even though I couldn't flex my fingers, I positioned my hands under her front and back legs, her belly resting against my forearms, and I lifted, trying to hold her to my chest. She cried out and even snapped at me, but then I just heaved and she squirmed a little but then settled in a resigned, helpless way that I didn't like. She was heavy. Oh my god, she was heavy.

"We're gonna be okay, Ang, I'm gonna take care of you," I

whispered as I staggered, carrying her away. I looked back once.

"I love you," I said, my voice rasping. I stopped, ready to return to my mother.

She still stood where I had left her. She nodded at me slowly and I turned away, a deep sob escaping from me as I squeezed my eyes shut and walked blindly through the trees. Angel whimpered a little and I felt a wetness from her. Was Angel crying, too?

I couldn't bear to think about it.

I trudged and stumbled to the trail that led most directly out of the park. My hearing was coming back, and I got into a pattern—listening to my steps and my panting breath. The focus allowed me to not think about what had happened and what was happening and what I was gonna do next. *Crunch-crunch-breathe, crunch-crunch-breathe, step over root. Crunch-crunch-breathe, crunch-crunch-breathe, crunch-crunch-breathe, watch out for rock.*

Just when I decided I couldn't go any further, that the dog was too heavy, and where was I going anyway, I caught a glimpse of the sidewalk in the sunlight. It was truly morning when we emerged from the woods. I was sweating and panting; Angel had begun wheezing, her head on my shoulder.

Once on the sidewalk, I slumped to the ground, Angel in my lap, and I wept.

I felt a shadow, someone blocking the sun and I looked up at a man standing over me. The sun was so bright behind him that I couldn't make out his face. "You okay?" he asked in a kind voice. I was aware then that traffic was going by.

I squinted up at the man and licked my lips. "My dog got hit by a car," I said. "I just need to get home."

"You should be taking that dog right to the vet," he said, crouching beside me. He was an older guy with wrinkles, dark-skinned with a nice, calm face.

"I will ... but I've got to get home first. It's only a few blocks away."

"Hey," he said. "My car is right here." I looked up to see a gypsy cab idling at the curb. "Can you carry him?"

"Her," I said. "Yeah. Yes."

The man hustled away, half walking and half jogging, and opened the back door of the long blue sedan. I caressed Angel's head, kissed her face. She watched me. She never took her eyes off me.

I picked her up again. She moaned. The few steps to the car seemed impossible. I wondered how I had made it through the woods. But then we were there and I slid into the back seat with her in my lap.

"Please just take us to 114th street. You can go up Myrtle," I said.

"Okay," he said. "But I think you should really get that dog to the vet. Like, immediately."

"I will," I said, "I will. Please just go."

As the car pulled away from the curb, the man turned around to look back at us, maybe to see if blood was getting all over his seat. "So, what happened?" he asked.

"She got hit by a car."

We stopped at a light. I listened to the directional blinking, the soft hum of the radio that he meant to turn off but only turned down. I hoped he knew I wouldn't be able to pay him.

The car smelled strongly of air freshener. A green cardboard pine tree hung from the rearview. I thought I might be sick.

"Was she on leash?"

"What?"

"Was your dog off her leash when she got hit?"

What did it matter? I thought. *It's a lie anyway*, I wanted to tell him. *What does it matter?*

"She got away from me."

Maybe the cabbie wasn't buying my story; maybe he was finally thinking, *what on earth did I get myself into? This kid is trouble and now her dog is gonna die in my car. Who's gonna clean that up?*

But Angel didn't die in his car.

We pulled up in front of the address Ann had given me, a small blue house with a big pine tree in the front.

I considered going to a different house, to a different address, just in case the guy, like, later got questioned by the police or something like that. But I didn't have the energy. I just wanted help. I needed someone else to help me with Angel.

"Thanks," I said, kicking the door open and sliding out, holding Angel like a baby. "I've got it from here." She cried out again as I awkwardly heaved us both out of the car, and I whispered, "Sorry, sorry, baby," and I was about to hurry away but I turned back, looked into the man's eyes. "Thank you," I said. "Really."

He looked back at me, frowning with concern. "You're welcome," he said. "I hope your dog is okay." I felt him watching me as I struggled up the driveway.

Once in the backyard, I laid Angel down on the grass. The back door was open. I could see into the kitchen. "Ann?" I called through the screen door, "Is anyone here?" A dog started yapping, a little white thing that came to the door, jumping and scratching and whining.

I tried the screen door, but it was locked. "Anyone?" I called again. What if she wasn't home? What would I do then?

But she was home. A moment later she was at the door.

"Iphigenia? What is it? What's wrong?"

I wasn't crying anymore at that point, I don't think. But I couldn't talk either. I just pointed at Angel on the ground.

"What happened?"

"Angel," I said, gulping air. "Please take her to the vet. Please don't let her die."

"Jeannie!" Ann shouted into the house, but there was already another woman standing in the door.

"What's going on?"

"We have to get her to the vet. Get a blanket. It's Lola. We have to get her to the vet."

I threw myself on the ground. I took Angel's head in my arms. I cried into her fur. I told her I loved her and I was sorry.

Then a different woman was there and she and Jeannie were putting the blanket on the ground and then putting Angel in the blanket and then carrying her away.

"You come in the house," Ann said, her hand on my shoulder. "They'll take care of Angel. You come in the house."

CHAPTER 39

Ann sat, her hands flat down on the small kitchen table. "Iphigenia, I have to ask you something."

I stood at the counter and kept my eyes on the humming toaster, looking in at the red coils. It was one of those industrial-sized appliances; it could hold eight slices total. I might have made eight slices if I'd been alone. Instead, I'd made four.

"What do you know about the shooting in the park?"

"Shooting?" I said. I moved to the fridge and opened it. Ann and Jeannie ate the fake butter that came in a tub. I'd never had it before coming to stay with them, and I found that I loved it—it was so easy to spread a thick layer on the bread, unlike the hard sticks of butter we'd always had in the apartment. I took out the tub and put it on the counter.

"A shooting of a young man. In a campsite. He's uh ... he's not cooperating with the police. But I think maybe you might know something about it?"

I nodded, looking at the closed refrigerator door. "Yeah," I said, turning back to the toaster.

"Is it?" Ann asked. "Not your boyfriend?"

I shook my head, no.

"But, you knew him? Not your ...?" she trailed off, maybe not wanting, really, to hear the answer.

"My stepbrother," I answered. "I didn't do it." I finally looked at her and I knew my eyes looked as dead as my words sounded. *Although, for a long time I wanted to,* I thought. I could feel my face, flat, impassive. You might think I was bored. But truly, I was holding on so tight. I knew that if I let myself start, I would never be able to stop.

The kitchen had yellow, brown, and orange paneling. Ann sat at a yellow-topped table that had matching chairs with yellow plastic cushioned seats that whooshed when you sat down and made a sucking noise when you got up. It was a large room and bright, but it was too clean, the counters uncluttered and spotless. I wondered, vaguely, if I would appreciate how clean this place was once they sent me to some overstuffed group home.

"We have to talk to the police," she said. "You understand that?"

"No," I said and the toaster popped.

Toast—that was all I understood anymore. Hot, buttered toast.

With my left hand I plucked each hot piece out, one by one, making a little pile on the plate.

Ann regarded me.

"What?" I asked.

"It's just ... we really should get out in front of this Iphigenia. You should talk to the police before the police decide to talk to you."

I didn't answer. Instead, I scooped a huge slab of the butter-type substance and slathered it on each piece of toast and then stacked the slices again. The ones near the bottom of the pile would have the butter melted in, soaked in, just the way I liked it.

After Jeannie and another person—a neighbor? a random unlucky visiting friend?—took Angel away, Ann had brought me inside the house. I suppose I was in shock, because the whole thing passed in a blur, Ann buzzing around, offering me water and bananas and wrapping my injured hand. Then I'd been led to a bathroom and my hand was in a Wonder Bread bag with ice in it and I remember that Ann had turned the shower on but still I found myself, standing, looking down at the dirty, bloody water and at the little swell of my tummy, wondering how I'd gotten there, exactly.

I was then led to a tiny room with a twin bed and a small window that looked out over the backyard. I glanced out once and then didn't look again. And then I'd slept, wearing a sweet-smelling gray sweat suit with the words "The Mary Louis Academy Hilltoppers" on the chest and "TMLA" down one leg.

I'd slept deeply and I don't know for how long, but I wasn't confused when I woke up. Instead, even half conscious, I woke and I instinctively knew *not* to feel. With my hand resting on my chest, it didn't ache so much and I'd noted the softness of the bed, the perfectness of the pillow, that my feet were cold in a way that made me enjoy the blankets even more. I woke up and decided I wouldn't think about my mother, even though it was all I wanted to do, to think about our time together in the tent. I wouldn't think about my stepbrother, about his face, and what I'd seen out of the corner of my eye, even though I was trying very hard not to look. I wouldn't think about Corinne and Anthony and whether or not either of them had come back for me.

Ann must have heard me stirring, because she was right

outside the door when I opened it, waiting to escort me downstairs.

"Angel?" I rasped. I realized my throat hurt.

"She's okay," Ann said. "They have to keep her while she recovers, but the vet says she is going to be okay."

I let myself feel relieved. And then I went back to not feeling anything.

And after two days, I was doing a pretty good job. Ann was always around, doing things for me: making phone calls and appointments, offering me a banana, asking how I felt. I focused on Angel, on her being okay, on keeping my hand very still and not bumping it against anything, and on my toast, and on the Gatorades Ann kept in the fridge. On air conditioning and ice cubes, on the slippers she gave me to wear around the house.

I didn't like being indoors. It was comfortable, but except for the kitchen the rooms in the house were small and if there was another person around I felt crowded. I thought maybe living in the park would make it hard to ever live indoors like a normal person again.

I ate my toast methodically, like getting through each slice was a job I had to complete perfectly. Ann watched me, and when I was done she rose and took a banana from the fruit bowl and handed it to me. What was it with these women and their bananas?

"Fruit is good for you," she said, as though reading my mind.

"Ann," I said and she watched me expectantly. I took the banana and put it to the side. "Can you keep Angel? I don't think I'm gonna be able to take care of her anymore."

I'd have thought it would have been harder to say.

"Of course," Ann said. "Of course."

I nodded, looking at the banana.

"Ready to go?" she asked.

"I want to do something first," I said, not meeting her eyes. "Actually."

She waited.

"Can I use your phone? Can I call information? It's long distance."

"That's fine."

I could tell she wanted to know who I was calling but she didn't want to come out and ask. "I need to call my friend, Corinne," I said.

She gestured, *help yourself*, toward the rotary phone on the wall.

There was a pad and a pen on a string next to the phone.

Ann stepped out of the room and I put the banana back in the fruit bowl.

I held the phone and dialed 411 with the same hand. I asked if there was a listing for Wales in Bayonne, New Jersey. There were two: Gary and Diane.

Cradling the phone against my shoulder, I took down Diane's number and then dialed it.

I was unaccountably nervous. Maybe I was nervous that it was the wrong number or, if it was the right one, she wouldn't be there or she wouldn't want to talk to me. But she might as well have been waiting because after the second ring, she picked up.

"Corinne!" I whispered.

"*Iffy?*"

"Yeah."

"Where are you?"

"I'm okay. I'm not in the park anymore."

"Where are you?"

"Ann's house."

"Wow. That's ... weird." She paused.

All I could say was, "Yeah."

"Is this gonna be like an *Annie* scenario after all?"

"I don't know what you're talking about."

"A joke. The movie, you know, *Annie*. The sun will come out tomorrow? Sorry. Never mind. But what happened?"

"A lot," I said. "Angel is ... Angel is in the hospital—you know, the animal hospital."

"Oh my god," she said. I wanted to tell Corinne everything but there wasn't time. I didn't know how to begin.

"What happened?" she asked again.

"I can't," I said.

"Oh my god," she repeated. I wondered if we'd just go on and on like this until it was time for me to go. "Oh, honey, I'm so sorry. But did you find her? Your mother?"

I couldn't answer. I held the phone to my face and squeezed my eyes shut so I wouldn't cry.

"Iff?" she asked.

I inhaled in a gasp. "I found her," I whispered.

I cried silently and she waited. I was so grateful for Corinne.

When I could, I asked, "Are you okay? Please tell me you're okay."

"Yeah," she said, her voice still aghast and high-pitched. She paused to see if I would say more and then went on. "Nothing unfixable, if you know what I mean. I mean, I'm still sore, and it's gonna be a while before my hair looks good again, but I'm fine."

"Good," I said.

"Is Ann's house nice?"

"I don't know."

"Is she a lesbian or what?"

"Yeah," I said, almost smiling. "I think so."

"So, are you going to live there?"

"No," I said. "I'm not sure what ... I have to go to a doctor today."

"Oh yeah? You okay?"

"I will be, I guess. I mean, I messed up my hand. But that's ... not the most important thing." I sighed. I curled myself around the phone. "I have so much I need to talk to you about, Corinne."

"Me too," she said. "He—Henry—he came up here. My mother called the police."

"Really?"

"Yeah. I actually couldn't believe it. I mean, she's still totally out of her mind, but she's been, like, weirdly great. Like, totally on my side and protective. And she hasn't even called me Corey once."

"Good," I said. "I'm glad, Corinne. I'm really glad to hear that."

"Yeah, back to you," she said. "What else do you need to see a doctor for?"

CHAPTER 40

After, they brought me to a room where other girls and women were sitting in a row of faux-leather recliners, lined up against a wall. Maybe the chairs were arranged side by side so that no one would have to look at anyone else. I appreciated that. The nurse guided me to my chair and gestured for me to take a seat and then she put some Oreos and a Dixie cup of water on a tray beside me. She walked away and then came back with a small green blanket and without asking, she tucked it in around my lap. I felt embarrassed but also grateful. The blanket was very soft.

There was a magazine on the tray, too, a well-worn summer issue of *Vogue*. On the cover a woman in a striped one-piece bathing suit eternally leapt in the air, her arms and legs at insane angles.

I sat like the others, holding the cup of water and staring straight ahead. And although it hadn't been good, it hadn't been too bad either, and then I felt a sudden welling of understanding that it was, at last and unmistakably, over.

I began to cry quietly, taking jagged breaths. I felt the girl in the next recliner cut a glance at me and I hazarded a look back at her. Her face was annoyed—she was pissed that someone couldn't hold herself together, and I could understand that. I whispered, "*Sorry,*" and gave her a little embarrassed half smile. After a moment she smiled back.

"You okay?" she asked, gruff, but not unkind. She had thin yellow hair and bad skin.

I nodded. "I feel a lot better, actually. Now."

"Me too," she said, sort of laughing through her nose. "They make you think that you're gonna be all sad and shit, but not me. I'm the opposite. Like, thank god, you know?"

I nodded. "I guess."

The girl handed me a box of tissues from her tray and I wiped my face and blew my nose. A nurse came over and took the girl's blood pressure and then told her she could leave. The girl untucked her soft green blanket and rose, moving gingerly.

"Good luck," she said to me.

I waved. "You too," I said.

I took a bite of a cookie and picked up the magazine, resting it in my lap.

I thought about Corinne, about what she had said.

She'd gasped and been shocked. "Isn't it the worst that characters on TV shows are always having these convenient miscarriages? Like, a girl gets pregnant and it's a problem and then she loses the baby and it's sad, but not *really.* But in real life you probably never have a miscarriage unless you really wanted to have a baby. I mean, why can't you ever get a miscarriage when you need one?"

We'd both laughed, though it was a little forced. Then Corinne had turned serious. "Wow, Iffy. That sucks. I wish I was there to go with you."

"Me too," I'd said.

"Look, you come here after. You can stay with me and my mom. Until I murder her. And then we can live in this amazing house. I mean, it is a *split-level ranch*."

When I didn't say anything she had added, "Ha, Iffy. That was a joke. I hate ranches. And we don't have to murder her. We could just save up and get an apartment."

I made myself smile wryly, as though she could see me. "Maybe."

"Iffy," she'd said, serious. "Iffy, you have people. Do you understand that? You don't have to do it by yourself. Think about that."

I thought about that.

Maybe I'd go to Corinne's mom's.

Maybe I'd go to Monticello.

But I knew it wouldn't be quite as easy as all that. My hand, the police, maybe even my father would have to be dealt with. And that was probably just the beginning.

But after that, I knew, I would go, for real and far away.

I looked at the magazine.

Maybe someday, that could be me in a candy-striped bathing suit, leaping at the beach. Taking flight.

Maybe I'd go ahead and follow the coast all the way to Florida, like I'd told Anthony I would.

I imagined myself, walking slowly at sunset, barefoot and tired.

And I knew I could do it too.

But maybe I didn't have to go alone. Maybe Corinne was right.

I imagined. The sea breeze soft on our sunburned faces as we walked in the reddish light.

EPILOGUE

Anthony held my good hand.

He seemed nervous. He kept getting up and looking at the subway map and then looking at the window and then coming back to sit next to me and hold my hand. I wondered if he was still feeling shy with me after being apart. It hadn't even been that long, only a few weeks. But maybe too much had changed.

Even the weather was changing, and as we rumbled through Queens on the 7 train, I saw that the leaves on the tops of the trees were already tinged yellow and orange.

I thought of my mother.

Corinne had found Anthony for me, had been able to track him down through his brother and pass on the phone number at Ann's. When we'd finally gotten on the phone together, Ann and Jeannie were nice about it and had gone upstairs so that I could really talk to him, sitting at the kitchen table to tell him, if not everything, as close to everything as I could. Speaking softly into the receiver I told him about my mother and then my stepbrother. I told him that I'd had an abortion. I told him that Angel was back from the animal hospital and that I thought my heart was going to explode the day she came home. I told him that Ann had found me a group home and that I supposed it was going to have to be okay.

I told him about my mother, that she'd been arrested, and that I was going to go and see her at Rikers.

"I'll go with you," he said right away. "I'll come down and I'll go with you."

He knew what it was to go see a parent in jail.

And so here we were, sitting next to each other in an almost-empty subway car, feeling shy with each other.

I was jumpy too. I hadn't ever been to somewhere like Rikers before. Someone from Ann's school, a nun who was some sort of prison specialist, had given me the rundown about what to wear and what to bring, how to act and what to say. She told me to be prepared, that the guards would be unpleasant, and that I might not even get to see my mother at all.

To see my mother at all.

Thinking of seeing her again had my hands shaking. I was gripping Anthony's hand, to still my own, when he jumped up again and looked out the window. The few people in the car had noticed and watched him in the way you watch people on the train, without looking at them directly. I knew that to them he could seem like a weirdo, maybe high on something, maybe dangerous.

But he began to smile widely and I couldn't imagine how anyone, especially me, could mistake that face for weird or dangerous. He put out his hand toward me. "Come quick! Get up!" he cried. "Come here and look!"

I stood and rocked as I walked to the opposite window. I grabbed the overhead pole and leaned forward. "What?" I asked.

"What am I looking at?" Brown and red apartment buildings coasted by; rooftops and laundry lines and fire escapes.

And then I saw it: my name, Iphigenia, in exuberant, enormous blue and purple letters, the lowercase *i*'s dotted with bursting red hearts, two huge white wings on either side, holding it aloft. *Iphigenia*, six feet tall on the side of the building.

"I did it last night," he said. "Do you like it?"

I couldn't answer because I couldn't take my eyes off it, my mouth open a little in wonder. I put my face close to the window to watch until it was out of view before turning back to Anthony, smiling and laughing, shaking my head.

"I can't believe it," I said. "You're crazy," I said. "I love it."

He nodded, so happy, too, and not nervous anymore, but bouncing on his toes, like the subway was a ride at an amusement park, and he laughed out loud and did a pull-up on the overhead pole before gathering me to his chest.

"I did it so every time you come this way, you'll think of me," he said. "And you'll know that I love you."

I buried my face against him and closed my eyes, smiling.

I didn't want to start crying again, so I didn't say anything. Instead we stood together like that, him holding the pole and me holding onto him as we rode, rocking back and forth, flying past the people and apartments and buildings, flying over the streets below, heading to my mother, hurtling toward ourselves.

ACKNOWLEDGMENTS

Thank you to Tavia Gilbert and Cathy Plourde: I am grateful not only for your keen eyes, but for your vision, your courage, and your unfailing support. I am so glad you are in the world. Thank you to Sarah Twombley for your generous attention. Thank you to the folks at Blackstone: Jeffrey Yamaguchi, Lauren Maturo, Josie Woodbridge, Bryan Barney, Greg Boguslawski, Mandy Earles, Josh Stanton, and Ember Hood. Thank you, Karen Hernandez for your enthusiasm and encouragement. Thank you, Lisa Modifica for your steadfast friendship. Thanks to my colleagues at Nassau Community College and to my students, particularly the students in my WST classes and in the WSA, many of whom have inspired the work I've done here: Hollis, Lucia, Shanice, Doug, Laura, JR, Gillian, Annie, Andi, Jaslin, Lindsay, Sam, Ibiene. It has been a privilege learning alongside you. Thanks to the teachers and staff at NCC's Children's Greenhouse Childcare Center—and in particular Janet Walsh—who have created a sustaining community, the likes of which should be available to all people. Thanks to my family: Mom, Dad, Jules, and Johnny. And thanks, always, to Jess, who is the Bert to my Ernie and, sometimes, the Ernie to my Bert.

If you or someone you know is in need of help, please reach out. The following organizations are dedicated to aiding individuals struggling with a variety of serious issues.

You are not alone.

RAPE AND INCEST NATIONAL NETWORK

(800) 656-HOPE (4673)
www.RAINN.org

NATIONAL COALITION AGAINST DOMESTIC VIOLENCE

(800) 799-7233
TTY (800) 787-3224
www.TheHotline.org

NATIONAL COALITION FOR THE HOMELESS

(202) 462-4822
www.NationalHomeless.org